BENEATH HIGHLAND STARS

SPECIAL OPS SCOTS
BOOK 3

KAIT NOLAN

TAKE THE LEAP PUBLISHING

CHAPTER 1

FINN

I nursed my whisky at the edge of the dance floor, watching my business partner, Alex Conroy, and his new wife, Ciara McBride—well, Ciara McBride Conroy now—sway together beneath the ancient wooden beams of Ardinmuir's great hall. If ever there was a setting for a happily ever after, the six-hundred-year-old castle turned event venue was it. Alex's bride looked like a bloody princess in the candlelight, and in his dress kilt and waistcoat, he looked like a character out of a romance novel. The kind with a guaranteed happy ending, and not a single landmine hidden under the floorboards. The pair of them glowed like they'd swallowed an ocean of stars. Alex—always so controlled, so measured—looked fair to bursting with happiness, his hand resting on the small of Ciara's back like it had always belonged there.

"Bloody hell, Echo," I muttered into my glass. "You've gone and done it properly, haven't you?"

The string quartet played something slow and sweet, notes floating up to the rafters where generations of MacKeans had celebrated their own unions. Alex whispered something in

Ciara's ear that made her laugh, her head tipping back, exposing the elegant line of her throat.

A knot formed in my chest. Not quite jealousy—I wanted this for them, Christ, did I ever—but something adjacent to it. Something like standing out in the cold and watching someone else's windows lit warm and golden. A recognition of something I'd convinced myself I didn't need. Didn't deserve.

My gaze drifted to my scarred hands, to the empty spot beside where I stood. I'd come alone, of course. Always did. For all my flirtatious ways, there was no one who mattered. Hadn't been in longer than I cared to remember.

This wasn't what I wanted for you.

I ignored the feminine voice that echoed from somewhere in the past—a past I wished was dimmer than it was. Instead, I focused on the couple on the dance floor. The music swelled, and Alex spun Ciara in a circle that sent her dress billowing. When she returned to his arms, the look that passed between them was pure, unguarded love. No walls, no defenses.

I tossed back the rest of my whisky, savoring the burn.

A hand clapped on my shoulder. "You're next, mate."

I shot Ciara's brother, Ewan, some side eye. "What are you on about?"

My former squad leader looked out at the newlyweds. "You're the last man standing, aye? Alex and I are both married. Callum will be right behind. Everyone has coupled up. So what the hell are you waiting for?"

I eyed the empty glass, wishing I had another. "It's no' like there's exactly a line of women who are waiting to become Mrs. Finley Patterson."

Callum Quinn, my other business partner, stepped up on my opposite side. "It disnae seem like you've been doing a whole lot of looking."

I shot a placid look in his direction. "I've been a little busy starting a business with you lot and making it a success." Out of Bounds Scotland, the outdoor adventure company we'd formed once Callum had retired, had taken most of our focus the past year and a half.

"Aye." Callum nodded. "That was a reasonable excuse for the first year. But we're well into the second now and growing by leaps and bounds."

"We have your fiancée to thank for that," I pointed out.

Parker Lawrence had strolled into our offices last year and saved our collective arses by becoming office manager when we needed one most. Somehow she'd tamed Callum's grumpitude, and the pair had fallen in love. I wouldn't have believed it if I hadn't been there to see the transformation firsthand.

"Just because you and Alex have gone and got yourselves sorted, disnae mean I need to rush." I tried to keep my tone light. "Some of us enjoy our freedom."

Ewan's eyes narrowed slightly. He'd always been too perceptive by half. It was what had made him such a good squad leader. "Freedom's one thing. But you've not even had a proper date since you moved up here and opened the business. Not even a fling."

"I've had dates." Even I could hear how weak that sounded. Not a single one of those dates had I let past the first pint. Casual was easy. Safe. Nothing to miss if it vanished in the morning.

Callum's one good eye fixed on me with uncomfortable intensity. "Aye, and how many second dates?"

I shrugged. "Just haven't found anyone worth the effort."

"Bullshite." Ewan's voice was flat. "You, who used to charm the knickers off half the women in any pub we walked into? The lad who once got three phone numbers in the span of ordering a round?"

I felt my smile grow tight. "Maybe I've matured."

Callum snorted. "Or maybe there's something else going on." His voice dropped. "Look, we all came back with baggage, Finn. If something's eating at you, we're all here to help."

That this came from Callum, who'd carried perhaps the most baggage of us all, hit me hard. What did it say that even he'd been able to process and heal, when I'd had far more time in civilian life?

Ewan moved in a little closer. "Look, I ken you took the news about Charlie hard."

At the reminder of the latest of our former squadmates to die in the line of duty, I wished viciously for another drink. One to drown the ache, then another to chase the ghosts.

The funeral had been almost two weeks ago. Swallowing down the lump in my throat, I nodded. "Aye."

We all lapsed into silence for a moment, out of respect for the man who'd save all our arses at one time or another. Didn't I owe it to him to do the one thing he'd asked of me?

"Charlie wanted me to have Ajax." The words spilled out before I could think better of them. I'd barely had time to process the news myself. Ajax was Charlie's military service dog. The Belgian Malinois had served with our squad for several years, becoming as much one of the team as any fellow two-legged Marine.

Callum paused, his glass hovering halfway to his mouth. "Truly?"

"Aye. I got contacted by the handler who took over for Charlie after he... after. The poor lad hasnae been functional since. Hasnae been able to do his job. He's listless and depressed. So they're retiring him. Apparently, Charlie left word that if anything happened to him, they should contact me." I sucked in a breath. "I'm going to take him."

Ewan and Callum exchanged a look. I couldn't blame them. I hadn't taken on additional responsibilities for a living thing other than my squadmates in years. Not even a plant. Not since my epic failure to keep *her* safe. But dogs were loyal, weren't they? They didn't leave unless someone gave the order. They didn't walk away when you failed.

Despite the weight of that, I couldn't leave Ajax to the whims of fate. There was no guarantee he'd end up in a good home. Better he stay with someone he knew than the alternative. No man—or dog—left behind.

"Well, I think it's grand." Was Ewan's voice a shade too forcefully cheerful? I couldn't quite decide. "When do you get him?"

"I go pick him up next week."

Callum chuckled. "Even from beyond the grave, Charlie's going to be your best wingman."

I frowned at him. "What?"

"There's nothing like a dog to get the attention of the ladies. Add in war hero to that, and you've got it made."

"Uh-huh. And what ladies would that be?" Did they imagine I'd be trolling the village with Ajax on a leash, extolling his virtues to any lass who'd listen?

"Maybe not ladies, but one specific lass, at least." Ewan looked pointedly across the great hall.

I knew exactly where he was looking, and I couldn't quite stop myself from following his gaze.

Dr. Saoirse MacGregor looked good enough to eat. Her spectacular dress was some sort of shimmery blue fabric that hugged her willowy curves and showed off her strong, sculpted back with a complicated series of laces that my fingers itched to pluck and unravel.

Of course, she'd show up looking like every mistake I wanted to make twice.

She was always gorgeous, but this was a big change from the jeans and wellies she habitually wore because of her veterinary practice. The hair she usually tamed into a tail was loose around her shoulders. A waterfall of honey blonde that looked like silk. That exquisite, fine-boned face had been enhanced by some sort of female magic that made those deep green eyes look like a siren's. Her bold red lips were currently curved into a smile I was seldom witness to. She was brilliant, talented, devoted to her friends. And for reasons that I didn't understand, she'd decided on-sight that she hated me.

Ever since that first meeting, we'd been clashing every time we were in the same room together. Which was more often than I'd like, given that we traveled in the same friend groups. She was besties with both Ciara and Parker. They were always hanging out together, so we saw each other often, which meant we needled each other all the time. Our collective friend group had decided that meant we were perfect for each other. Or at least that we needed to go to bed to work out our differences in a more constructive manner than bickering. In the privacy of my own head, I could admit that her posh London boarding school accent absolutely worked for me.

The snobby attitude, however, did not.

Realizing that my mates were still waiting for a response, I rocked back on my heels. "I dinna think the dog would make a difference with that one. She'd be more likely to date him than me, if I were even interested."

"Aye. Right," Callum murmured.

I fixed him with a flat stare. "She disnae like me."

Ewan huffed. "Every woman likes you."

"Exactly. Which just goes to show there's something wrong with her."

The pair of them actually snickered.

"So glad I can be of amusement to you."

Callum thumped me on the shoulder. "Why dinna you go

work on rectifying whatever shite impression you've made? Go ask her to dance."

Knowing they weren't likely to leave me be until I gave in, I shrugged and set my glass on the tray of a passing server. "Fine."

Saoirse sat at a table with Parker and two of their other friends, Skye Stuart and Pippa Wallace. Like Parker, who originally hailed from Tennessee, Skye was also an American ex-pat who'd made her home in Glenlaig because she'd fallen in love with her Scottish penpal. Pippa was a local whose claim to fame was making cheese so good it had prompted more than one marriage proposal. She hadn't said yes, but it turned out that was because she was in love with a cowboy. That cowboy had relocated here a few months ago to be with her, and we all expected the proposal to happen by the end of the year.

Damn, I really was the last man standing.

I headed in their direction. I wasn't in the market for anything real. But the second Saoirse smiled at Parker—really smiled, not the sharp little smirks she gave me—I felt something in my chest shift.

Dangerous territory.

I should've walked away. Instead, I turned on the charming smile that worked on almost everyone. "Hello, ladies. You all look lovely this evening."

Parker grinned at me. "You don't look so bad yourself. There is so much Scottish hotness in this room, I hardly know what to do with myself."

Saoirse crossed her legs, revealing a slit in her dress that showed a long stretch of muscled thigh. "I expect if you took your own piece of Scottish hotness home, he would have plenty of ideas."

Bloody hell. I had quite a few ideas of my own, starting

with finding out exactly how high I could slide my hand beneath that dress.

Focus, Patterson.

The music changed.

"Pippa, darlin', they're playin' our song." Zeke Shaw, a tall, dark-haired chap in the incongruous combination of a kilt and a cowboy hat, extended his hand.

There was a flurry of movement as Callum collected Parker, and Jason McKinnon swept Skye onto the dance floor. Then Saoirse and I were alone, with no friends as buffer.

Right. I'd come over here on a mission.

I held out my hand. "Would you care to dance?"

Saoirse looked at me like I was something stuck to the bottom of her shoe—which, considering she was a vet who routinely dealt with all manner of animal messes, was saying something. Her green eyes narrowed slightly, lips pursed as she weighed her options. I could practically see the war between good manners and genuine distaste playing out across her face.

"All right." Her posh accent clipped the words short.

She placed her hand in mine with visible reluctance. Her fingers were cool and slender, and a little jolt of awareness shot up my arm at the contact. I led her to the dance floor and placed my hand at her waist, careful to keep a respectable distance between us. She smelled incredible. Something citrusy and fresh that tempted me to lean in closer.

"I'm surprised you're not already paired up with someone." Her tone implied she couldn't fathom why any woman would voluntarily spend time with me.

"Maybe I was waiting for you." It was audacious, ridiculous, and... maybe a wee bit true.

Her eyebrow arched. Classic Saoirse. One part ice, one part fire, all wrapped in posh vowels sharp enough to draw blood. I'd been flirting with women my whole life, and this one? She parried like it was an Olympic sport.

"Do lines like that actually work on women?"

"Occasionally." I grinned. "Though not the clever ones, apparently."

"At least you recognize your limitations."

I spun her smoothly, bringing her back with perhaps a touch more force than necessary, closing the gap between us momentarily. Her breath caught, and for a split second, something flashed in her eyes that wasn't annoyance—that flicker of heat, quick and gone like a match strike. What would it take to make it burn longer?

My voice dropped lower. "I'm not as limited as you seem to think."

She recovered quickly. "I've yet to see evidence to the contrary."

"You've barely given me the time of day since we met. Hard to demonstrate my many talents."

"Talents?" She huffed a laugh that was dangerously close to a snort. "Like your talent for avoiding responsibility?"

I guided her through a turn. "I'm reliable where it counts."

"I'm sure your definition of 'where it counts' is quite convenient."

The music shifted tempo, and I adjusted our steps. Her body moved in perfect time with mine, despite her obvious discomfort. The friction between us was building—and not simply the argumentative kind. Why was it *this* woman who incited this reaction in me?

"You know—" I kept my tone conversational. "—most people actually like me."

"I'm not most people."

"Clearly."

She stepped back suddenly, breaking our connection.

"Thank you for the dance." She offered the words with the stiff formality of someone completing an unpleasant obligation. "I believe I'll get some air."

Before I could respond, she turned and walked away, her back straight as a board. I watched her go, admiring the view despite myself. Once she'd disappeared out the side door, I shook off whatever spell she'd cast.

Get a grip, Patterson. She wasn't for you. Not then. Not now. Not ever.

But that didn't stop me from wanting to follow her out the door.

I'd been polite, done the thing. Now I deserved another drink.

CHAPTER 2

SAOIRSE

I kicked off my heels the moment I crossed the threshold of my cottage, sighing as my bare feet met the cool wooden floor. Ciara and Alex's wedding had been beautiful, and I'd loved getting to see them take this next step, but five hours in those torture devices was my absolute limit. Give me wellies or other boots any day.

I dropped my clutch on the side table. "Home sweet home."

A clatter from the kitchen announced Isla's presence before she appeared in the doorway, curly dark brown hair piled messily atop her head, wearing my oldest flannel pajama bottoms and a faded university t-shirt. It reminded me so much of our uni days, I almost ached. Between my veterinary practice and her field research on rewilding efforts in the Scottish Highlands, our careers kept us both busy, so these visits were few and far between, and incredibly cherished.

"Look who finally escaped!" She grinned at me and brandished a steaming mug. "Want a cuppa?"

"I'd love one. Put the kettle on while I go change?"

"On it!"

I strode down the hall to my bedroom, where I found Pippin, my polydactyl ginger cat, curled up in his favorite spot amid the mound of colorful pillows.

"Hello, my handsome boy," I cooed, sitting on the edge of the bed. Pippin raised his head, yawned widely, and then stretched his three legs before hopping up to bump his head against my hand. "Did you miss me? Or were you too busy being spoiled by Auntie Isla?"

He purred in response, the rumble vibrating against my palm as I scratched under his chin. I'd found him as a kitten four years ago, his back leg mangled beyond repair after being caught in some kind of trap. The surgery to amputate had been one of my first procedures after finishing vet school.

"You're not even going to ask how the wedding was, are you?" I shook my head, unclasping my necklace. "Typical man."

Pippin blinked his golden eyes lazily and settled back into the pillows.

I untied the bow at the base of my spine, loosening the multitude of laces criss-crossing my back enough to shimmy out of the fancy gown, careful not to snag the delicate fabric. It really was beautiful, and I so seldom had reason to dress up, but I was beyond ready to be out of it. I hung it carefully in my wardrobe before digging through my dresser for my second-oldest pajama bottoms—soft blue flannel with little sheep printed on them—since Isla had already claimed my favorite pair. The tank top I pulled on was well-worn and comfortable. Perfect loungewear.

I twisted my hair up into a messy bun and wiped off my makeup with a cleansing cloth, watching my "done up" self disappear in the mirror. There was something unsettling about seeing that reflection—the polished, proper woman who looked so much like my mother's daughter. Like a ghost of the girl they raised, still trying to crawl her way out through my skin. The girl my grandmother still hoped I'd become, hosting garden parties in Chelsea rather than mucking out stalls in the Scottish countryside.

Pippin bumped against my ankle, begging for cuddles and the inevitable treats that went along with them when I'd been gone for a while. Scooping my boy into my arms like a big ginger baby, I scratched at his belly and carried him into the kitchen, where Isla was popping the top on my insulated tea mug—both because distracted vet was often distracted, and also because Pippin liked to be a stereotypical feline arsehole and knock open beverage containers off tables and counters. We relocated into the lounge and curled up on opposite ends of the sofa.

Isla set my mug within arm's reach. "So, how was the wedding? Did you dazzle them all with your posh accent and killer dress?"

"The dress worked its magic. The accent, as always, marked me as an outsider." No one would know I had half-Scottish roots by hearing me open my mouth. My English mother had done her best to see to that. I took a long sip of tea, savoring the warmth as it slid down my throat. "The wedding was lovely. Absolutely perfect. The castle looked like something out of a fairy tale with all those tiny lights strung everywhere. And Ciara was stunning. That dress was made for her."

"And Alex? Was he a proper mess watching her walk down the aisle?"

"Complete disaster. Tears everywhere. It was adorable." I laughed, tucking my feet under me. "They're so in love it's almost nauseating." And if I let myself think too long about how much I wanted something like that—how far away it felt—I'd drown in it.

Isla raised an eyebrow, her expression knowing. "Do I detect a little pinch of envy?"

I sighed, absently stroking Pippin's fur. "Maybe a little. The single gig is getting a bit old." There. I said it out loud. And maybe that was the first real thing I'd said in weeks. I hadn't meant to admit it, but if I couldn't be honest with my oldest, dearest friend, that would be a sorry state, indeed. "Not that I have *time* for anyone. Not even an uncomplicated shag."

Isla snorted into her tea. "Lass, when was the last time you got laid? Six months ago? A year?"

I grimaced. "Fourteen months, if you must know." God, when had that happened? How had time slipped by so fast without anyone to share the days with? "And if there's one thing I've learned since moving to Glenlaig, it's that there's no such thing as an uncomplicated shag in a village this size."

"Ah, the small-town curse. Sleep with someone and suddenly everyone knows your business."

"Exactly." I nodded emphatically. "And then you run into them at the post office, and the bakery, and the pub... and before you know it, Mrs. MacDougal is asking when the wedding is while you're trying to vaccinate her terrier."

That dragged out another snort laugh. God, I missed that sound.

Isla managed to sober slightly. "Okay, but there has to be someone. What about that flirty mechanic?"

"Toby Byrne? His mum runs the bakery. I'm not doing a bloody thing to imperil my supply of pastries."

"Okay." She considered. "Oh, how about Fergus Hughes? I know how you like a man in a tool belt."

"Darling, you need to get your eyes checked. When we ran into him at the pub last time, it was you he was giving the eye."

Isla brightened. "Was he really?"

"He was."

"Something to remember on my next break from the field. What about Lachlan Reid?"

"The only thing I want with the likes of Lachlan Reid is an advanced reader's copy of his latest tartan noir thriller. Besides, I'm pretty sure he's got something going with Zo Bassey."

Isla arched a brow, interest piqued. "Really?"

"That's the rumor, anyway. There was something about him testing out an escape from handcuffs and getting stuck, and the only number he could manage to hit on his mobile was the pub. Zo was the one who came to his rescue, and they've been spending a fair amount of time together ever since."

Isla waggled her eyebrows. "Handcuffs give an entirely different vibe to his thrillers."

It was my turn to snort into my tea.

Isla finished her tea and set the mug on the coffee table. "What about Alex's other business partner? The not grumpy one."

"Finley Patterson?" My voice came out sharper than intended, and I immediately busied myself with scratching behind Pippin's ears. My sweet boy began to rumble under my hand.

"That's the one." She leaned forward, suddenly interested. "The one who's always out in the wilds on the overnight expeditions?"

I nodded, trying to keep my expression neutral. Neutral was safe. Neutral didn't invite questions I wasn't ready to answer. "What about him?"

"I don't know. He's fit, isn't he? I've seen pictures of the Out of Bounds crew on their website."

"I suppose some might think so," I muttered, feeling heat creep up my neck. Because apparently my hormones had no interest in aligning with my standards.

Isla's eyes narrowed. "Oh, there's a story here. Spill it."

"There's nothing to spill."

"Saoirse MacGregor, I've known you since our first day at uni. I can tell when you're hiding something."

I sighed, knowing she wouldn't let this go. "Fine. He asked me to dance at the wedding."

Isla's eyes widened. "And? How was it?"

It had been horrible. A man like him had no right to have that much sex appeal. He'd looked so damned good in his kilt as a groomsman, and now I couldn't unknow how those muscles felt beneath my palms. And, damn it, he could actually lead. That was such a rarity these days. I was attracted. To *him*, of all people. And I hated that I couldn't fully control my reaction.

"I walked away from him as soon as the song ended."

She looked genuinely confused. "Why?"

"Because he's just... a lot. Always trying to be charming and funny."

"The horror," Isla deadpanned.

"I'm serious."

"Exactly why you could use some charm and funny in your life." She pointed at me with her poppy red painted toes. "You spend all your days being responsible and taking care of everyone else. A bit of lightness wouldn't kill you."

I frowned. "You know I don't trust that kind of thing. And I could never be with someone who doesn't like animals."

That made her pause. "He doesn't like animals?"

"Not long after I moved here, there was this abandoned kitten situation. He refused all responsibility, point blank." I stroked Pippin's fur, remembering how Alex had been the one to take Saffron. He'd carried the little thing around in his pockets until she'd outgrown it. "Anyone who rejects a helpless animal like that..."

Even as I said it, unbidden memories surfaced—Finley giving Parker's service dog, Falkor, a good scruff around the ears. How he played tug with Ciara's maniac Aussie shepherd, Maeve. The way he wrestled with Ewan's massive dog, Havoc. Maybe it wasn't animals in general. Maybe it was specifically cats? Or maybe it was responsibility he was avoiding?

The trouble was, that last one hit a little too close to home. Because what if it wasn't indifference, but fear? And how the hell was I supposed to handle that?

Isla echoed my own thoughts. "So he's not a cat person. That's hardly a crime."

In my lap, Pippin yowled.

"His majesty disagrees." I scratched under his chin. "It doesn't matter. Finley Patterson is not for me. He's all surface charm and jokes. I need substance." *The kind of man who shows up. Who stays. Who doesn't make everything a joke because feeling things is hard.*

The kind of man I'd stopped believing existed.

Isla studied me for a long moment. "You know, for someone you claim to dislike, you've put an awful lot of thought into analyzing him."

"I have not."

"Have too. Your face goes all pinched when you talk about him." She mimicked my expression, scrunching her features with great exaggeration. "Like you're trying very hard to convince yourself."

I laughed, too loud, too fast. Because if I didn't, I might actually start to believe her. Then I tossed a pillow at her head. "You're ridiculous." But something fluttered uncomfortably in my chest. "Let's talk about something else. Tell me how the rewilding project is going."

Her entire face lit up. "Saoirse, it's incredible! We've documented seventeen new species just this month. The pine marten population is thriving, and there's evidence the red squirrels are expanding their territory." She gestured wildly with her mug. "I'm setting up motion-sensor cameras tomorrow to try to capture the beaver activity near the eastern loch. The ecosystem is regenerating faster than our models predicted!"

"That's amazing." I knew seeing the Scottish wilds returned to their natural state was truly her passion project. That she'd been able to get in on the ground floor of a study utilizing huge, remote swaths of the estate at Ardinmuir—where Alex and Ciara had gotten married—had been a point of great pride and excitement.

I drank my tea and listened as she chattered on about the details I didn't entirely follow. But it didn't matter. It was simply good to be here with her. I couldn't remember the last time I'd felt this content.

"It's getting late," Isla announced. "We should probably head to bed."

Realizing I was halfway to dozing already, I couldn't disagree. "You are not wrong." I shifted, dislodging Pippin, and stretched.

Isla scooped up our mugs. "I really appreciate you letting me use your place as a base of operations to reset and do laundry. You have no idea how glorious that shower felt after three weeks of field stations and wet wipes."

"Please, mi casa es su casa. Always. I just wish you could stay longer."

"I should be able to stay at least a few days when I come back from this next excursion. Meanwhile, you'll be getting my check-in texts on the daily."

"I look forward to them." I pulled her in for a hug. "I'm glad you're here."

She gave me a squeeze. "Bit like old times, aye?"

"The best of times."

CHAPTER 3

FINN

The miles disappeared under my tires as I drove further from the Scottish Highlands, each kilometer taking me closer to a responsibility I wasn't sure I deserved, let alone wanted. Charlie's final request echoed in my mind like a persistent ghost. Not that he'd asked it of me while he'd still been living. It had been part of his will, and a request left with his superiors. Honestly, I was surprised they'd agreed to it. But without Charlie, it was possible that Ajax could or would no longer perform his duty. Which would make him a tool that they'd consider broken. Better they retire the dog than push him to function under circumstances that would get him or anyone he was with killed.

I gripped the steering wheel tighter. What the hell had Charlie been thinking? Me, of all people, to take his service dog? The man knew my history. Knew why I avoided attachments like live wires. Because everything I touched either left or broke. Yet here I was, driving to collect a Belgian Malinois who'd lost his handler and probably had more emotional baggage than I did. Which was saying something.

The military kennel came into view—a modest farmhouse with outbuildings that had been converted for training and housing service dogs. My stomach knotted as I pulled into the gravel driveway.

I killed the engine. "This is a mistake."

Before I could talk myself into turning around, a stocky man with a weathered face emerged from the main building. Sergeant Donovan. We'd met at the funeral. Well and truly caught now, I slid out of my 4x4.

"Patterson." He nodded, extending a hand. "Right on time."

"Traffic was light." I shook his hand, scanning the property. "How's he doing?"

Donovan's expression softened. "As well as can be expected. Hasn't eaten much since Charlie passed. Keeps looking for him."

My chest tightened. "Maybe this isn't the best idea. I'm not exactly a dog whisperer."

"Charlie was specific. Said you'd try to back out." Donovan's eyes crinkled. "Also said you were the only one he trusted to understand what Ajax needs."

"I dinna even have a proper garden. I mean, not a fenced one anyway."

"Ajax doesn't need a garden. He needs purpose." Donovan gestured for me to follow. "Charlie said you'd give him that."

I had no idea how he thought I'd manage that for Ajax when I'd barely managed it for myself since my own retirement.

We walked toward one of the kennels, and I caught my first glimpse of Ajax. The Belgian Malinois sat at perfect attention, ears forward, eyes alert. Unlike the other dogs who barked or wagged tails, Ajax remained perfectly still, watching us approach with an intensity that felt uncomfortably familiar.

Like looking in a mirror with four legs and a service record.

I recognized that look. The thousand-yard stare of a soldier who'd seen too much.

"He's been waiting for someone," Donovan said quietly. "Maybe he's been waiting for you."

I couldn't imagine anyone waiting for me. What did I have to offer anyone other than a quick joke to lighten the mood?

I crouched down, keeping my movements slow and deliberate. Ajax's ears twitched forward, his amber eyes studying me with an unnerving intelligence.

"Hey there, lad. Remember me?" I kept my voice low, letting him catch my scent.

For a moment, nothing happened. Then Ajax's tail gave a single, tentative wag. He took a step toward me, nose working overtime as he processed who I was.

"I think he does remember you." Surprise laced Donovan's voice.

"We spent two years in the same hell together." I extended my hand, palm up, letting Ajax make the choice. "This dog saved my life in Kandahar."

Ajax sniffed my hand, then pressed his muzzle against my palm—a gesture so unexpected it nearly broke me. Trust, so freely given. And I didn't know what to do with it. I scratched behind his ears, exactly where Charlie had shown me he liked it.

"Remember that night outside the village? When those bastards had us pinned down?" I spoke directly to Ajax now, not caring if Donovan thought I was mental. "Charlie couldn't see shite through his scope with all that dust. But you knew. You always knew."

God, I'd forgotten what it felt like to speak to someone who listened without judgment.

Ajax's posture changed subtly, as if the memory was registering.

"You broke position before Charlie gave the command. Took off like a bullet." I smiled at the memory. "Charlie was cursing up a storm, but you'd already locked onto that sniper. Gave us the precious seconds we needed to reposition."

Ajax's tail wagged again, stronger this time.

"Charlie always said you were smarter than half the brass giving orders." My throat tightened. "He was right."

I glanced up at Donovan. "We lost two men that night, but it would've been all of us if not for this dog." And that knowledge had sat under my ribcage like a second heartbeat ever since.

Ajax moved closer, pressing his body against my leg in a way that felt like recognition. Not quite trust—that would take time—but acknowledgment of our shared past. Of Charlie.

"I didn't realize you'd served together that long."

I jerked my shoulders in a shrug, as if it would shed the memories circling like smoke. "Charlie, Ajax and I—we saw the worst together. And somehow made it home."

I straightened up, keeping my hand on Ajax's head. The weight of responsibility settled on my shoulders, heavier than any pack I'd carried through Afghan mountains. Time to get down to it. "What's he going to need? I've been around military dogs, but never had to transition one."

Donovan leaned against the kennel fence. "First thing to understand is he's not only grieving Charlie. He's lost his purpose. Military dogs are workers. They need jobs."

"So I should find him work?" I frowned. "I'm a wilderness guide, no' exactly K-9 unit material."

"That tracking ability could be useful in your line, couldn't it?" Donovan raised an eyebrow. "He's trained to follow scent trails through the most inhospitable terrain on earth."

I hadn't considered that. "Suppose he could help locate lost hikers." Maybe that was enough. Purpose didn't have to mean war anymore.

"Exactly. Don't try to make him a pet, Patterson. He's not built for it. Keep his mind engaged." Donovan handed me a worn leather folder. "Charlie's notes on his commands, routines, training exercises."

I flipped through pages of Charlie's cramped handwriting. "Jesus, this is detailed."

"That's why he's alive. Charlie was meticulous." Donovan's voice softened. "Stick to the routine at first. Same feeding times, same exercise schedule. Structure will help him adjust."

Ajax sat perfectly still beside me, as if he understood we were discussing his future.

"What about the nightmares?" I asked quietly. I hadn't meant to say it out loud. But the words were already in the air, bare and cold.

Donovan's eyes met mine. "You have those, too?"

I nodded. They weren't as bad or as often these days, but I had them.

"Then you already know what he needs. Someone who understands. Someone who won't panic when he's having a bad night." Donovan gestured between us. "That's why Charlie chose you."

I swallowed hard. "I'm no' sure I can be what he needs."

"Charlie thought otherwise." Donovan crouched down, giving Ajax a final pat. "He'll have good days and bad days. Some mornings he'll wake up looking for Charlie. Just be patient. And remember, he's reading your emotions constantly. If you're anxious about him, he'll sense it."

Fantastic. One more living soul I had to lie to with a smile and steady hands. "No pressure then," I muttered.

"One last thing." Donovan straightened up. "Don't baby him. He's a soldier. Treat him with respect."

I nodded, understanding completely. Ajax wasn't a pet to be coddled. He was a veteran who needed purpose, structure, and dignity.

I looked down at Ajax. "Ready to come home with me, lad?"

Ajax's ears perked up at my question, his amber eyes locked on mine with an intensity that made my skin prickle. I'd swear he understood. With a soft whine, he rose to his feet, muscles tensed as if waiting for a command.

Donovan uncrossed his arms. "I'd say that's a yes."

I clipped the lead to Ajax's collar, feeling the weight of responsibility settle even heavier. "Come on then, soldier. Let's get you sorted."

Ajax followed at perfect heel position—not too close, not too far—as we walked to my 4x4. I'd spent the previous evening preparing the back seat, installing a proper dog sling that would keep him secure without restricting his movement too much. I'd also picked up a specialized harness that doubled as a seat belt attachment.

"Up you go," I said, opening the rear door.

Ajax hesitated, sniffing at the unfamiliar setup. For a moment, I worried he might refuse, but then he gracefully leaped into the back seat, turning once before settling onto the padded sling.

"Good lad." I secured his harness to the seat belt anchor, checking twice that it gave him enough slack to adjust position but would keep him safe if I had to brake suddenly.

Donovan handed me a duffel bag. "His kit. Food for the first week, his favorite toy—though he rarely plays with it—his service vest, and his medical records."

I nodded, stowing the bag in the back. "Anything else I should know?"

"Only what's in Charlie's notes." Donovan extended his hand. "Good luck, Patterson. He's a special one."

I shook his hand firmly. "I know. I'll do right by him."

"Charlie would appreciate that."

With a last nod, I slid into the driver's seat and started the engine. In the rearview mirror, Ajax lay perfectly still, not relaxed or anxious, his eyes fixed on the back of my head. Waiting for what came next.

"It's you and me now, lad," I said softly as we pulled away from the kennel. "I know I'm not Charlie. I know I never will be. But I promise I'll do my best."

The long drive stretched ahead of us, five hours back to Glenlaig. Five hours to wonder if I'd made the biggest mistake of my life. Five hours to worry about all the ways I might fail this dog who'd already lost too much.

I glanced in the rearview again. Ajax hadn't moved, but his eyes met mine in the mirror.

"Dinna worry," I told him, though the reassurance was probably more for me. "I willnae fuck this up."

Because I couldn't. Not again.

CHAPTER 4

SAOIRSE

ISLA:

:photo of sunrise over the mountains:

ISLA:

Miss you to pieces, but the view does not suck.

SAOIRSE:

Indeed it does not. Miss you, too. Be safe.

I slid my phone into my back pocket, knowing Isla would reply when she could. Probably tomorrow. Mobile signal was nonexistent where she was on the back side of the 12,000 acre Ardinmuir estate, and she didn't abuse the satellite phone, though her messages did become more frequent the closer it got toward the end of her trek, when the lack of other people started to get to her. I had to be content with her daily check-ins. It wasn't the same, but it was something. And I'd learned to survive on scraps when it came to connection. At least until she came back through in a couple of weeks for her next supply run.

It was early yet, and my first appointment wasn't for

another forty-five minutes, so I planned to catch up on some paperwork. Since I'd come up here last year to help Grandda out after he had hip surgery, I'd been on a crusade to drag him into this century with a proper computer system.

He'd fought me every step, but not because he didn't trust the technology. Because he didn't trust letting go. It was an uphill battle. But the vet techs were on my side. Probably because they could barely decipher the chicken scratch Grandda called handwriting.

I was finishing some charting when Emily popped her head around my door, her curly hair escaping from its ponytail as usual.

"Dr. MacGregor? Sorry to interrupt, but we've got a nervous horse outside. Mrs. Campbell just pulled up with Willow. Says she's been off her feed the last couple of days."

"I'll be right there." I grabbed my stethoscope and followed Emily through the clinic.

Aileen Campbell was a worrier, but I couldn't fault her dedication. She'd rescued Willow, a lovely chestnut mare with a white blaze, from a neglect situation last year. The poor thing had understandable trust issues, and we'd seen a lot of her, mostly at the Campbell farm. But last I knew, she'd been making really good progress. I hoped nothing had set her back too far.

Outside, Aileen was already at the back of her van, speaking in hushed tones to her horse.

"Good morning, Aileen." I approached at an angle so Willow could see me coming.

"Oh, Dr. MacGregor, thank you for seeing us. I ken it's probably nothing, but I needed to be sure, aye?"

"Never apologize for being cautious." I smiled, noting how Willow's ears flicked anxiously. "Let's get her settled in the examination stall, shall we?"

Between the three of us, we managed to coax Willow down the ramp and across to our barn. The mare's steps were hesitant, her eyes wide and nostrils flared at the unfamiliar surroundings.

Once in the stall, Willow immediately retreated to the far corner, head high.

"She's barely touched her grain for two days." Aileen wrung her hands. "And she seems, I dinna ken, just not herself. More jumpy than usual."

I nodded, keeping my movements slow and deliberate as I approached the horse. "Hey there, beautiful girl," I murmured, letting her catch my scent. "No need to worry. We're going to have a wee chat, you and I."

Willow's muscles quivered beneath her glossy coat, but she didn't shy away as I gently placed my hand on her neck.

"Has there been any change in her routine lately?" I ran my hands along her sides, feeling for any abnormal heat or swelling.

"Well, the neighbor started some construction last week. Quite noisy. And I did try a new hay supplier."

I nodded, continuing my examination while maintaining a steady stream of gentle nonsense talk to Willow, who was gradually relaxing under my touch. I felt along her flanks and checked her gums. Her temperature was normal, and I didn't feel any obvious blockages or tenderness in her abdomen. The mare had relaxed considerably, her head lowering as I worked.

"That's it. There's a good girl. I suspect it might be the combination of the construction noise and the new hay," I said quietly. "Horses are creatures of habit. Let me check her teeth to rule out any—"

The barn door creaked open, and a booming voice called out, "Where is everyone this morning?"

Willow's head jerked up, eyes wild with panic. I tried to

maintain my hold on her halter, but it was too late. The mare reared, her head catching me square in the face with enough force to send me flying back against the stall wall. Stars exploded across my vision, and for a moment, all I could do was *survive it*. Breathe through the pain, force my body to move. I'd learned how to keep going. I always did.

"Saoirse!" Emily started to rush inside, but I lifted a staying hand.

"I'm all right." I was conscious. That counted. "Stay back. More people in here will rile her up more. Everyone back up."

I dragged myself to my feet, ignoring how the stall seemed to spin. Then I started all over with calming the mare. It took longer than I wanted, and the coffee I'd downed before coming in this morning was threatening to come back up, but eventually she settled enough that I could lay a hand on her shoulder.

"There now. It's all right. You're all right."

The mare quivered in obvious terror, but she didn't shy away.

Drawing on every ounce of stubbornness imbued in me by the Scottish half of my ancestry, I stayed on my feet and finished the exam, because that's what you did.

You didn't sit down. You didn't stop. You didn't let anyone know you were hurting until everything was handled.

By the time I'd finished, I was satisfied there was nothing seriously wrong with Willow. Her vitals were normal, her teeth were fine, and aside from being anxious, she seemed healthy.

"I think it's exactly what we suspected," I told Aileen, keeping my voice low and steady for Willow's benefit. "The combination of construction noise and the change in feed has her unsettled. Horses are incredibly sensitive to routine disruptions."

Relief flooded Aileen's face. "So she's no' ill?"

"No, but she is stressed." I stroked the mare's neck, pleased when she leaned slightly into my touch. "I'd recommend moving her to the paddock furthest from the construction, if possible. And perhaps mix the new hay with what you have left of the old for a gradual transition."

"I can do that." Aileen nodded eagerly.

"And perhaps some chamomile in her water? Just a bit to help take the edge off until she adjusts. We've also got a calming supplement that might help. Nothing strong, just something to ease her anxiety. Emily knows the one. She'll get it for you."

Only after I'd finished giving my recommendations and my instructions to our vet tech did I turn to face my grandfather, who hovered awkwardly in the aisle of the barn. His weathered face was creased with guilt, his bushy eyebrows drawn together in concern.

"What the hell are you doing here? You're not supposed to be in until ten." If there was more bite in my tone than I'd meant, I was blaming it on the pounding in my skull and face that was squarely his fault.

"My bloody hip is good as new. I'm fine, and there's work to be done. No reason for me to have a lie about when I dinnae need one." His face pinched. "Are you all right, lass?"

I was not, in fact, all right. There was absolutely no question that I'd have a black eye by noon, and maybe a concussion to go with it. But I'd be damned if I'd admit it to him. That wasn't what mattered. What mattered was no one else had gotten hurt. What mattered was staying upright, staying useful. What mattered was control.

So I strode past Grandda without a word, prowling back to the clinic and into the staff kitchen. Maybe by the time I'd finished treating my own injuries, I could trust myself to speak.

I filled two plastic bags with ice. Pain spiked bright and hot as I pressed the first against my cheek. Good. A sharp edge to focus on. Easier than the mess of guilt and fear and generational pride waiting outside the kitchen door. The cold sent a fresh wave of pain through my face before beginning its numbing work.

Grandda hovered in the doorway, his weathered hands fidgeting with his cap. "I didnae mean to startle the poor beast."

"I know you didn't." I winced as I adjusted the ice pack. "But that's not the point."

"What is the point, then?" His voice had that defensive edge I'd come to know well over the past year.

I took a slow breath. "The point is that if that had been you instead of me, we wouldn't be having this conversation in the kitchen. We'd be having it in A&E while they set your broken bones."

"Pish. I've been kicked by horses before."

"Yes, when you were forty. Not seventy-three." I grabbed the second ice pack and pressed it to the back of my head where it had connected with the stall wall. "I came up here to help you recover from hip surgery, and I stayed because I'm worried about you."

His chin jutted stubbornly. "I dinnae need a nursemaid."

"No, but this practice needs a vet who won't get killed trying to treat a nervous horse." I met his gaze directly. "I'm not trying to push you out, Grandda. This is your legacy. But I want you to consider that maybe it's time to step back from the more physical parts of the job."

His eyes narrowed. "And do what? Sit about with my thumb up my arse while you do all the work?"

"No. Consult. Mentor. Share all that knowledge you've accumulated over forty-five years instead of risking your neck with skittish horses and bulls with attitude problems." I lowered the ice pack, wincing at how tender my face felt. "I didn't come up here to steal your practice. I came because I care about you."

The fight seemed to drain out of him a bit. He sagged against the doorframe, suddenly looking every one of his seventy-three years.

"I dinnae know how to be anything but what I am, lass."

I knew that feeling too well. Of being built for one thing and terrified of what happens if that identity slips.

"I'm not asking you to be something else. Only... a slightly safer version." I attempted a smile, then regretted it as pain shot through my face. "We MacGregors are too stubborn to go down easy, but we're not actually immortal."

"True enough." He huffed a breath. "I'll... consider it."

"That's all I'm asking." I paused. "And for you to take this morning's appointments so I can deal with this."

"I can do that. And I truly am sorry."

"I know." Lowering the ice packs, I stepped in to give him a hug, pressing a kiss to his grizzled cheek. "Go on. The next appointment should be here any minute."

With a gentle squeeze, he let me go.

I waited until he'd gone to hiss out a long breath. My face *hurt*. Heading down the hall, I stepped into the loo and checked my reflection in the mirror. Christ, I looked like someone who'd gone ten rounds and lost. But what caught me wasn't the bruising—it was the familiar hollowness in my eyes. That flicker of a girl who always had to prove she was strong enough. Tough enough. Unbreakable enough.

The flesh around my eye and the ridge of my cheekbone was swollen and already purpling. It was going to be one hell of a shiner before it was through. Damn it.

If Mum heard about this, she'd have an absolute fit.

It was a bloody good thing she was all the way in London, and I had absolutely no intention of seeing her anytime soon.

Not that I didn't love my mother, but the familial expectations of her side of the family were far easier to tolerate from several hours away. Rothwell-Penningtons were not supposed to spend their days in jeans and wellies with four-legged patients who didn't know the meaning and importance of the name. They were supposed to marry well and smile politely and never raise their voices in public. But I'd never fit that mold, no matter how hard they tried to press me into it. It was a point of particular contention that I'd always been far more a MacGregor, despite my blue-blooded upbringing.

Maybe that was a big part of why I'd always preferred my summers and holidays up here in Scotland, visiting my father's parents. Even after my grandmother had died too soon from cancer, I'd stayed close with Grandda. He understood me in a way no one else in my family actually did. So I'd stick around to make sure he wasn't a danger to himself, whether he liked it or not.

Because that's what MacGregors did. We didn't run. We stayed. We carried what had to be carried, even if no one saw the weight.

CHAPTER 5

FINN

I eased the Land Rover around another bend in the Highland road, glancing in the rearview mirror for what must have been the hundredth time. Ajax sat perfectly still in the back seat, his amber eyes fixed on some distant point beyond the window. The Belgian Malinois hadn't made a sound since we'd left the handler's place. Not a whine, not a bark, not even a sigh. It was like riding with a ghost. One I wasn't sure I deserved to bring home.

"Almost home, mate." The conversation had been one-sided the whole drive, but I couldn't seem to accept straight silence. "You'll like it at Out of Bounds. Plenty of space to run. Good people, too."

The mountains rose around us, bathed in late afternoon light. The sight never got old, no matter how many times I drove this road.

"Callum's a bit of a grumpy bastard, I'll warn you now. Lost his eye in service. But he was with you and Charlie on that last deployment in Helmand, remember?" I tapped my fingers on the steering wheel. "And Ewan owns the pub in the village.

The place makes a decent cottage pie. His sister, Ciara, recently got married to Alex. You'll remember Alex, too, I reckon."

Ajax's ears twitched slightly at the familiar names, the first reaction I'd seen from him in hours.

"That's right. The whole gang's here." Encouraged by that tiny response, I mustered a smile. "They'll be glad to see you. We all miss Charlie something fierce."

My voice caught on the last words. Charlie had been the best of us. Steady, dependable, with a quiet strength that had saved our arses more times than I could count. The image of his grin flashed in my memory, that day he'd introduced us all to his new canine partner.

"He loved you, you know. Always going on about how you were the smartest dog in the regiment."

I slowed as we approached a viewpoint overlooking the valley. On impulse, I pulled over.

"One more quick stop before we get there."

I got out and opened the back door. Ajax looked at me, unmoving.

I snapped on his lead, just in case. "Come on, boy. Let's stretch those legs."

After a moment's hesitation, he stepped carefully from the vehicle, his movements precise and measured. I didn't reach for him or try to pet him. Donovan had warned me to give him space. Instead, I walked slowly to the edge of the viewpoint. Ajax followed, ears pricked, eyes scanning the terrain for threats.

"At ease, soldier," I murmured. That wasn't the proper command. I'd have to go through the lengthy list the handler had given me. But I hoped Ajax would get the gist.

The valley sprawled below us, a patchwork of greens and

purples fading into the blue-gray mountains beyond. The breeze carried the scent of heather and pine, clean and sharp.

I stayed quiet, standing with my hands in my pockets, trying to breathe in enough of this place to keep me standing upright. The Highlands had always known how to hold my broken pieces better than I could.

After a minute, Ajax's rigid posture softened. His nose twitched, sampling the unfamiliar scents. When a red deer appeared at the edge of the distant treeline, his focus locked onto it with laser precision. No sign of aggression, simply the tracker in him awakening.

I knew that feeling. The way nature pulled you back into your body when your mind was spinning off into dark places. How the mountains had their own way of putting things in perspective.

I nodded toward the jagged peaks. "Charlie and I used to climb those ridges. Whenever we got leave. Said it helped clear his head after deployment."

Ajax's ears flicked back at the sound of Charlie's name, then forward again.

"It helped me, too."

The deer moved on, disappearing into the trees. Ajax watched it go, then surprised me by sitting down properly, his weight settling as if he'd decided this spot was acceptable—for now. Maybe that was all either of us needed. Somewhere to sit with our ghosts without having to explain them.

We stayed like that for ten minutes. Not friends yet, just two broken pieces of Charlie's life, finding some common ground in the wild open space.

When the wind picked up and clouds started gathering over the peaks, I clicked my tongue. "Time to go, boy."

This time, Ajax jumped smoothly into the back seat without hesitation. Progress.

The last twenty miles to Glenlaig wound through increasingly familiar territory. The village appeared around the final bend, nestled between mountains and loch, stone cottages with smoke curling from chimneys.

"Home." I said it more to myself than to Ajax. It still felt like a borrowed word. Like something I'd been given without earning.

My cottage sat on the edge of the village, a sturdy stone building with a small garden out back that ran right up to the forest edge. Not much, but it was mine. A place to land after years of having nowhere permanent.

And as I pulled into the drive, I spotted a couple of familiar vehicles parked by the kerb.

I cut the engine and eased out of the Land Rover, stretching my back after the long drive. Callum leaned against his 4x4, arms crossed, while Ewan pushed himself away from the fence he'd been perched on.

"What's this then?" I jerked a head at the pair of them. "Welcoming committee?"

Callum shrugged, his one good eye fixed on the backseat of my 4x4, where Ajax sat peering out the window. "Figured we'd come pay our respects."

"And to welcome Ajax home," Ewan added.

Something caught in my chest at that. These lads never ceased to surprise me. Even after all we'd bled and buried and bottled up together, they still showed up. No explanations or request needed. Which was sometimes the only thing that mattered.

"Well then, let's not keep him waiting." I moved to the back door and opened it slowly. "Ajax, come. Meet some old friends."

The Malinois hesitated only briefly before jumping down

with minimal expenditure of energy. His ears perked forward as he took in Callum and Ewan, nostrils flaring.

Callum crouched down and held out his hand, palm down. "Remember me, you daft mutt? Helmand Province. You found that IED before I stepped on it."

Ajax's tail gave a single, tentative wag.

"That's right." Callum's voice was gentler than I'd heard in years. Well, at least as applied to anyone other than Parker. "Good lad."

Ewan stepped forward next, keeping his movements slow and deliberate. "Hey there, Ajax. Charlie showed me all your tricks that time in Cyprus."

The dog's posture changed subtly—still alert, but something in him seemed to relax. He sniffed Ewan's outstretched hand, then looked back at me as if seeking permission.

"It's alright. They're pack." Again, probably not the right order, but we'd sort it out.

Smart lad that he was, Ajax got the idea, moving forward to press his nose against Callum's knee. Not exactly exuberant, but recognition. Connection.

"There he is." The ghost of a smile crossed Callum's face. I still hadn't gotten used to how readily he used it since Parker came into his life. "Still in there somewhere."

I felt something unclench in my chest. Maybe this hadn't been such a mad idea after all.

Callum moved toward his Land Rover. "We got him a few things."

I watched as he opened the back hatch, revealing several bags and packages. My eyebrows shot up as he and Ewan began unloading what looked like half a pet shop. Ajax observed the proceedings with cautious interest.

"Christ, did you leave anything for other dogs in Scotland?"

Callum pulled out a large, plush dog bed in forest green.

"This one's for the office. So he can be comfortable while you're working."

In the wake of this matter-of-fact announcement, I stared at him, momentarily speechless. My battle-hardened friend had been turned into an utter marshmallow by the power of love. Or, more specifically, the power of Parker Lawrence. And maybe I envied him a little. Not the softness—but the safety it took to allow it.

Ewan hefted another small bag. "These are a couple dozen of the organic dog treats from the bakery. Isobel's got Havoc addicted to them."

"And this is from Alex." Callum handed me a package wrapped in brown paper.

I opened the paper to find a new collar embroidered with Ajax's name. My contact information was etched on a little metal plate attached to one side. Genuinely touched, I shook my head. Trust Alex to make something practical feel like a goddamn heirloom. "He's on his bloody honeymoon."

"Ciara helped him sort it before they left." Ewan's lips quirked. "We were given strict instructions."

Callum watched Ajax with the assessing gaze he had never quite lost after leaving the service. "The girls all wanted to come, but we thought too many new people might overwhelm him."

I nodded, swallowing the unexpected lump in my throat. My mates had shown up. Not only shown up—they'd seen what was needed.

Not for me. For Ajax. For Charlie.

And somehow, in the middle of it, I didn't feel like I was drowning anymore.

Ajax had ventured closer to investigate a rope toy Ewan was holding. Not grabbing it yet, but interested. Progress.

"Thanks, lads." I meant it more than they probably knew. "Really."

Sucking in a steadying breath, I jerked my head toward the house. "You lot want to come in for a beer?"

Ewan picked up another bag. "Wouldn't say no."

I pushed open the front door and let Ajax step inside first. The Malinois paused on the threshold, nose working overtime as he took in his new surroundings.

"Go on, have a look around." I unclipped his lead. "Make yourself at home."

Ajax moved cautiously into the cottage, his nails clicking against the hardwood floors. His ears swiveled in different directions as he absorbed every sound and scent.

Callum and Ewan followed behind me, arms laden with their haul of dog supplies. I directed them to set everything in the corner of the lounge for now.

My cottage wasn't much to look at. Only the essentials. A worn leather sofa faced a small fireplace, flanked by a couple of mismatched armchairs. I hadn't bothered with a telly, as I rarely sat still long enough to watch one. Instead, I had a bookshelf with a handful of paperbacks and a decent collection of maps. The coffee table was actually an old wooden crate I'd found and sanded down.

What the place lacked in furniture, it made up for in gear. My climbing equipment hung neatly on wall hooks—ropes, carabiners, harnesses. A pair of well-worn hiking boots sat by the door next to my trail runners. My mountain bike was propped in the corner, and fishing tackle occupied a basket near the back door.

Ajax seemed particularly interested in my backpack, which probably carried the scents of every hill and glen I'd traversed in the past month.

I headed for the kitchen and snagged three bottles of lager

from the fridge. Back in the lounge, I passed them around, and we settled onto the mismatched furniture, the silence comfortable as we watched Ajax continue his methodical exploration.

"He seems to be settling in all right," Ewan observed.

Callum nodded. "Give him time. Took Falkor a few days to get used to the office."

Remembering back, I thought it more likely that it had taken Callum a few days to get used to the dog when Parker had shown up with him, unannounced.

I twisted the cap off my beer. "Donovan said he hasn't been himself since Charlie..."

The words trailed off. Ajax had circled back to us and now sat at attention, watching our little gathering with those intelligent eyes.

"Well, then." I raised my bottle. "To Charlie. The best of us. May we do right by his memory—and his dog."

"To Charlie," my friends echoed.

At the sound of his former handler's name, Ajax's ears pricked forward. His soft whine was the first voluntary sound I'd heard from him all day. He padded over to sit directly at my feet.

I reached down slowly and rested my hand on his head. He didn't pull away.

It might not have been much, but it was a start.

And after the past few years, I'd take a start over silence every damn time.

CHAPTER 6

SAOIRSE

I tried not to wince as Mrs. Dunne's eyes widened at the sight of my face.

"Good heavens, Dr. MacGregor! What happened to you?"

"A minor disagreement with a horse." I forced a smile that pulled painfully at my swollen cheek. "Nothing serious."

The elderly woman clutched her tabby cat carrier tighter. "That looks quite serious to me, dearie."

"Occupational hazard." I reached for the carrier. "Now, what seems to be troubling Marmalade today?"

As Mrs. Dunne described her cat's symptoms, I caught my reflection in the metal cabinet behind her. Christ. The bruising had deepened overnight into a spectacular purple-black crescent that spread from my cheekbone to my eyebrow. No wonder everyone kept staring.

Three more appointments followed Marmalade's, each beginning with shocked expressions and concerned inquiries about my face. By midday, I'd perfected my explanation down to a brief, "Spooked horse, wrong place, wrong time," delivered with a professional smile that didn't reach my eyes.

In the break room, I pressed a cold compress to my face and checked my phone. Three missed calls from Mother. Brilliant. Ignoring those, I flipped to my texts to find one from Isla checking in for the day.

ISLA:

Cripes, I hope the other guy looks worse.

I'd sent her a selfie of my face this morning.

SAOIRSE:

I'm all set for my cosplay as a prizefighter. And the horse is okay. Love you. Stay safe.

Across the room, Jenny, another of our vet techs, popped her lunch in the microwave. "You really should have put something on that."

"And have people think I'm covering up domestic violence? No thank you." I winced as the cold hit a particularly tender spot. "Besides, makeup on an open wound is asking for infection." Not that the scrape that went along with the bruise was bad. Not in the grand scheme of the injury. But still.

"Fair point. Mr. MacDougal has arrived with his new puppy for vaccinations. And there've been four more walk-ins this morning."

I sighed. "Thank God Grandda's here, even if he is the reason I look like this."

"He seems to be enjoying himself," Jenny offered.

"That's what worries me." I tossed the compress into the sink. "He'll never retire if he thinks he's still indispensable."

Emily knocked on the doorjamb. "New patient in three."

I squared my shoulders and prepared for another round of explaining my black eye to startled clients.

I glanced at the chart in my hand as I walked toward exam room three. Belgian Malinois, eight years old. Uncommon breed for our practice. The working dogs we saw were usually herding or flock guarding varieties.

"Let's see what we've got here," I murmured to myself, pushing open the door.

The dog lay on the floor, alert but subdued. His rich brown coat looked healthy enough, but there was a heaviness in his posture. A lack of the usual Malinois energy. His watchful, intelligent eyes tracked my movement as I entered.

I immediately lowered into a crouch beside him, my voice softening automatically. "And who do we have here today?" I extended my hand, palm down, letting him catch my scent. "Hello, handsome."

The dog's nose twitched as he sniffed my fingers, then he gave them a gentle lick. I got no tail wag, but no growl either. I'd take the middle of the road tolerance of my presence to the alternative any day. I ran my hand gently along his head, noting the barest hint of gray around his muzzle.

When I finally looked up to address the owner, the words died in my throat. Finley Patterson stood at attention, arms crossed over his chest, watching our interaction with an unreadable expression.

My professional demeanor snapped back into place like armor as I straightened. My bruised face throbbed as I tensed my jaw. "Finley. I didn't realize you were Ajax's owner."

But he didn't say a word. Before I could even process, he'd shifted from that odd, military stillness to looming intensity. One moment he'd been standing across the room, and the next he was right in front of me, close enough that I could smell the faint evergreen scent of his soap and feel the heat radiating from his body.

His hand hovered near my face, not quite touching the bruise but close enough that I could feel the warmth of his skin. His hazel eyes had darkened to the color of storm clouds, his jaw clenched so tight I could see a muscle jumping beneath the stubble.

"Who do I need to put in a body bag?"

The words hit like a slap—not because I was afraid, but because I wasn't. Because some primitive part of me believed him. He looked like he'd already started the mental list, and the only thing stopping him was the lack of a confirmed name.

The protective rage in his eyes didn't match our dynamic at all. We weren't friends. We weren't anything. But in that moment, Finley Patterson stood there like a man willing to go to war for me. And I didn't know what to do with that.

I'd read the books. The over-the-top touch-her-and-die nonsense that always made me roll my eyes. But standing there, face-to-face with it in real life, I understood why readers swooned. Because when he said it, my heart pounded like I'd just sprinted uphill, and my body betrayed me with a heat I had no business feeling.

This close, I could see the flecks of gold in his eyes, the slight scar above his left eyebrow, the fullness of his lower lip. My gaze dropped to his mouth, then jerked back up to his eyes.

God help me, I wanted him to kiss me. To find out if those surprisingly sensual lips were as talented as I imagined. To see what all that intensity would be like directed toward something a lot more satisfying than a beating.

The exam room suddenly felt too small, too warm.

I should have been offended by his presumption, irritated by his caveman response. Instead, I found myself fighting the inexplicable urge to close the distance between us.

I swallowed hard, trying to regain my composure while my body betrayed me with a rush of attraction so intense it left me dizzy. This was Finley Patterson. The man who couldn't be bothered with a helpless kitten. The eternal joker who never took anything seriously. The man who drove me absolutely mad.

And yet, in this moment, with his eyes blazing and his entire body coiled with protective fury on my behalf, I couldn't remember why I disliked him so much.

I managed to find my voice, stepping back to create some distance. "I appreciate the defense, but it's really not necessary to hurt the horse because she got scared."

My voice came out even, but inside I was spiraling. The man had cracked open something I didn't know I'd locked down. And now he was pretending like it hadn't happened.

"A horse did this?" Finn's expression shifted from murderous to bewildered.

My back went up immediately. "I'm a large animal vet. They are occasionally unpredictable. I get the odd injury."

I watched as Finn visibly reeled himself in, his shoulders dropping incrementally, his breathing evening out. It seemed to take him a long time to regain his composure, as though he were physically wrestling his rage back into some internal cage. The intensity of his reaction both unnerved and fascinated me.

When he finally managed to speak again, his voice was carefully controlled. "Arnica cream will help with the swelling and the pain."

Of course, he would know what would help with bruises. Royal Marines probably collected injuries like I collected veterinary journals.

"Um. Thank you." I smoothed down my lab coat, determined to get this interaction back on a professional keel. "Why don't you tell me about this fellow here?"

I gestured toward Ajax, grateful for the excuse to look away from Finn's face. The dog had watched our entire exchange with those dark eyes, his head tilted slightly as though trying to understand the sudden tension in the room.

Finn's expression softened as he looked at the Malinois. "This is Ajax. He was my friend Charlie's service dog. Military working dog, specifically. Charlie died three weeks ago."

The matter-of-fact way he said it didn't hide the undercurrent of raw grief, and my chest tightened in sympathy. Whatever else Finley was, I recognized legitimate pain. I knelt beside Ajax again, running my hands gently over his head.

"I'm sorry for your loss." I lifted my gaze back to the man. "Both of you."

With uncharacteristic sobriety, Finn nodded. "Thank you."

I cleared my throat and focused on Ajax, who sat perfectly still under my examination. His coat was healthy, eyes clear, but there was a stillness to him that spoke of more than physical ailments.

"So, he was a military working dog?" I gently checked his teeth. "What was his specialty?"

"Tracking, mostly." Finn crouched beside us, his voice softening when he addressed the dog. "He and Charlie were deployed together for six years. They were inseparable."

The tenderness in his tone caught me off guard. This wasn't the flippant charmer from the wedding dance floor. This was someone else entirely.

"Has he been eating properly?" I ran my hands along Ajax's ribs, noting he was slightly underweight but not dangerously so.

"I got him home yesterday. The handler who's had him said he's not eaten as much as normal since—" He cut himself off, swallowed, and tried again. "Since it happened. I've got the food that was sent home with him. Didnae think I was supposed to change things too quickly."

I nodded, continuing my exam. "Depression affects dogs much like it does humans. Loss of appetite, lethargy, withdrawal. He's grieving."

"That's why I brought him in." Finn's eyes followed my hands as I checked Ajax's joints. "I know he needs time to adjust, but I wanted to make sure there wasn't something else wrong."

The earnestness in his tone made something shift inside me. This wasn't someone fulfilling an obligation or carrying a burden he resented. This was genuine concern.

"You really care about him." The words slipped out before I could stop them.

Finn's eyes met mine, no trace of his usual mischief. "Charlie was family. Which makes Ajax family too. Besides, I wouldn't be here if not for this animal. He saved my life several times over. It seems only fair I do the same."

Well. That was unexpected. I felt my walls crumbling slightly. The man who'd refused a helpless kitten was now taking on responsibility for a grieving military dog with determination and care. It didn't fit my neat mental categorization of Finley Patterson.

I gave Ajax a gentle scratch behind the ears. "He's physically healthy. The weight loss isn't critical yet, but we should monitor it. The rest is going to take time and patience."

Finn nodded, relief evident in the slight loosening of his shoulders. "I was also hoping you might have suggestions for helping him transition from military to civilian life. He's been through enough. I dinna want to fuck things up any worse than they already are."

Would wonders never cease? Those walls crumbled a little bit more. "I can see you're committed to helping him through this, so let's talk about your options."

CHAPTER 7

FINN

"You ready for this, lad?" I swiveled in the driver's seat to look back at Ajax in the back.

At the word "ready," he rose to his feet, ears at attention, body braced for action.

Not quite what I'd been going for. But then, he and I both had trouble separating readiness from tension. We were built to brace. There'd been a lot of this kind of thing over the past three days as we'd begun getting used to each other. I supposed the signs of vigilance were better than the depression, but as I'd been warned, he didn't know how to simply... dog. It would take a long time to teach him that he didn't have to be on alert all the time. But I knew plenty about that. We were two creatures wired for watchfulness, still waiting for the next command that wouldn't come.

I slid out of the 4x4 and opened the door to the backseat. "Come on, then."

Ajax leapt neatly down and immediately took up a heel position. I clipped on his lead. Today was his first day at the office. I had the new bed in the boot, but I didn't want to bring it inside until I saw how he did with the rest of the staff and with Parker's mobility assistance dog, Falkor, who'd effectively become the Out of Bounds mascot. I hadn't yet seen Ajax around other civilian dogs. I didn't think he'd be aggressive, but the concept of a canine friend wasn't exactly part of his life experience up to this point.

I considered taking him around the outside of the building to sniff everything, but that smacked too much of patrol. I wanted him to learn that this was another safe place for him. So I let us in the back door. It was early yet, and I didn't expect anyone here but Parker and Imogen Ross, one of our recent hires. Callum had done me a solid and taken the overnight guided hike that had originally been on my schedule. According to the electronic calendar that Parker maintained religiously, Kieran Stevenson, our other new hire, was out with a group of intermediate kayakers, and Parker's bodyguard, Jade Washington, should already have left with the mountain biking expedition booked for the morning. Parker's need for an active bodyguard had been more or less eliminated last year, but we still made sure that one of us was around as much as possible, just in case.

The empty equipment bays told me what I needed to know, even if I hadn't heard the two quiet female voices from the front office. It was only the three of us.

Ajax tensed beside me, his posture shifting from alert to rigid, like his spine had turned to steel. His ears flicked forward, then back, processing the unfamiliar sounds and smells of the office. I could feel the tension in the lead. Not aggression, but the heightened awareness of a dog trained to assess threats in new environments.

"Easy, mate." I kept my voice calm and steady. "The office. Safe place."

The click of nails on hardwood announced the white blur

that bounded down the hallway, tail wagging like a metronome gone haywire. Falkor, Parker's Great Pyrenees, all sunshine and enthusiasm as always.

Ajax went completely still beside me, muscles coiled tight. I kept the lead loose but stayed ready.

"Falkor! Come back here!" Parker's Southern drawl echoed from down the hall.

Falkor skidded to a halt about ten feet away, head tilted in confusion. His tail kept wagging, but slower now, as he looked between Ajax and me. The poor lad seemed genuinely perplexed. His entire job description was essentially "be friendly to everyone," and here was a new someone he wasn't immediately allowed to greet.

Parker appeared around the corner. "Sorry, Finn. I heard you come in and was trying to intercept him before he rolled out the welcome wagon." She paused, taking in Ajax's stiff posture. "Oh, this must be Ajax." She smiled, and I saw her hands twitch before curling in on themselves. Parker holding back her innate desire to get down and love on the newest arrival with fur. She wanted to reach out. Of course she did. She just had to wait.

"Aye. First day. Thought we'd start with a short visit, see how he does."

Ajax hadn't moved, but I noticed his ears had perked up at Parker's voice. He was tracking everything—Falkor's movements, Parker's approach, the sounds from outside—but not reacting. For now, he was taking his cues from me.

"Falkor, stay with me." At Parker's soft command, the polar bear masquerading as a dog reluctantly backed up to her side, though his eyes never left Ajax. He let out a small, confused whine that seemed to say, "But I'm supposed to say hello to everyone."

"Good lad." I gave Ajax a gentle scratch behind the ears. "That's Parker and Falkor. They're friends."

Imogen peeked down the hall. "Oh, he's gorgeous, Finn. How do you want us to do this?"

"Let's take it slow." I gave Ajax's lead a gentle tug to keep him close. "He's still learning that not everything's a threat."

Parker nodded, keeping her distance. "Maybe let's do this out front, in the lobby, where he's less likely to feel cornered."

"Good idea. Ajax, heel." I moved forward slowly, and he matched my pace perfectly, staying precisely at my left side. His eyes never left Falkor, but his posture had relaxed slightly from battle-ready to merely vigilant as we moved into the lobby.

"Parker, if you dinna mind, have Falkor sit and stay. Let Ajax approach on his terms."

"Of course." She guided Falkor into a sitting position, though the big white fluffball was practically vibrating with the effort of containing his excitement.

I crouched beside Ajax. "Easy, lad. Friends."

His ears twitched at the word "friends," a concept Charlie had surely taught him, though probably in a different context. I let the lead slacken further, giving him enough freedom to move if he chose.

After a moment's hesitation, Ajax took a tentative step forward, then another. I moved with him, keeping my hand near his collar, just in case. When we were about three feet from Parker and Falkor, he paused again, nostrils flaring as he took in their scents.

Falkor whined softly, tail thumping against the floor.

"Good boy, Ajax," I murmured. "Good lad."

To my surprise, Ajax lowered his head slightly and continued forward until he was nose to nose with Falkor. The two dogs sniffed each other carefully. Then Falkor, unable to contain himself any longer, gave Ajax's muzzle a quick, friendly lick.

Ajax startled, backing up a step, but didn't growl or show any aggression. He looked confused, as if he'd never encountered such enthusiastic friendliness before and didn't know how to receive it. Aye. I knew that look, too.

Parker laughed softly. "That's Falkor's way of saying hi. He flunked service dog school for being too friendly."

"He's doing brilliantly." Pride surged through me, and I gave Ajax's ears a careful scratch. "Better than I expected, honestly."

Imogen had been watching from a respectful distance. "Can I say hello, too?"

I nodded. "Let him come to you. Dinna reach over his head."

Imogen approached slowly, hand extended low, palm up. "Hey there, handsome." She crouched down to Ajax's level without making direct eye contact. "Aren't you a beautiful boy?"

Ajax's ears twitched forward with interest. He glanced up at me, as if asking permission. Looking for reassurance that he was safe doing something unfamiliar. Trust—earned in inches.

"It's alright," I assured him. "She's one of our guides. Friend."

He took a tentative step toward Imogen, stretching his neck to sniff her outstretched hand. After a moment's consideration, he allowed her to gently stroke under his chin. The tension in his shoulders eased slightly.

"There you go," Imogen murmured. "Not so scary, is it?"

I felt a surprising lump in my throat watching him. This was the most relaxed I'd seen him since bringing him home. Charlie would be proud. And if I didn't choke on the lump in my throat, it'd be a bloody miracle.

"I've got something for him." Parker moved slowly to a drawer in the nearby desk. She pulled out one of the fancy dog biscuits she kept for Falkor. "May I?"

"Aye, go ahead." I was entirely in favor of anything that got him to eat.

Parker knelt down, holding the treat flat on her palm. "Ajax, would you like a biscuit?"

His ears perked up at the word "biscuit." Oh, he knew that word. He looked to me again for confirmation.

I gave him a gentle nudge. "Go on, then."

It felt like I was giving him permission to hope for something small and sweet. I wasn't sure I knew how to do that for myself.

Ajax stepped forward and delicately took the treat from Parker's hand, retreating a step to eat it. His tail gave a single, hesitant wag.

"There's a good lad."

Parker beamed. "Sometimes the way to a man's heart really is through his stomach."

Falkor, not wanting to be left out, nudged Parker's hand hopefully.

"You already had two this morning." There was absolutely no heat to her scolding as she reached for another biscuit, anyway.

I watched as Ajax finished his treat, looking marginally more at ease in his new surroundings. He couldn't be called relaxed, but the rigid vigilance had softened to cautious observation.

It was a start.

I retrieved the big fluffy bed and bag of supplies from the boot of my car, Ajax trotting faithfully at my heel. He'd done better than I'd expected with the initial introductions. It was a promising start.

"Come on, lad. Let's get you settled."

My office was little more than a glorified storage closet with a desk wedged in. When we'd renovated this place, it had been more important to us to have plenty of storage for gear, as we still spent most of our time on expeditions. But it had a perfect corner where Ajax could observe everything without feeling exposed.

I tucked in the plush bed Callum had brought over. "What do you think?"

Ajax circled the bed three times before finally settling with a sigh I hoped was some shade of contentment. He rested his chin on his paws, dark eyes watching me intently as I booted up my laptop.

"Make yourself comfortable. I've got reports to catch up on."

I'd barely started reviewing the risk assessments for next month's expeditions when a soft knock interrupted. Parker peeked around the door, her smile brightening when she saw Ajax curled up.

"He looks like he's settling in."

"Aye, better than expected." I leaned back in my chair. "What's up?"

"I wanted to let you know Kieran's group will be back early. The wind picked up on the loch." She handed me a folder. "And here's the updated itinerary for the corporate retreat next week."

"Thanks." I flipped through the papers, intending to ask about the T-shirt order she'd been putting together last week. But what came out instead was, "Have you seen Saoirse since the wedding?"

I told myself it was a casual request for information. Not the thing I'd been pretending I wasn't wondering since I saw her bruised face and felt that split-second, blood-red urge to destroy whoever had hurt her.

Parker's eyebrows shot up, a smile spreading across her face. "Why, Finley Patterson. Are you asking about the lovely Dr. MacGregor? I couldn't help but notice the sparks you two were throwing off at the reception."

I had to nip this in the bud. "She despises me, as you well know. I was wondering how she's healing up. Call it professional curiosity."

But it hadn't been professional curiosity that had driven me to the brink of violence in 0.2 seconds at the sight of her injured face. It hadn't been professional curiosity that had made her almost the exclusive topic of my thoughts when they weren't tuned entirely to my new dog.

"Mmhmm." Parker leaned against the doorframe, not even trying to hide her amusement. "That black eye was ferocious, wasn't it? I think it's in the worse before better phase, but starting to fade."

"Good to hear."

She was improving. That was what I'd needed to hear. Now I'd be able to let all those obsessive thoughts go.

"Just checking." I turned back to my computer, hoping to end the conversation before Parker could dig deeper.

No such luck.

"She doesn't despise you, you know."

I couldn't stop myself from going brows up. "Could have fooled me."

"Oh, you definitely somehow step all over some nerve with her. But I kinda don't think it's personal to you. I think you confuse her."

I leaned back in my chair. "I confuse *her?* I'm a simple man. What's there to be confused about?"

Parker snorted. "Oh, please. You want people to think

you're simple. That you're this happy-go-lucky, flirty, fun, charming guy. But that's all an act so they don't look closer."

The observation struck way closer to home than I liked.

I put on a bland face. "I think you're complicating the rest of us because you fell in love with Mr. Enigma."

"Oh, of the two of you, Callum *is* the simple one. He was never able to hide his pain. You're the one who has everyone fooled. Except me."

That was the thing about Parker. She didn't stab. She scalpeled. Quiet. Precise. And always straight to the truth.

She tapped the side of her nose. "Anyway, Saoirse doesn't like the mask. But I think she'd actually really dig what you hide underneath. My two cents, for whatever that's worth."

With one last wink, she disappeared back to her command center in the lobby, leaving me staring at the space where she'd been standing.

At last, I looked over at Ajax, who blinked at me in a "Well, what are you gonna do with all that?" kind of way.

He was getting very good at asking the questions I didn't want to answer.

"Not a bloody thing," I told him, and turned back to my paperwork.

CHAPTER 8

SAOIRSE

I tucked my hair behind my ear and checked my reflection in the pub's bathroom mirror one last time. The concealer was doing its job. I could barely see the yellowing edges of the bruise—except when I looked too long. Then it pulsed like a warning light. Or a memory.

I tugged my hair a little further forward and tried to stop checking. After a week of explaining to every client, delivery person, and random villager exactly how I'd gotten my black eye, I was thoroughly sick of the whole affair.

"Saoirse! There you are!" Ciara pounced on me as I emerged from the bathroom. She looked radiant, her skin glowing with a light tan from her Greek honeymoon.

I accepted her enthusiastic hug. "Look who's back from paradise and looking fabulous."

"God, I missed everyone." She looped her arm through mine and led me outside to the patio where the others were already gathered, their various canines in tow.

Falkor sat beside Parker's chair, his feather duster of a tail cleaning the cobblestones behind him as he spotted me. Walter,

Skye's sheepadoodle gave a cheerful bark from where he sprawled behind her chair. Maeve immediately lunged for Ciara with a happy bark, dragging the chair her leash was attached to at least two feet.

I pointed at the Australian shepherd. "You. Sit."

She plopped her bum down and panted up at me, eyes bright.

"Good girl." I offered up one of the training treats I kept in my pocket.

"Bribery will get you everywhere," Ciara sang.

"So will consistency." I crouched down to give Falkor a rub and accepted his lick hello. "Here's a good lad."

"He's the best, as always," Parker announced.

"Naturally." I kissed his nose before turning to lavish some attention on Walter.

"Wine?" Skye asked.

"Yes. God, please." I dropped into a chair beside Pippa and gave her a side hug.

Jade leaned back in her seat next to Parker. "How's the eye?"

I reached for the glass Skye offered me. "Better, and thankfully covered. I've had quite enough of wasting time explaining to everyone why all their outlandish theories of how I got it are entirely wrong."

Parker winced. "Got some doozies, huh?"

"The number of alleged secret abusive affairs people assume I'm having makes me sound far more exciting than I actually am."

"People and their gossip." Skye rolled her eyes. "Walter knocked me flat on my ass last week chasing a squirrel, and I swear Jason had to give three separate explanations at the bakery."

Pippa raised her own glass. "To better stories, then. Ciara, tell us everything about Greece."

"I'll drink to that." I clinked my glass to hers.

As Ciara launched into tales of crystal-clear waters and ancient ruins, I found my mind drifting. Isla hadn't checked in yesterday.

Not a red flag. Not yet. But it fluttered uneasily in my chest all the same.

She always checked in. Even with a satellite phone, there were places so remote she couldn't get enough of a signal to get through. But when that happened, she made sure to hike to a previous location she *knew* she could get signal to send a brief check-in, even if only to say she couldn't check in properly. Which meant I should have heard something from her today. But we were well on into the dinner hour, and I hadn't heard a word. She still had a few hours of daylight this time of year, but the lack of contact left me feeling uneasy.

Her silence was starting to feel loud.

"—and Ajax is finally starting to adjust to being around Falkor."

At the mention of Ajax, I tuned back into the conversation, focusing on Parker. "How is Ajax doing?" I'd thought of him often in the past few days.

"A little better each day, I think. Finn's been bringing him to the office, and Falkor has decided they're best friends now." Parker reached down to scratch the pup in question behind the ears. "Poor Ajax doesn't quite know what to do with all that enthusiasm. He just sits there looking confused while Falkor tries to get him to play."

"But no signs of aggression?" I leaned forward, genuinely concerned. "Military dogs can sometimes struggle with the transition." I hated the idea that Parker's friendly floof might get bitten, or worse, for his trouble.

Parker shook her head. "None at all. He's more... reserved?

Like he's waiting for commands or something. But Falkor's persistence seems to be good for him."

"Pretty sure Falkor can wear down anybody. Has Ajax been eating better?" His lack of appetite had been a concern during our exam.

Ciara picked up her pint. "Alex and I got him some puzzle feeders that Finn says he seems to be enjoying."

"And for better or worse, Isobel and I have got him hooked on the fancy dog treats I buy for Falkor." Parker shrugged with a grin. "Sorry. Not sorry. Good boys deserve cookies."

Falkor woofed in agreement, and we all laughed. He stared at his mum in clear expectation.

Parker scruffed his ears. "You'll have to wait until we get home, pal. I don't have any more in my purse."

With a beleaguered sigh, he settled back on the ground, resting his head on his paws.

Pippa snickered. "It's hard to be a dog."

"So hard," Skye agreed. "I think I'd like to be this one when I retire."

I couldn't resist dragging the conversation back to Ajax. "How is Ajax doing when Finn has to leave him for work?"

"Well, he's only *just* tried it yesterday." Jade stabbed a fork into one of the haggis balls she'd developed a fondness for since she'd moved to Glenlaig. "The rest of us have been trading off, picking up some of the excursions he'd usually do, so he can ease Ajax in more slowly."

Parker picked a loaded chip out of the basket in the center of the table. "Yeah, he's only done a couple of short trips. Two hours, max. Ajax stayed at the office with me and Falkor, and we kept him in a quiet room in the back so he didn't get over-whelmed by any clients."

"How did that go?" This poor dog would no doubt have some abandonment issues.

"Pretty well, I'd say. Falkor stayed with him the whole time, and Ajax was less anxious today than yesterday. It's a start."

Leave it to Falkor to be the emotional support animal for Ajax, too.

I snagged a chip myself. "That all sounds positive. Poor boy has had so much to adjust to."

"Finn's doing everything he can. Lots of long walks where Ajax can sniff anything he wants. And he's designing an obstacle course for his back garden."

That surprised me. "He's actually doing all that?" The mental image hit unexpectedly hard—Finley Patterson out in his garden, hammering agility equipment together for a dog he barely knew a week ago.

I'd mentioned agility work as something that would be a good way to engage Ajax, but I hadn't expected Finn to jump on it. Certainly not this soon.

"Oh, aye." Ciara grinned. "Alex has gotten way too into that, though he'd deny it on pain of death."

"Nice of Alex to help out." That wasn't surprising in the least. Alex Conroy was usually the first to volunteer help for anything. Maybe he was the one behind the agility course.

"All of them have stories about how Ajax saved their lives," Parker added. "So they all want to help him make this transition as easily as possible."

"Good of them." I'd been impressed before at how these men still functioned as a unit, even as civilians. "Are they trading off with him?"

Jade shook her head. "Not really. Finn's in this a hundred percent. Won't even let anybody else take him out because he says they need to bond."

I sat in silence for a few long moments, processing this avalanche of information. "That's... actually perfect. Consistency and patience are exactly what Ajax needs right now."

And I was shamed to admit, even to myself, that I hadn't expected him capable of that.

"Finn's been reading up on canine grief too," Parker added. "He asked me to order some books."

The image of Finley Patterson studiously reading about dog psychology wasn't one I'd expected. I felt a small, reluctant smile tug at my lips. "Good. That's... That's really good."

More than good. Admirable. Unexpected. Inconvenient.

I hated when people didn't stay in the boxes I'd built for them.

Pippa nudged my shoulder. "See? He's not so bad."

I fought the urge to stiffen up. "What does that have to do with anything?"

"Oh, what was it you said?" Skye gripped her chin as if trying to remember. "That you wouldn't date Finn if he were the last man on earth?"

"I'm not trying to date him. I'm inquiring after his dog purely out of professional concern..."

And if I'd spent a little too long imagining him with that dog—his hand gentle, his voice low—that was entirely beside the point.

"The lady doth protest too much," Ciara pointed out.

"Admit it," Jade prodded. "All this surprises you. You were convinced he was some kind of irresponsible ass."

Heat rose to my cheeks, because that was exactly what I'd thought. It seemed that maybe I'd misjudged the man, at least a little. That bothered me more than I was willing to admit. I'd been judged enough in my own life, and I generally made it a point *not* to jump to conclusions about people. And yet Finley Patterson had rubbed me the wrong way straight out of the gate.

Gathering together the shreds of my dignity, I conceded, "It does appear there is more to the man than I gave him credit for."

Which wouldn't be such a bitter pill to swallow if I hadn't built my whole personality around not jumping to conclusions.

Apparently, he brought out the worst in me. Or maybe the parts I'd tried hardest to ignore.

"Like the fact that he looks smashing in a kilt," Ciara muttered into her drink.

"Again, what does that have to do with anything? I never denied he was hot."

Parker dimpled. "Hot was how you two were looking at each other during that dance at Ciara's wedding."

"It was nothing. You've got on love-colored glasses." I took a long drink of wine—not because I needed it, but because I needed to do something that wasn't looking too closely at what that dance had stirred up.

Finn Patterson in a kilt should be a crime. So should the way I kept thinking about it.

Compulsively, I glanced down at my phone. Yet again.

"Okay, what gives?" Jade nodded toward the phone. "You expecting a call, or are you secretly texting with someone more interesting than our Finn?"

Ignoring that, I took the change in topic. "I'm expecting a check-in text from Isla. A few of you met her on a previous visit to Glenlaig. She's a scientist researching the results of the rewilding project at Ardinmuir. She's out on a two-week expedition, and usually she manages to send me a text from her sat phone every day, but I haven't heard from her since the day before yesterday. I'm getting a little worried."

"Could be in an area without signal. It's pretty bloody remote out there," Ciara suggested.

"True enough. But she never goes more than two days without checking in." That was the rule. And rules were there for a reason. They were structure. Reassurance. Control. Without them, my brain went to places it shouldn't.

"If she can't get through, she'll hike back to somewhere she knows she has signal."

Jade considered. "Sat phone could be lost or busted."

"Certainly. And she's meant to be back in Glenlaig on Sunday next. It's probably nothing, and I'll hear from her tomorrow. I'm just..." I lifted my shoulders in a helpless shrug that encompassed the whole array of terrible outcomes my brain was starting to spin up.

"There's nothing wrong with being concerned about her," Parker soothed. "Honestly, if you're truly worried, come in and talk to the guys. They'd be the best ones to go check on her."

"I don't think we're to the point of needing to mount a rescue mission. She's not that far off her schedule yet. But I'll certainly keep that in mind, thanks."

As conversation drifted to other topics—not my potential interest in one frustrating former Royal Marine, thank God—I did my best to reassure myself that Isla was fine. She was an experienced outdoorswoman, and she could handle whatever came at her.

But I couldn't stop thinking about how she was out there completely alone. And how helpless I felt not being able to do anything about it.

CHAPTER 9

FINN

I stood outside the Out of Bounds Scotland office, Ajax's lead loose in my hand. After a little over a week together, we were still finding our way. The Belgian Malinois sat at attention beside me, his dark eyes alert but not quite engaged. Not yet.

I held out a hand, giving him a moment to register it before I gently scratched the top of his head. "Ready for a wee adventure, lad?"

Ajax's ears twitched, but he maintained his disciplined posture. Charlie had trained him well.

Alex had slipped out during lunch to lay a trail through the woods behind our office. Before heading out, he'd handed me one of his gloves with a grin. "Think he'll remember how to do this?"

"Only one way to find out."

Now I crouched beside Ajax, holding Alex's glove. "This is different from our walks, boy. This is work you know." I held the glove under his nose. "Find Alex."

The transformation was immediate and stunning. Ajax's entire body tensed, his nose working furiously at the glove. On deployment, I had, of course, seen Ajax at his peak. I knew what he was capable of. During the past week, I'd seen glimpses of his training, but watching him shift from depressed companion to focused military asset was like watching someone wake up. Maybe I was doing something right.

"Find Alex." I repeated the command Charlie had used countless times.

Ajax circled, nose to the ground, working through the confusion of Alex's scent being everywhere near the office entrance. He paused, head lifting to test the air, then dropped back down. After three tight circles, his body language changed. He'd found the trail.

With a low whine, he pulled forward, and I let the lead run through my fingers. This wasn't about control. This was about letting him remember who he was.

As he moved with purpose toward the treeline, I murmured quiet encouragement. "Good boy, that's it."

His tail wasn't quite wagging, but it had lifted from its perpetual droop. His steps were purposeful, his body language confident for the first time since I'd brought him home. This wasn't the dejected shadow who'd been following me around. This was a working dog doing what he was born and trained to do.

I kept pace behind Ajax as he worked the trail, his movements becoming more fluid with each passing minute. The path Alex had laid took us up a gentle slope, winding between evergreen trees and moss-covered boulders. The scent must have strengthened, because Ajax's pace quickened, his nose never leaving the ground as he navigated the twisting route with absolute certainty.

"That's it, lad. You've got this." I did nothing to interfere with his work, merely keeping a steady pace behind him.

The trees thinned as we crested the hill, opening to the

meadow high above the village proper with its secret cache of ancient standing stones and the cadre of roaming sheep that always seemed to be here. Ajax paused at the treeline, head lifting to test the air. Something shifted in his posture, and I knew he'd caught Alex's scent on the breeze.

With renewed determination, Ajax pulled forward, leading me straight across the meadow toward one of the massive stones. He circled it once, twice, then stopped abruptly on the far side, where Alex stood waiting with a broad smile.

Eyes locked on his quarry, Ajax let out two sharp barks and sat.

"Well done!" Alex dropped to one knee, already pulling treats from his pocket. "Bloody brilliant work, Ajax."

I released the lead, letting Ajax move forward to collect his reward. Alex scratched behind his ears as he fed him treats, murmuring praise in that soft voice he reserved for animals and his wife.

"Look at you, remembering all your training." I leaned against a nearby stone. "Charlie would be proud, mate."

Alex produced a rope toy from his pocket and gave it a little shake. Ajax's eyes tracked the movement, and for a moment, he seemed unsure what to do.

"It's all right. This is for you." As Alex shook the rope again, the dog hesitantly reached for it.

"That's it." Alex engaged in a gentle tug. "Good boy."

The hesitant pull became slightly more enthusiastic. Not the exuberant play of a happy dog, but progress nonetheless. When Ajax released the toy, I swore I saw the faintest wag of his tail.

I exchanged a glance with Alex. "Did you see that?"

"I did." Alex grinned, making a show of scratching Ajax's chest. "Who's the best lad? You are! Absolute champion tracker!"

I joined in the praise, perhaps overdoing it a bit, but the sight of that tentative tail wag felt like a breakthrough worth celebrating.

As we started back for the office, I glanced at my friend. "Maeve's going to lose her mind when she smells him on you later."

"Aye. And Saffron's likely to avoid me for a week. But it's worth it."

The wee kitten we'd found hiding in our building during renovations had turned into Alex's very opinionated cat and still only tolerated Ciara. Maeve was terrified of her.

Ajax maintained that slight lift in his demeanor on our way back to the office, occasionally glancing up at me or Alex as we descended through the trees. His stride had more life now, different from the mechanical plodding of our previous walks.

Alex emerged from the trees at the back of our building first. "We should do these tracking exercises regularly. Maybe even get him back to some of his search work, eventually. He'd be an asset to mountain rescue work."

"Aye, I think maybe he'd like that." I watched Ajax navigate a fallen log with an ease that belied his middle age. "He's not likely to go quietly into retirement."

"None of us did." Alex tugged open the back door, and we headed inside.

The sound of female voices drew us toward the front. I expected to find Parker and Jade, but I didn't expect Saoirse to be with them at the desk we referred to as the Command Center. Her green eyes met mine, and I came to an immediate halt. Her face was calm—polished, even—but I'd seen behind that veneer once already. The way her hand slipped up to tuck her hair back wasn't for neatness. It was nerves.

My brain threw me back to that moment in her office a week ago when I'd been ready to commit violence in her name.

The black eye that had ignited the reaction had faded considerably. She'd managed to cover the lingering bruise with cosmetics, such that anyone who didn't know what to look for wouldn't notice a thing. But I still saw the slightest puffiness in her cheek.

Realizing everyone was staring, I cleared my throat. "Dr. MacGregor. Are you coming by to check on Ajax?"

Saoirse paused. "Yes, and no. How is he doing?" She knelt as she asked the question, extending a hand toward Ajax, who'd stopped when I did.

He glanced up at me, and I nodded. "Go ahead. You can say hello."

With less hesitation, Ajax padded across to Saoirse, his tail giving another tiny wag as she scratched beneath his chin and cooed.

"He's coming along." I watched Saoirse's gentle examination of Ajax. "Better than I expected, if I'm honest."

"He looks more alert." She ran her hands along his sides, checking his condition. "Has he been eating properly?"

"The puzzle feeders worked wonders. He's not exactly enthusiastic, but he's getting there."

Ajax leaned slightly into her touch, another small but significant sign of progress. A week ago, he'd barely tolerated being handled by anyone but me.

"Falkor's been the real breakthrough. He basically appointed himself Ajax's emotional support dog from the moment they met." The gentle giant had simply flopped down next to the grieving Malinois and stayed there, offering silent companionship that somehow bypassed all of Ajax's defenses.

"They've become inseparable at the office. We keep them both in the back room while I'm out. I'm still not comfortable having him interact with clients yet. But those two curl up together on that ridiculous dog bed Callum bought and stay that way for hours."

Saoirse's eyebrows lifted. "Callum bought a dog bed?"

"Right? The man now has strong opinions about orthopedic support for aging military dogs."

"To be fair, he has strong opinions about orthopedic support for all of us," Parker pointed out.

"Still, that's sweet." Saoirse's smile seemed genuine, and something in my chest loosened at the sight.

"We're all spoiling him rotten." I shifted from foot to foot, not sure what to do with myself. "He's got more toys than he knows what to do with, though he's only just starting to play with them."

Ajax glanced up at me, then back at Saoirse, his posture more relaxed than when we'd entered. The difference between the heartbroken shadow I'd brought home and the dog standing beside us now wasn't dramatic, but it was *real*. Like watching someone remember how to breathe after holding it for far too long.

Or maybe that was me projecting again.

"He's still got a long way to go, but there's progress." I reached down to scratch behind his ears. "The tracking exercise we did was the most engaged I've seen him. Like watching him remember who he is."

"Tracking exercise?"

I couldn't put my finger on what, but something changed in her expression as she said it. Something beyond professional interest as Ajax's vet.

"Aye. A quick scent drill. He tracked Alex up to the high meadow behind the village."

Saoirse looked reluctantly impressed. "That's all excellent progress."

I folded my arms. "Okay, so that's the checking on the

patient portion. Why else are you here?" I could tell she was off somehow. "Something's bothering you."

Her gaze shot to mine, her eyes widening faintly in surprise. Her professional demeanor slipped, and I caught a glimpse of genuine worry in her eyes.

"Actually, I came because I need help."

I blinked. Of all the reasons I thought she might've shown up—professional concern, curiosity, sheer bloody stubbornness —this one hadn't made the list.

And yet it hit me like a gut punch.

The woman who always had an answer was here to ask me for help?. Okay, maybe not me specifically. Alex was here, too. But still...

The admission seemed to cost her something. "I have a friend, Isla Grant. She's a biologist working on the rewilding project at Ardinmuir Estate."

"The biodiversity study?" I asked. "I've seen some of the research stations when I've been guiding out that way."

Saoirse nodded. "That's her work. She's been documenting the changes since they introduced the wild cats and reduced the deer population." Her fingers twisted together. "She has a satellite phone and always sends a check-in text every day. It's been four days since I've heard from her."

Alex frowned. "Maybe her phone died?"

"That's what I thought at first, but Isla's meticulous about her equipment. She carries solar chargers, backup batteries— everything."

"Could be out of range?" Jade suggested.

"She knows the dead zones by now. If she can't get a signal, she hikes to higher ground." Saoirse's voice tightened. "She's never gone more than a day without checking in."

I watched her carefully. This wasn't simply professional concern. "Have you contacted anyone else?"

"Everyone. The MacKeans, her department at the university. No one's heard from her since I did." She took a deep breath. "It's another three days before she's due back in the village for supplies."

"Is there anyone else out there with her?" I asked.

"Not this trip. She prefers working alone." Saoirse's voice caught slightly. "Look, I know it probably sounds ridiculous. There are a dozen rational explanations. But something feels wrong."

I'd learned long ago to trust that kind of instinct. "It's no' ridiculous."

Her eyes met mine, relief flickering across her face at not being dismissed.

"What are you thinking?" I asked.

"I need to go check on her. I know her research sites, her usual camping spots." She hesitated. "But some of those areas are pretty remote. I don't know them well enough to go alone."

And suddenly I understood why she'd come to us specifically. Out of Bounds Scotland specialized in remote wilderness guiding.

"You need someone who knows the back country of Ardinmuir." I nodded slowly.

"I was hoping one of you could come with me to try to find her, to reassure me."

"Of course we'll help." Alex's calm voice seemed to soothe her a little, and I had to bite back a surge of irritation. This wasn't about a popularity contest. A woman might be in danger.

"Have you contacted Police Scotland? Mountain Rescue?"

She shook her head. "I don't have enough proof of something being wrong, and I didn't want to waste a lot of resources if this is merely a case of her phone being damaged and she's absolutely fine."

Alex and I exchanged a look. He inclined his head. "Nomad, I believe you're up." Turning back to Saoirse, he added, "Finn is the best tracker of all of us."

"And there's Ajax."

She shook her head. "I don't want to set him back in his recovery."

"This is what he was trained to do. Find people. And other things. This won't set him back. It'll probably liven him up a wee bit to give him something more challenging than chasing Alex up a hill."

Saoirse caught that lush lower lip between her teeth in another show of uncharacteristic anxiety that had me thinking about all the ways I'd like to soothe that little hurt with my own mouth.

At last, her shoulders dropped—in acceptance or defeat, I didn't know. "If you don't mind, I would appreciate it if you could help me find my friend."

"Of course." I paused. "You dinna have to come with me." I could move a lot faster on my own.

That look of resignation turned mulish. "She's my friend. I'm the reason you're going out there. I'm the one who'll know if something's wrong. I'm coming."

Her voice didn't waver, but I heard the fight in it. The kind you only use when you're terrified and trying not to be.

I'd been wrong about her. She wasn't an ice queen. She just kept all her emotions buttoned down tight. But I'd gotten a glimpse of what lay underneath, and now all I could think about was keeping that fire burning.

It was my turn to incline my head. "Okay. Then let's make a plan."

CHAPTER 10

SAOIRSE

I glanced at my watch as Grandda's ancient Land Rover rattled to a stop at the trailhead. Five-thirty in the morning and Finn was already there, leaning against his vehicle with Ajax sitting patiently at his feet. The dog's ears perked up at our arrival, though his posture remained disciplined.

Grandda killed the engine. "I've told you a dozen times, I'm perfectly capable of managing the practice." He turned in his seat to scowl at me. "Forty-six years I've been at it. Think I can handle a few days without you hovering."

"I'm not hovering. I'm being practical." I'd had to prepare for far more than a multi-day hiking expedition last night, trying to line up additional coverage for the time I was gone. "I've written down the contact information for Dr. Campbell and Dr. MacIntyre. Either of them can—"

He waved a hand in dismissal. "I know who to call if I need help." Affection softened the gruffness in his voice. "Focus on finding your friend."

I sighed. "Promise you'll take it easy? No wrestling with any bulls?"

"Aye, and I'll be sure not to challenge any horses to a boxing match either." He nodded toward Finn. "That the lad with the military dog?"

"Yes. Finley Patterson. That's Ajax with him."

Grandda studied him with narrowed eyes. "Looks capable enough."

That was, of course, why I'd hired him, despite our inherent personal friction.

I climbed out. Finn straightened as we approached, Ajax alert beside him.

"Dr. MacGregor." Finn greeted me with a nod, then extended his hand to my grandfather. "And you must be Dr. MacGregor the elder. Finn Patterson."

"Liam." Grandda gave his hand a firm shake. "You're the tracker, then?"

"Yes, sir. Former Royal Marine."

While the two of them sized each other up, I hauled my pack from the boot, and mentally checked my inventory against the five-day supply list we'd agreed upon before I'd left Out of Bounds Scotland yesterday. Water purification tablets, first aid kit, emergency blanket, protein bars, dehydrated meals, extra clothes and wool socks, my sleeping bag, and, of course, a bag with the pajama bottoms Isla had worn when she'd visited to use as a scent article. Everything was meticulously organized. Finn was providing the tents and some of the other gear.

Grandda eyed him with the same scrutiny he used on questionable radiographs. "Military training's one thing, but these mountains have their own rules. Weather can turn in minutes."

Unruffled, Finn only nodded. "I respect that. It's why I've packed extra supplies and emergency gear."

Ajax sat quietly at Finn's feet, his intelligent eyes following our conversation. The dog looked markedly more alert than when I'd first examined him at the clinic.

Grandda's gaze shifted between us. "How long were you in service, then?"

"Twelve years, sir. Special Forces for most of it."

I'd known Finn was Special Forces. Alex, Callum, and Ewan had been, too. But somehow I hadn't really thought about what it meant. For all the man rubbed every last nerve the wrong way, that kind of capability would be an asset if Isla really had gotten into some kind of trouble.

"Hmm." Grandda gave that noncommittal Scottish grunt that could mean anything from approval to deep suspicion. Then he surprised me by extending his hand again. "Take care of my girl."

"I will, sir."

Because of course he'd say that. As if I were some fragile vase in need of chaperoning. And yet... the way Finn answered —quiet, steady—sent a little pulse of something through me. Not comfort, exactly. Something warier. Like a door creaking open.

Still, I rolled my eyes at this patently male exchange. "I can take care of myself, thank you very much."

Grandda turned to me, his weathered face softening. "Aye, but even the best of us need backup sometimes. At least, that's what someone keep telling me." He pulled me into a hug, the familiar scent of antiseptic and wool enveloping me. "Find your friend, then come home safe."

I squeezed him tight. "I will. And you—"

"I know, I know. No wrestling with bulls." He winked. "Pippin will be fine. We understand each other."

Meaning they both spoke cantankerous. God help them both. They deserved each other.

With a final wave, Grandda climbed back into the Land Rover. The ancient engine sputtered to life, and then he was gone, leaving me alone at the trailhead with Finn and Ajax, the mountains looming before us.

Finn was the one to break the silence. "Who's Pippin?"

"My cat." The one who'd known I was about to be gone for a few days by the packing I'd done last night and had taken himself off to sulk well before bed. I hadn't even seen him when I'd poured out his breakfast kibble this morning. The furry little traitor.

"Ah."

I glanced at Finn. What the hell did "ah" mean? That single syllable seemed loaded with judgment.

After a moment, he looked back at me. "You only have the one?"

"For now." I frowned slightly. "Why?"

He jerked his broad shoulders in a shrug. "It surprises me, is all. Dinna vets usually have a whole menagerie?"

"Often, but I've basically inherited my grandfather's menagerie since I've moved up here. So that doesn't leave a lot of room for adding to my own at the moment." Even if I did have the time. Which I didn't. So far, I'd been able to find new homes for all of the "project animals" I'd taken on. Falkor had been one of them before I'd convinced Parker he was exactly what she needed.

"Fair enough."

Finn straightened and gave me a once-over, his eyes lingering on my well-worn hiking boots, water-resistant walking trousers, and the top-of-the-line pack I'd had since uni. His eyebrows lifted slightly, and I could practically see the recalculation happening behind his eyes.

"What?" I raised an eyebrow. "Did you think I'd show up in designer wellies and spritzing dry shampoo into my crown braid?"

He had the decency to almost look sheepish. Almost.

Men like him never knew what to do with women like me.

Too polished to be rustic, too muddy to be ornamental. Heaven forbid I inhabit both worlds.

He held up his hands in surrender. "I didn't peg you as the outdoorsy type."

Heat rose in my cheeks. Of course he hadn't. For all that I'd judged him, he'd clearly judged me right back for exactly the half of my life and upbringing that I'd been trying to escape. The posh English boarding school girl with the trust fund and the polished accent. The privileged princess who couldn't possibly know how to pitch a tent or navigate with a compass.

I opened my mouth to snap back at him, a defensive tirade ready to spill out. But I stopped myself. This wasn't about me or my wounded pride. This was about Isla.

"Look." I reined in my temper. "I've been hiking these hills since I was seven. I spent every summer with my grandparents, and Isla and I have done multiple multi-day expeditions together. I wasn't exaggerating my capabilities when we planned this."

Finn nodded, his expression shifting to something more professional. "Good. That'll make this easier." He popped the back hatch of his 4x4. "Let's double-check our supplies before we head out."

We methodically went through everything. Finn had brought additional first aid supplies, a satellite mapping device, and extra rations. I added my wilderness medical kit, which contained specialized equipment for treating injuries in remote locations. I sent up a prayer that we wouldn't actually need it.

He didn't say anything as he redistributed the weight in my pack, but I saw the faint lift of his brows.

What? Had he expected a lipstick and heels situation? I'd lived out of a tent for ten days straight without a mirror once. I didn't need his approval. I really didn't.

Except that a tiny traitorous part of me liked that he looked surprised.

"You're well-prepared."

"Foolish not to be." I was many things, but foolish wasn't one of them. It was why I'd gone to Out of Bounds Scotland for a guide instead of trying to do this on my own.

Ajax stood patiently nearby, already fitted with his own custom harness and small saddlebags containing his food, collapsible water bowl, and a few specialized items.

"He's carrying his own supplies?"

"Military dogs are trained to carry up to thirty percent of their body weight. This is nothing for him." Finn pulled out a satellite phone from a padded case. "We'll be checking in with base twice daily. Morning and evening. Standard procedure."

"Base?"

"Out of Bounds. We always maintain contact during wilderness expeditions."

There it was again—that shift. Gone was the joker. This version of Finn moved with quiet precision and military clarity. He was probably like this when bullets were flying. God help me, I found it reassuring.

He dialed and held the phone to his ear. "This is Nomad checking in for mission start, over."

I was surprised to hear a response so early in the morning.

"Copy that, Nomad." Alex's voice came through clearly. "Weather report shows clear conditions for the next 48 hours. What's your ETA to first checkpoint?"

"Estimating 1800 hours at base camp. Will confirm position then. Over."

"Copy that. Echo out."

Finn tucked the phone away, and I found myself staring. The easy-going flirt had vanished, replaced by someone focused and methodical. Of course he was. He'd been Special

Forces, for God's sake. The man had probably conducted actual search and rescue operations in war zones.

He caught me watching him. "Something wrong?"

"No," I admitted. "Just... adjusting my perspective."

He nodded once, then gestured toward the trail. "Are you ready?"

I tightened the straps on my pack, fastened the chest strap into place, and squared my shoulders.

I looked up at the mountains, the early morning mist curling around the treetops like smoke. Somewhere out there, Isla was alone. Or worse.

And I was walking into the wilds with the one man who made my skin prickle—for reasons that had nothing to do with danger.

Let's find her and get this over with.

"Let's go."

CHAPTER 11

FINN

The woods had begun to thicken an hour before we stopped. Twilight settled into the trees like breath on glass. Thin, grey, and quiet, but for the distant scold of a jay and the soft crunch of boots over loam and moss.

We'd made good time. Eight, maybe ten miles, and not once had Dr. Saoirse MacGregor slowed me down.

Not that I'd say that out loud. I liked my head where it was, thanks verra much.

She hadn't said much all day as she hiked with steady, efficient purpose, eyes forward, focus tight. Every now and then she'd kneel to check Ajax's paws or refill our water filters at a stream, but otherwise she was all business. Coiled like a wire, waiting for tension to snap it.

I didn't blame her. I'd seen that kind of determination before. The kind that came from knowing someone you loved was missing and not wanting to speak the fear aloud in case that made it more real.

Now, at the edge of a sheltered hollow framed by black pines and half-ringed in stone, I knelt to pitch the tent. We were far enough from the trail to avoid curious hillwalkers—not that we'd seen a soul all day—and close enough to the treeline for wind protection if the weather turned.

Saoirse was kneeling a few meters away, coaxing a small fire to life. It wasn't for heat—we'd sleep warm enough—but for comfort, for light, and maybe a sense of control. She'd scavenged dry wood like she'd done it a hundred times, and she lit the kindling with practiced ease.

I didn't offer to help. Didn't need to. She had it handled.

And she was damned good. Better than I'd expected, if I was honest. But again, didn't say it. One compliment and she'd probably torch me with whatever flint and steel she had in her kit.

The tent snapped taut under my hands, lines drawn, pegs secure. Ajax patiently watched the proceedings, curled beside my pack, head resting on his front paws, eyes always moving.

Once the fire caught fully and started licking up through the kindling, Saoirse rose, brushing off her palms and walking over. She pulled her hair back into a bun with a tie from her wrist, expression set in that composed mask she wore like a second skin.

Her gaze dropped to the tent. Then lifted back to me.

A beat.

Then, "Where's mine?"

I didn't flinch. But I also didn't meet that gaze dead-on, because there was fire behind it now, and not the campfire kind.

"We've got one." I kept my tone level. "Ultralight."

Silence. The kind that didn't belong in nature—too sharp, too heavy.

"One," she repeated.

"Aye."

Another beat. "For both of us?"

"Only made sense. We had to cut weight. Food for five days, gear, med kits, sat phone. Couldn't spare the bulk for two shelters." I shrugged. "Didn't think it'd be a problem."

"You didn't think to mention it before now?"

I finally looked up. Her arms were crossed, her expression schooled tight, but I could see the flickers behind it—irritation, discomfort... something else she probably didn't have a name for yet. Maybe didn't want to.

"I didn't think we'd be discussing sleeping arrangements like it was a five-star booking."

That earned me a look that could've frozen the loch.

"It's not about that," she said, voice low. "It's about expectations."

"And it's a tent," I replied. "Not a honeymoon suite."

A flash of something crossed her face. Not embarrassment. Not quite. But surprise, maybe, that I'd go there—cut through the tension with dry humor instead of apology.

Ajax let out a quiet huff like he was already tired of our nonsense.

I gestured to the setup. "It's double-length. Two separate bags. You'll have space."

She didn't answer right away, instead walking past me to look inside. She ducked her head through the opening, inspecting every seam as if maybe she expected to find me hiding an ulterior motive in the mesh lining.

Finally, she stepped back and gave a curt nod.

"Fine," she said. "But I'm not spooning you if it drops below freezing."

I blinked. Then laughed. Couldn't help it.

"There's a first aid kit in the side pocket," I said. "You might need it after that ego wound."

She didn't smile. But she didn't scowl either.

Progress.

Ajax rose and stretched, then ambled toward the tent and flopped down squarely in front of it, like a bouncer barring the door. His tail gave a single *whump* against the ground before he settled.

I eyed him. "Diplomatic as ever, mate."

Saoirse crouched down beside him, ran a hand over his shoulder. "He doesn't want to listen to us bicker all night."

"Canna blame him." I grabbed the cook kit and set about unpacking our no-frills dinner. "You want curry pouch one or curry pouch two? One has a picture of a mountain goat. The other's a mystery."

"Surprise me."

"Bold choice."

Ajax had flopped down like a soldier on leave. His nose twitched toward the wind, tail giving the occasional lazy flick as Saoirse crouched beside him, running her hands gently over his shoulders, his flanks. A check for injury, sure—but there was more to it. The way she moved with him, slow and steady, like she'd been doing this for years. Which, of course, she had. I had to keep reminding myself she was a lot closer to my age than I'd originally thought.

"Still good?" I flicked the fuel tab under our pot of boiling water.

"He's not showing any soreness or fatigue." Her fingers traced the edge of one of his saddlebags. "Gait's clean. Appetite was decent. He seems... happy."

"Good to hear," I murmured.

Happy wasn't a word I'd expected to associate with Ajax. Not yet.

Saoirse shifted to sit cross-legged beside him, letting the dog use her thigh as a pillow without a word. His eyes blinked slowly and then closed. Lucky bastard.

I pulled the satellite phone from my pack and gave her a quick glance. "I'll check in."

She nodded, but didn't move. Ajax's ears twitched once. I stepped a few paces away from the fire to make the call.

"Nomad to base, check-in one." I kept my voice low but clear.

Alex's voice came back almost instantly. "Copy that, Nomad. How's the weather?"

"Calm and clear. We made good progress today. About ten clicks in, give or take. No visual on anything yet."

"Any signs of the camps?"

"None. Should hit Isla's first station by mid-morning tomorrow."

"Understood. You two all good?"

I glanced back. Saoirse hadn't moved, still petting Ajax with soft, rhythmic motions that seemed unconscious. "We're fine. She's holding up."

"Keep us posted. I'll expect check-in two around 0900. Echo out."

"Copy that. Nomad out."

I killed the call and dropped the phone back into its pouch. Dinner was ready. Two steaming pouches of vaguely curry-scented mush. Gourmet, it was not. But hot food was hot food.

I stirred the contents. "Dinner."

Saoirse rose smoothly, brushing dirt from her trousers, and took the offered pouch with a small nod of thanks. We ate in relative silence at first, side by side near the fire. Ajax settled in at our feet again, radiating heat and canine serenity like some kind of four-legged Switzerland.

I was halfway through my meal when I made a play for conversation. Neutral territory. "Tell me about Pippin."

She glanced up, startled. "My cat?"

"Aye. What's he like?"

Something shifted in her expression—not softening, exactly, but loosening. Her brow smoothed, and she looked down at her food like she was debating whether to answer.

"He's cantankerous. Moody. Possibly plotting my death for leaving him with Grandda. But he's family." A beat. "I found him when he was a kitten. Someone had set an illegal snare. His back leg was a mess. The surgery was one of the first procedures I completed on my own after I finished school."

I watched her as she said it, how her voice dipped subtly— warm, sure, almost proud.

"He never really forgave me for it. But he lets me cuddle him sometimes at his command, so I consider that a win."

"Sounds like he's got a healthy sense of boundaries."

"He's a cat." She gave the barest twitch of a smile. "They invented boundaries."

There was a lull—comfortable, for once—so I let myself ask, "Did you grow up with animals?"

Her face twisted in something between a grimace and a laugh. "God, I wanted to. Dogs, cats, horses—everything. It was like a wildlife rescue center every summer at my grandparents'. But my mother—" She broke off with a shake of her head.

Mother, I noted. Not Mum.

"Not a fan?" I guessed.

"My mother kept a Bichon frisé named Celeste. Wore little jumpers. Ate boiled chicken and rice off a china saucer. She thought animals were for showing off, not for *touching*." Saoirse stabbed her fork through a chunk of congealed chickpea. "She used to lose her mind when I brought home injured birds or hedgehogs. Said it was *unsanitary*."

"And becoming a vet?"

"Oh, she loved that." Dry sarcasm practically steamed off the fire with her breath. "Said it was a perfectly *filthy* profession. Bodily fluids and ungrateful clients and unseemly country types. *Very* glamorous."

I studied her profile—how her jaw tightened, the glint of old friction in her eyes. Too dim for rage. Not hard enough for bitterness. Merely... exhaustion. The kind of weathering you got from years of being told your instincts were wrong.

Her fingers brushed unconsciously over the fading bruise along her cheekbone.

"Some days she calls to ask if I've found a 'nice small animal clinic in a proper city yet.'" She gave a tired laugh. "As if mucking out stables and dodging pissed-off horses wasn't exactly the point."

I said nothing, unable to tear my eyes off her. And in the firelight, with her eyes rimmed in smoke-shadow and the last of the bruise yellowing along her cheek, I realized I'd had her pegged all wrong. She had the voice of Mayfair and the posture of a woman raised in gardens with hired staff. But underneath?

Underneath, she was grit and soft-spoken rebellion and worn-in boots she didn't give a damn about scuffing.

"Hell of a mismatch," I said before I could stop myself.

She looked over. "What is?"

"You and her."

A pause. Then she nodded once. "Yes. But I got lucky. I had Grandda. He taught me that loving animals wasn't childish or foolish. It was a kind of calling."

"Smart man."

"Stubborn as hell."

"Still smart."

And then, finally, a real smile broke over her face. Crooked. Small. But real.

"Thanks." The word came out a little rough.

Ajax thumped his tail once against the dirt between us.

"Think he approves," I said.

"Probably just wants a bite of your dinner."

"God help him if he does."

She laughed. Actually laughed. A quiet thing that came from her chest instead of only her mouth.

And in that moment, sitting cross-legged in the firelight, I knew I was in more trouble than I'd realized.

Because this wasn't professional respect anymore.

This was intrigue.

And that was always a bad idea.

CHAPTER 12

SAOIRSE

I woke to the sound of birdsong threading through canvas and the quiet warmth of breath that wasn't mine.

For a disoriented half-second, I didn't remember where I was. The air inside the tent smelled like damp nylon and campfire smoke, and something woodsy and faintly citrus beneath that—Finn's soap, probably. I shifted slightly, the ache of yesterday's miles flaring in my calves, and that's when I registered the shape between us.

Ajax.

Flat on his side, legs twitching in some half-remembered dream, he took up the center of the tent like he owned the place. Finn and I had curled around him in our sleep like two parentheses. I had maybe a foot of space between myself and the tent wall. Less, if I wanted to breathe fully.

Ajax snorted, rolled onto his other side, and in doing so nudged Finn's arm.

Finn stirred with a low grunt, then froze. I could feel the awareness wake in him like a tide. His breathing changed—slow, then sharp, and then a little too careful.

"Morning." His voice was still graveled from sleep.

I cleared my throat, unsure why the sound of it made me feel like I'd been caught doing something I shouldn't. "Morning."

Silence stretched. I heard the faint chirr of insects outside. The air was cool, but not unpleasant, carrying that sharp-edged smell of moss and turned earth.

Finn exhaled. "Guess ultralight is code for *awkward proximity.*"

I shot a look toward the lump of fur between us. "You could've warned me."

"I did. Yesterday. When you asked where *your* tent was."

"That's not the same as saying, 'By the way, we'll be sleeping like sardines.'"

He grinned sleepily, not bothering to open his eyes. "Could've said you snore."

"I don't."

He cracked one eye open. "You twitch."

"I was dreaming."

He smothered a yawn with the back of his hand. "Hope it was a good one."

I didn't dignify that with a reply. Instead, I sat up, nudging Ajax's back end with my hip as I untangled from the sleeping bag. The dog opened one eye, seemed to weigh the cost of moving, and promptly decided against it.

Outside the tent, the morning was silver and soft, low mist coiling between the tree trunks like something out of an old storybook. Behind me, I heard Finn zip open the tent flap and emerge into the chill, yawning wide enough to scare off birds. He glanced at the sky, then reached into his pack for the stove and coffee kit. I found my way into the trees, locating a private spot for morning necessities. Within minutes, I was back, and the rich scent of brewing coffee filled the clearing.

He handed me the first cup. I didn't miss the way he slipped it into my hands without flourish or commentary.

"Thanks," I murmured.

"No problem."

We drank in silence. Ajax finally heaved himself up, stretched with a groan, and shook out his coat in a cascade of dust.

Finn crouched to check the dog's gear before slipping it on him, inspecting each strap and pouch with quiet focus. He didn't coo or baby-talk, just moved with a kind of practiced, unshowy care.

I watched him from the corner of my eye. Still barefoot, hair rumpled, hands sure.

Annoyingly competent. And—fine—attractive in a rugged, casually dangerous sort of way.

I sipped my coffee, then said, "So... is it that you don't like cats?"

His hands stilled on Ajax's harness. "What?"

"The kitten," I said. "From last year. The one you found during renovations at the office."

He blinked. "What about it?"

"You were very quick to disavow yourself of any responsibility of it. I wondered if you didn't like cats."

A flicker of something crossed his face—amusement, maybe, but something darker beneath it. "It's not the cat. I like cats fine."

"Then why the 'not my problem' attitude?"

He straightened and gave a noncommittal shrug. "I've lost people. Men under my command. Friends. Squadmates. I dinna do well with responsibility that has a heartbeat."

I raised a brow. "And Ajax?"

He didn't look at me when he answered. "No man left behind. No dog either."

The words were quiet, but they carried weight. More than I expected. Like it was a motto—or a promise.

Something in his tone stopped me from pushing further. For now.

We finished breaking camp. There was no need to coordinate; we moved in an odd, synchronized rhythm, like two dancers performing a routine they hadn't rehearsed but somehow knew anyway. It was... disconcerting to feel connected to him like this.

As we double-checked the site and shouldered our packs, Finn glanced toward me, brow slightly raised. "You ready?"

I tightened my straps. "Let's go find my friend."

We moved through the forest in near silence, Ajax ranging ahead in wide loops, nose low, body loose and efficient. His every step was measured, purposeful—a living metronome set to the scent trail.

I stayed behind Finn, letting him lead. Not because I couldn't have managed the route myself, but because it was... enlightening. He didn't need dramatic gestures or barks of command. The two managed to communicate through a series of quiet murmurs, occasional hand signals, and a deep, mutual trust I envied. Did Finn realize how much he'd already bonded with Ajax? I didn't think he did.

At one point, he knelt to check a patch of disturbed moss. Ajax waited, muscles taut but still. Finn glanced at a bend in a broken fern stalk, then up at the canopy.

"No new signs." He straightened. "But the scent's still holding. Wind hasn't shifted."

I nodded, though I wasn't entirely sure what he meant by all of it. I knew enough to let him work. My job was to keep up and keep alert—and to try not to get lost in my own thoughts, which wasn't going especially well.

For hours, the path rose and fell beneath our boots, knotted with roots and stitched with leaf-littered gullies. Ajax tracked with almost eerie consistency. Occasionally he'd pause, look back at Finn as if to say *you seeing this?* then move on.

And then, somewhere past midday, I broke the silence.

"You're good at this."

Finn shot me a quick look over his shoulder. "Thanks."

"I mean it," I said. "You and Ajax. It's like watching a search-and-rescue documentary with better biceps."

That got a faint laugh out of him, which he mostly smothered with a hand. "High praise."

I shrugged, eyes on the terrain. "So your friend Charlie trained him?"

"Yeah." His tone changed so subtly I almost missed it. The humor drained out, leaving something quieter. "They were paired not long after Kandahar. Served together for years."

I glanced over, waiting.

After a moment, he went on. "Charlie was the one who said it." His gaze stayed fixed on the trail ahead. "'No man left behind. No dog either.' Used to spout it off with this daft grin, like it was a joke."

"But it wasn't."

"No." Finn's voice dipped, rougher now. "It wasn't."

He slowed slightly, hand falling to Ajax's back as the dog paused to sniff the base of a pine. Finn's fingers moved in a small, unconscious pattern—comfort more than correction.

"When Charlie died, he left Ajax to me," he said finally. "Because apparently I was the only one he trusted not to treat him like broken equipment."

I didn't know what to say. So I said nothing, only kept walking beside him.

After a minute, he forced a chuckle. "Christ. Sorry. That got bleak fast."

"Don't apologize." My voice was quieter than I meant it to be. "You're allowed to miss him."

He looked at me then—really looked. And for a moment, I saw all of it. Not only the smooth charm or the competence, but the raw edge beneath. The weight he carried and the way he'd learned to carry it with a smile, so no one would ask too many questions.

I recognized that look. I'd seen it in the mirror more times than I cared to count.

"Grief's a weird thing." I said it mostly to the trees. "Sometimes it feels like a shadow. Other times, like someone's cracked your ribs open and is pressing on your heart just to see if it still hurts."

He blinked. Then nodded.

"I like to think it means we loved them properly," I added, softer.

For a while, we simply walked.

Eventually, Finn cleared his throat. "So... still think I'm just a charming pain in your arse?"

"Yes." I maintained my straight face. "But now I think you're a *complicated* charming pain in my arse."

He grinned. "I'll take it."

And for the first time since we'd set foot on this trail, it felt less like we were two strangers thrown together and more like we were becoming something else entirely.

CHAPTER 13

FINN

The light changed first.

It was subtle—a shift in temperature, the sun slipping lower behind the ridgeline, bleeding warm gold across the canopy. The trail underfoot softened into loamy moss and pine needles, the crunch of rock giving way to a muted hush that swallowed our steps.

We were getting close.

I let Saoirse take point, not because I couldn't have led— hell, I'd mapped this section myself for excursions before we'd even opened the doors to Out of Bounds Scotland—but because watching her work was... enlightening. She hadn't spoken much all day beyond little check-ins here and there about pace, water, direction. But with every step, she impressed the hell out of me.

She carried herself like someone who knew her place in the wild. Not as a tourist, not as someone trying to prove something, but someone who belonged. The terrain hadn't fazed her once. Steep inclines, ankle-snapping divots, damp ground slick with leaf mold. She handled it all with easy, unflinching awareness.

If I hadn't known better, I'd have thought she was leading me.

Behind us, Ajax worked his loop. Nose to ground, breath steady, every movement economical. He'd fallen into that razor-sharp headspace I recognized from deployment, where the world narrowed to scent and instinct. And I'd started to do the same until a rustle of map paper snapped me out of it.

Saoirse stopped up ahead, one hand steadying her compass, the other unfolding her worn topo map. She studied it for all of three seconds, then adjusted her heading without comment, stepping off the trail onto a game path I'd completely missed because I'd been too focused on her.

I quickened my pace to catch up. "You always this good with a compass, or is it only when you're trying to impress me?"

She didn't look up. "If I were trying to impress you, I'd have let you get us lost first."

I barked out a surprised laugh. "Fair."

She kept walking, but a second later—*there it was.* A smile. The real kind. Quick, a little sideways, but it lit up her face like someone had pulled back the clouds.

I stumbled on a root.

Ajax gave me a look like, *get it together, mate.*

She surprised me. Constantly. And I hated how much I liked it.

"Pretty sure that smile added an extra mile to the hike," I muttered.

"What was that?"

"Nothing." I adjusted the strap on my pack and tried to focus.

We crested a small ridge, the trees thinning to reveal a clearing ahead. The gentle slope, mossy undergrowth, a half-circle ring of stones blackened from old fires told me this was Isla's first station.

Saoirse stepped into the space like someone walking into a cathedral. Reverent. Searching.

"She was definitely here," she said softly.

I nodded, moving to check the perimeter. "Tent broken down. No signs of struggle or distress. Looks like she packed out properly."

"She always does." She knelt near the fire ring. "She's methodical. Stubborn as hell, too, but she wouldn't leave this place a mess."

I circled the site slowly. Nothing screamed "emergency." But something still felt... off. Like the echo of a presence, just out of reach.

Ajax moved through the clearing like he was cataloguing it. No alerts, but his posture was different. Not the confidence he'd had earlier. More like anticipation. Like he was waiting.

"She's not here." Saoirse rose to her feet. "But she was. And recently."

I nodded, casting another glance across the clearing. It felt like walking into a room still holding someone's breath. The quiet buzzed faintly with what had *almost* been.

"Trail's still readable," I said. "Subtle, but there. She headed northwest, same as her last report. If we push hard, we'll make it to her second camp by nightfall."

Saoirse adjusted the strap on her pack. "Let's do it."

I crouched to unclip the sat phone from Ajax's gear, thumbing the antenna out with a practiced motion. "Give me two minutes. Check-in window's about to close."

She gave a short nod and moved to sit on a mossy stone at the edge of the clearing, pulling her water bottle from its holster. Ajax padded over, nosed at her knee, and flopped down with a grunt that said *five hours is enough, thank you.*

I keyed in the frequency.

"Nomad to base, come in. Over."

A pause. Then Callum's dry, unmistakable tone crackled over the line. "This is Ghost. You're behind schedule."

"Good to hear you too, sunshine." I crouched, keeping my voice steady and low. "We reached Isla's first research site. Camp was packed out clean. No signs of distress. We're following the expected heading to the second site now."

Static, then: "Any deviation in trail?"

"Nothing major. Ajax is confident. Wind's in our favor."

Callum grunted. "Weather's holding through evening, but expect a cold front to move in late. Watch your elevation."

"Roger that. Estimated arrival at second camp by 2100 hours. Will update then."

"Copy that. Keep your head down, Nomad."

"Always do. Nomad out."

I tucked the sat phone back into my pack and stood, rolling my shoulder until it popped. When I looked over, Saoirse was watching me.

Not merely looking—*watching*. Like she was trying to line something up in her head.

I raised a brow. "What?"

She didn't blink. "I thought you'd talk more."

That caught me off guard. "Now or in general?"

"In general." She took a sip from her water bottle, then capped it slowly. "I don't know. I assumed you'd be more of a running commentary type. You know—jokes, banter, class clown with a compass."

I let out a short breath that wasn't quite a laugh. "Class clown?"

She lifted an eyebrow right back. "I've seen you in town, Finn. You hold court with a grin and a pint in your hand like it's your full-time job."

Touché.

I could've deflected. Should've, maybe. But I adjusted the strap on my pack and said, "Maybe I'm conserving energy."

Her gaze didn't waver. "Or maybe that's not actually who you are."

That landed harder than it should have. Not because she was wrong. Because she wasn't. Parker had said much the same, hadn't she? But somehow, I hadn't expected Saoirse to see through the act. And I certainly hadn't expected that to come without judgment or challenge.

And I couldn't decide if that made me want to let her in or throw up another wall.

I swallowed, shifted my weight. "Sometimes you need someone to keep morale up."

It wasn't the whole truth. But it was enough for now.

"I appreciate you managing mine." Without further comment, Saoirse stood to hoist her pack onto her shoulders. "Come on. Long way yet."

I watched her for a second longer than I meant to. Then I followed.

And for the first time since this whole thing started, I wondered what else she'd seen that I hadn't meant to show.

CHAPTER 14

SAOIRSE

We should've heard birds.

Even in the most remote parts of Ardinmuir, the woods were never truly still. Wind whispering through pine boughs. The peep of small birds. The distant rush of water. Even the low rustle of some unseen creature in the underbrush. This place, though—Isla's second camp—felt muffled. Heavy. Like the forest itself was holding its breath.

My stomach twisted the moment we stepped into the clearing.

Isla had been here. Recently. That much was obvious. Her tarp shelter still clung to the trees at a crooked angle, the anchor lines tangled like they'd been yanked rather than unknotted. The fire ring was scorched dark, half-ringed with charred stones, and the pot she'd used for boiling water sat tipped on its side in the ash, as though it had been knocked over in a hurry.

I crouched beside it, brushing my fingers against the cold metal. The underside was blackened, but the soot looked fresh. Rain hadn't had time to wash it away.

"She didn't pack out properly," I said quietly.

Finn didn't answer right away. I looked up to find him already moving in a slow, deliberate circuit of the camp's perimeter, Ajax ghosting behind him like a silent second shadow.

"She's methodical," I said. "She'd never leave a camp like this. Not on purpose. She's a huge proponent of leaving things as good as or better than you find them."

Finn's voice came low, steady. "Any chance something spooked her? Animal activity?"

I shook my head. "Not unless it was human. She's not scared of wildlife." I glanced at the surrounding trees. "She's slept in the open in bear country, for God's sake." Not that we had that sort of predator here. There were no large predators in Scotland anymore except the two-legged variety.

I was already moving toward the edge of the tarp when I spotted her backup boots. Mud-caked and unlaced, sitting off to one side like they'd been stepped out of and forgotten. But Isla didn't forget. And she would never abandon gear unless—

I stopped that thought dead. Couldn't follow it.

I moved on instinct, scanning the mess for something—anything—that would explain why she'd leave without breaking camp. My breath caught when I saw the corner of a familiar weathered notebook tucked beneath the collapsed edge of her sleeping pad.

Her field journal.

I dropped to my knees and slid it out, brushing off bits of leaf and pine needles. The leather cover was scratched, the edges damp, but it was intact. I flipped through quickly, fingers trembling.

The early pages were classic Isla. Everything recorded in her tiny, neat hand—notes about tree species, scat samples, paw prints near the river. Sketches of a nesting site she'd been excited about. Observations of small shifts in ecosystem behavior, the kind of thing most people would miss, but she lived for.

And then, halfway through, something changed. The tidy entries became clipped. Less detail and fewer drawings. One page was no more than a single line, jagged and rushed:

Unidentified prints near western perimeter. Not feline. Not deer. Not sure.

And then the rest of the journal went blank.

Nothing after that.

No closing entry or summary. Only pages of silence.

The clearing tilted around me. I sat down hard on the nearest log, the journal open on my lap, air clogging in my lungs.

This was wrong.

Isla didn't stop writing. Not unless something forced her to.

Ajax padded over and rested his chin against my thigh. I didn't even realize I was shaking until the weight of his head pressed me back into my body. I tangled my fingers in the thick ruff of his fur and held on.

I didn't hear Finn's approach, but I felt his presence settling beside me like a counterweight. He didn't touch me or offer pointless platitudes, but his nearness reminded me that I wasn't alone.

"I can't lose her." It came out hoarse, barely a whisper. "Not her, too."

Silence.

With someone else, it might've felt awkward or uncomfortable. But somehow Finn's quiet offered space. And I felt compelled to fill it.

"I was eighteen when my father died." The words pulled loose like threads from a frayed seam, one that had been stretched to the breaking point. "It was right at the start of my first year at uni. Isla and I were assigned as roommates, total strangers. She was loud, and weird, and had about a dozen different tea tins she kept offering me like they were a personality quiz."

A breathless, bitter laugh escaped me.

"But when I came back from the funeral, she'd cleared out half her wardrobe to make space for my things. Bought my favorite biscuits, even though I'd never told her what they were. And then she just... sat. No pressure. No questions. She let me not talk. She let me fall apart and didn't try to tape the pieces back together."

Finn was quiet, but I felt him shift enough that his shoulder brushed mine. A gentle lean. I didn't move away.

"My mother..." I swallowed. "She didn't handle the grief well. She turned it into a performance. All clipped tones and proper mourning attire. When I started crying at the service, she handed me a tissue and told me to pull myself together. Stiff upper lip, and all that."

I was aware of the sound of my own breathing. Of Ajax's slow, patient exhale.

"I've had people I cared about disappear on me," I murmured. "Some by choice. Some not. But Isla's the one who's always stayed. The one who knows the difference between who I am and who my family wants me to be."

"She's not gone." Finn's voice wasn't soft—it was steel. Quiet, but unyielding. "She left us a trail."

I looked down at the journal again, flipping to the last filled page. There was something about the way the pen lifted halfway through a sentence. Like she'd been interrupted. Like she'd meant to come back.

I stood, suddenly desperate for something to do. "She was running motion-detection trail cams near here. Tracking wildcat movement and deer population clusters. She might've left memory cards behind."

Finn was already moving. "You check the east edge. I'll take the south tree line."

We split the clearing in silence, scanning bark and branches. He spotted the first camera near a thick birch, its casing half-obscured by lichen. The second I found behind a cluster of ferns, mounted to a pine.

Then I saw it. Tucked into the base of a tree, under a camouflaged flap of moss and bark, was a small waterproof case. I snatched it up and flipped it open with shaking fingers.

Three SD cards, each labeled in Isla's precise hand. Locations, dates—last week. Which meant they were likely the final pieces of her data collection before whatever had happened... happened.

I stared at them, the weight of those tiny plastic rectangles suddenly enormous.

"We'll have to wait until we're back in Glenlaig," I said quietly. "I don't have anything out here that can read them."

Finn didn't answer right away. When I looked up, he was already crouching by his pack, unzipping a side pocket and pulling out a small device.

Stunned, I could only stare. "You brought a card reader?"

"Card reader, rugged tablet, and about three thousand spare battery packs." He didn't look up as he kept digging in his pack. "Didn't think we'd need it for cam footage, but I never leave on a backcountry op without it. Learned that lesson the hard way."

I blinked. "You carried a tablet into the Highlands?"

"It's military grade. Shockproof, waterproof, and lighter than my coffee press."

"Wait. You brought a coffee press too?" Of course, he'd handed me coffee this morning, but I hadn't seen him make it. I'd assumed it was instant.

He glanced over his shoulder, deadpan. "What kind of monster do you think I am?"

I huffed a sound that was halfway between a laugh and a sob. "I don't even have a response to that."

Dropping the teasing, he held out a steady hand for the cards. "We'll check them tonight, after camp's up. It's too late to go anywhere else."

And that was it.

His quiet competence and foresight were starting to make me rethink everything I thought I knew about Finley Patterson.

I passed him the cards, one by one. "Okay."

Because maybe we wouldn't have to wait for answers after all.

CHAPTER 15

FINN

The fire had burned down to a cradle of coals, just enough heat to keep the chill at bay. Above us, the canopy swayed in the breeze, pine needles whispering. The quiet had changed from the earlier suffocating stillness of a disturbed camp, to a more natural hush, like the woods had decided to keep their distance.

Ajax lay stretched out beside me, his chin resting on his paws, ears twitching with every shift of the wind. Not tense. But not asleep either. Like he knew we weren't done yet.

Saoirse sat across from me, cross-legged, her hands curled around a mug of weak tea like it was the only thing keeping her tethered to the present moment. She hadn't said much since we found the journal. I'd stayed close but quiet, giving her space without giving her distance. She hadn't pushed me away. That felt like a win.

I powered on the tablet and dug out the first of the SD cards from the waterproof case. Saoirse watched, her gaze sharp now—ready for answers even if they hurt.

"This might take a minute." I didn't really expect a

response. The tablet chugged as it registered the card, directories loading with all the urgency of molasses.

Still, it worked.

Rows of image files appeared, sorted by timestamp. I selected the first and let the tablet do its thing.

She shifted, taking a closer seat, shoulder almost brushing mine. I didn't move away, and tried my best to ignore the fact that she now sat close enough I could feel the heat of her. I sensed her unease and squashed the urge to wrap an arm around her. Saoirse wasn't a woman who'd accept easy comfort.

Together, we waited as the first photo flickered to life on screen: a deer mid-step, partially blurred, eyes glowing in the flash like something mythic.

Saoirse let out a breath. "Well, at least the camera's working."

Another image loaded—badgers this time, two of them bumbling through undergrowth. A red squirrel. A fox with a half-missing tail. This was Isla's world. Data and dirt. Wild things. Patterns. And we were walking through it like ghosts.

I tapped to the next image, and the world started to shift.

The next frame was darker. Not a trick of the lighting. Something about it made my skin pull tight across my shoulders.

It was time-stamped four days before Isla's last check-in. Same angle. Same camera. But instead of wildlife, it had caught something else.

Movement. A flash of fabric. Dark, too dark for the usual hikers who passed through in their neon jackets and bargain-bin rain gear. A figure, mostly turned away from the lens, only the blur of a shoulder and arm visible. But it wasn't the shape that got my attention. It was the stance. Something about it felt wrong in a way I couldn't put my finger on.

The figure reappeared in the next burst—clearer this time,

half-turned toward the lens. He wore earth-toned gear: technical fabric, high-end. Nothing flashy, but efficient. The kind of setup someone might use for stalking deer in the hills or photographing rare wildlife in poor light.

Except something about it made the hairs lift on the back of my neck.

Then I saw it. The gleam of metal.

A rifle slung across his chest. Not a hunting shotgun. Not something weather-beaten and decades old. This was newer. Sleek. Low-profile.

Saoirse leaned in, eyes narrowing. "Is that a scope?"

"Yeah." I tapped the screen to zoom in. "Looks like a Blaser. Modular build. Lightweight. You don't see many of them here."

"In Scotland?"

I shook my head. "Not outside of game estates. And not in a conservation zone. That's not something you carry on a hill walk."

She didn't say anything, but I watched the realization settle in. She understood what it meant—how tightly firearms were regulated here, how few excuses there were to be armed this far out. Especially without clearance.

I flipped to the next image. Same man. Head turned. Looking directly into the lens. He wasn't startled or caught mid-motion. If anything, he looked like he'd paused enough for the flash to catch his face.

And he was smiling. Just the barest twist of the mouth. Like he knew exactly what he was doing. Like he saw the camera— and chose to let it see him back.

My stomach sank, slow and deliberate. It wasn't fear yet. Only a shift in weight. As if gravity had tilted the wrong way. A premonition of the bad to come.

The next photo showed a different man passing through from another angle. Same type of clothing. Another rifle—

angled a little differently, but carried with casual ease. Neither of these men looked hurried or disoriented. They weren't stumbling through the woods. They weren't lost.

They were there with purpose.

Then came another shot. Slightly off-center, almost missed. A third man, visible only from the waist down. He was moving past the edge of the frame, but a large, curved knife was clearly visible on his belt. It wasn't oversized or theatrical, but it was... deliberate. Something you strapped on because it served a purpose, not because it looked impressive.

Not a souvenir. Not casual camping gear.

Saoirse sat frozen beside me. She hadn't touched her tea in minutes. Her eyes were locked on the screen, and I could see her brain working, running the same silent calculations I was.

"They're not hikers," she said. Flat. Certain.

"No," I agreed. "They're not."

"Not legal hunters either."

"Not with that kind of kit," I said. "Not in this zone. This is protected land."

She finally looked away from the screen, blinking hard. "Jesus."

"Aye."

We sat in silence for a moment, letting the implications settle in.

These weren't people who'd taken a wrong turn. This wasn't some wayward stag hunt bleeding into conservation ground.

They were here. Armed. Moving quietly. Confident enough not to hide from trail cams. And that smile—God, that smile—had said everything I didn't want it to. Illegal hunting at best. I didn't want to consider the worst.

I tapped the tablet and began compressing the images. "I'll send these to Alex. See what he can dig up."

Saoirse nodded slowly, her face unreadable. "He'll find something."

"Or at least confirm this isn't simply someone screwing around with illegal kit."

She was still watching the screen as I worked, and even in silence I could feel the weight of her thoughts. Not panic. Not even fear. But something beneath the surface. A tension she hadn't shown when we'd started this trek. Not even when we found Isla's notes.

This was different.

"Do you think they know we're here?" she asked.

"I doubt it."

"But they could."

"They could," I said. "Depends how long they've been out here. How alert they are. Whether they saw Isla or only her cameras."

"Either way, she saw them."

"Aye."

"And she knew it mattered."

I looked at the fire, now burned down to nothing but orange coals and a faint rim of ash. The light flickered, catching on the lines of her face as she stared into the dark.

"They weren't just poachers," she said, voice low.

"No," I agreed. "I dinna think they were."

She rubbed her thumb along the edge of her mug. "This wasn't an accident."

"No," I said again. "It wasn't."

The stillness between us held, heavier now. A different kind of weight. Not dread. Not quite.

"So what does that make this?" she asked.

I studied her in the fire's flickering edge-light as I considered my answer. She wasn't fragile. But she wasn't untouched, either. I could see it in the set of her shoulders. The way she hadn't asked what if—only *what now?*

"This might not be a wilderness rescue," I said. "Might be something else entirely." Time would tell whether that was a hostage situation or a body recovery, but I sure as bloody hell wasn't saying that aloud. Not without incontrovertible proof.

Her gaze met mine—clear, unwavering. She understood. Even if we didn't have the full shape of it yet.

I glanced out toward the trees. The sun hadn't fully set. It hovered beyond the ridgeline, low and gold, casting long shadows that stretched over the undergrowth like reaching fingers. The forest wasn't dark yet—but it felt like it wanted to be.

"We'll move early," I said. "Try to locate where those shots were taken. Get eyes on the ground."

"And Isla?"

"If she saw them, she might've left more than photos. A trail. A note. Something we haven't turned up yet." I kept quiet about the more likely possibility that she'd fled without being able to leave anything at all because these men, whoever they were, had come after her. Saoirse needed whatever scraps of hope I could provide in order to keep going.

She nodded once, firm. "Whatever this turns out to be, I'm not backing off."

I held her gaze for a beat. Didn't offer comfort. Didn't try to pull her back. "Good."

Because we weren't looking for a path anymore. We were following one Isla had already found.

I just hoped we found her at the other end of it, and that she was in one piece when we did.

CHAPTER 16

SAOIRSE

The trees pressed in like sentinels, their branches crowding the overgrown path as we hiked single file through the woods. I'd lost track of how long we'd been moving, but my calves burned, and my shirt clung damply to the small of my back. Ajax moved ahead of us, silent and sharp-eyed, nose to the ground. Finn followed behind him with a focus that had narrowed to a single, forward line.

We hadn't spoken in a while.

The silence hadn't grown uncomfortable, merely taut. Coiled. As if the wilderness around us was holding its breath again, the same way it had at Isla's camp. Something was off in the air. Maybe it was the way the light filtered green-gold through the pines, or the way the birdsong had gone scattered and infrequent. We weren't being watched. Not yet. But we weren't alone out here either. I could feel it.

Or maybe that was my own paranoia.

Ajax's ears twitched. Finn slowed slightly, gesturing for me to drop back a pace as he moved forward to examine a scuff in the moss. He crouched low, fingertips brushing the earth, eyes scanning the underbrush. His lips parted, as if he might say something, then closed again. Not worth speculating aloud.

I didn't interrupt. I knew better than to talk when someone like Finn was working. Not because he couldn't multitask, but because every ounce of him was in the process of building the story the trail told him. You didn't ask a surgeon to explain while they were cutting. You let them cut.

Still, I studied him as he moved. The careful, deliberate way he shifted his weight. The faint limp he didn't think anyone noticed when he thought no one was watching. The way he clicked his tongue once—softly—and Ajax immediately pivoted to the left, redirecting their arc.

This wasn't hiking anymore. This was a pursuit.

The adrenaline that had carried me through yesterday had long since burned off, but a new kind of energy had taken its place. Something slower. Heavier. Determined.

Isla had run from something here. That much was obvious now. We were following her last known path—the one she hadn't meant to leave behind. The forest swallowed signs quickly out here, but Finn and Ajax moved with unshakable focus, reading broken twigs, disturbed moss, and minute impressions in the soil like breadcrumbs only they could see. Every step took us farther from Isla's deserted camp and deeper into terrain she must have fled through. And the farther we followed, the more certain I became that she hadn't run blindly.

She'd run because someone was chasing her.

We crested a low rise without a word, the incline giving way to a gentle dip in the terrain. Ajax stopped first, posture going rigid. Finn was only a breath behind, lifting a hand in a signal to halt.

The air had gone wrong again. That too-quiet stillness that made the hairs lift at the back of my neck. I dropped into a crouch beside Finn, following his gaze down the slope.

Past a tangled copse of rowan and pine, across a shallow ravine, was a clearing. In it, was a cluster of tents.

I froze.

They weren't like Isla's. These weren't scrappy, weather-beaten things patched and repurposed with years of fieldwork. These were clean. Sturdy. Angled tents in muted, matte fabric that caught no light. Set up in careful rows, evenly spaced. Not military, exactly, but structured in a way that didn't belong in a place like this.

Finn passed me the binoculars without a word. I adjusted them with damp fingers and focused in.

Four men. Maybe more beyond the trees.

They didn't look like hikers. Nothing about them suggested casual or even rugged outdoorsmanship. Their clothes weren't matching, but they were all of the same ilk—practical, stream-lined, dark in tone. Jackets cut to move in. Durable trousers. New-looking boots. Everything they wore looked chosen with purpose, not thrown together from a kit list or bargain shelf. No bright colors, no reflective strips, nothing that would catch the eye on a trail.

Each man carried a heavy pack. Larger than necessary for day trekking, and far too full to suggest they were only passing through. They'd come prepared to stay.

And then there were the weapons.

Not long-barreled hunting rifles. Not anything I could picture on a licensed stalker's shoulder during deer season. Which it currently wasn't. These were compact. Clean lines. I didn't know enough about guns to name them, but even I had the immediate, visceral understanding that whatever they were carrying, it didn't belong here. Not in these woods. Not under any lawful pretense.

One of the men stepped forward, adjusting something at his chest—maybe a strap or a small pack-mounted device. I couldn't see the details, only the ease of the motion. Like someone accustomed to wearing that kind of kit. Like muscle memory.

He turned slightly toward another figure beside him, head angled in conversation. Calm. Comfortable. Like there was nothing unusual about any of it.

My breath caught.

I knew that face.

Not well. Not personally. But well enough.

I'd seen it across linen-covered tables, at banquets and black-tie galas my mother insisted I attend during the school holidays. Usually standing beside a son who was even more unbearable. He'd been loud. Opinionated. Laughing about game stocks and fox hunting and how conservation was "good PR" but bad business.

Victor Sandhurst.

That was his name. I hadn't thought of him in years.

There was no reason for him to be here.

And yet... he was. On this slope. In the heart of protected land. Armed and at ease, like he owned the place.

I lowered the binoculars, hands gone cold despite the sweat at the back of my neck.

"Finn." I jerked a chin in the direction of the camp. "That man. The blond. I know him."

He turned his head enough to catch my tone. "How?"

"Fundraisers. My mother's friends. That sort of circle."

A pause. I didn't need to say more. Finn's jaw ticked once. He nodded, already backing us down the rise, into the trees again. Once he was satisfied we had sufficient cover, we dropped to a crouch behind a fallen log slick with moss. My legs ached from the hike, but the pressure in my chest made it hard to feel anything else. Finn slung his pack off and pulled out the satellite transmitter—sleek and matte like most of his gear, with a stubby dish antenna and a scuffed casing that spoke to heavy use. Not a phone. A data unit. Built for uplinks, not conversation.

He crouched beside me, fingers moving fast and sure as he pulled out the tablet and connected the two devices with a short cable. He slid in the memory card from his camera, not one of the old trail cams from Isla's study but his own—likely loaded with the zoomed-in binocular photos he'd snapped right after I identified Sandhurst.

"We'll try to send these," he murmured. "High-res is too risky with signal this thin, but compressed stills—maybe we get lucky. Echo might be able to work with faces, gear, timestamps."

That made more sense. The trail cam footage had gone through last night. This was something else—new, urgent, immediate. Not proof, exactly, but evidence. And something to chase.

I didn't ask what Echo—Alex—could do with it. At this point, I didn't need a breakdown of whatever hacker capabilities he possessed. I needed someone who could take what we had and make it mean something.

Finn tapped quickly through a few menus, then adjusted the antenna, angling the dish toward a narrow break in the canopy. The trees here were dense, and the terrain had begun to slope again, pinning us against the low forest rise. He shifted to one knee for elevation, bracing with one hand as the other adjusted the orientation. I could see the tension in his shoulders, the frustration in the tight set of his jaw.

He wasn't panicking.

But he was trying very, very hard to keep ahead of whatever clock had started ticking.

And *him.*

Victor Sandhurst turned half toward the lens, the faintest

trace of a smirk on his face like he knew no one would stop him. Like he *never* had to worry about consequences.

My stomach twisted.

This wasn't some stranger in tactical gear. This was a name I'd seen on donation plaques and hospital wings. This was a man who'd once waxed poetic about the "thrill of the chase" while sipping a thousand-pound bottle of Bordeaux.

He was here. With a gun. On protected land. And Isla was missing.

I tried to slow my breathing. Inhale. Exhale. But the forest tilted, and I couldn't tell if it was the altitude or the memory or the sudden collision of past and present that knocked something loose inside me.

They *couldn't* be connected, could they?

And yet... how else did someone like him end up out here?

Finn made a sound low in his throat. A curse, maybe. The communicator flashed red—**UPLOAD FAILED.**

"Signal's bouncing. Too much interference," he muttered. "Might be topography, might be weather. Or both."

He stood, lifting the dish slightly, trying to aim it toward the clearest strip of sky.

I stared at the screen, fists clenched around my knees.

Victor Sandhurst was a walking emblem of everything I'd left behind. Everything I thought I'd severed when I chose muddy boots and animal breath over clean pearls and white wine smiles. He didn't belong here.

Except clearly, in some sense, he *did*.

And that terrified me more than I was willing to admit.

Because if men like him had found a playground in this forest—this wild, sacred place—what hope did Isla have?

Finn dropped back beside me, one hand bracing the device against the uneven earth as he tried another angle. I watched his brow furrow, saw his lips press tight in frustration.

We were trying. Working. Moving fast. But I couldn't shake the feeling that we were already too late.

Ajax went still.

Not scenting something interesting. This was different. Frozen, hackles barely raised, ears sharp and forward. Every muscle in his body hummed like a live wire.

Finn noticed it the same second I did.

Without a word, his body shifted—low, tense. Hand sliding automatically to the side of his pack, where I knew his emergency gear was stashed.

Then I heard it.

A voice.

Distant. Too distant to make out the words, but definitely male, and far too confident for someone on a casual hike. No accent I could place, but the rhythm was wrong. Not hurried. Not confused. Someone used to being obeyed.

Then came the unmistakable crunch of boots on forest debris. Not the quiet press of someone walking carefully, but the heavy cadence of someone moving with purpose.

They were close.

My breath caught. Finn met my eyes for half a second, and that was all it took.

Run.

He yanked the communicator and the tablet in one smooth motion, shoving them into his pack with practiced speed. His voice was a whisper, fast and tight: "Stay close. Don't stop."

We moved.

Ajax surged ahead of me, silent but swift, slipping through the trees like a shadow. I followed him, barely aware of the branches that slashed at my arms, the uneven ground clawing at my boots. Behind me, I could hear Finn—barely. Not the sound of panic, but of control. Focus. Movement.

But also urgency.

I didn't look back.

I could *feel* the space behind us narrowing.

Another voice rang out, sharper this time. A word I didn't understand, but the tone didn't need translation.

They'd seen us.

Or heard us.

Or sensed enough to know something was out of place.

My lungs burned. My thighs screamed. The pack on my back suddenly felt like a boulder. But I kept going, because the alternative was unthinkable.

The forest blurred into streaks of green and shadow, light flashing through the canopy like strobe effects. Somewhere ahead, Ajax barked once—short and sharp—and then I was stumbling down a slope, half-controlled, half-tumbling. I slid the last few feet into a shallow gully, landing hard on my hands and knees in the wet moss.

Finn hit the ground behind me a second later, his pack slamming into the dirt beside him. The sat transmitter skidded out in the impact, bouncing once before coming to a stop against a rock with a dull, final-sounding crack.

I scrambled toward it, but he was already reaching, already swearing under his breath.

The housing was split along one side. The screen—small and embedded into the side panel—was spider-webbed with fractures, the dish antenna half-sheared from its hinge. He didn't waste time trying to turn it on. One look was enough.

"It's dead," he said, voice tight. "That was our uplink."

Ajax growled low and deep, planted firmly at the top of the slope above us, watching the tree line.

They hadn't followed yet. Not that we could see.

But they would.

And without the transmitter—and with no time or cover to risk a sat phone call—we were cut off.

No backup, and no way to reach anyone.

I pressed the heel of my hand to my chest, trying to calm my pulse. It wasn't working.

They weren't just out there now.

They knew we were here.

And they weren't the kind of people who left witnesses.

CHAPTER 17

FINN

The trees blurred past in streaks of green and shadow, branches clawing at my sleeves, my pack snagging on undergrowth I couldn't afford to slow down for. My lungs burned with each inhale, but I barely felt it.

Ahead of me, Saoirse moved like the devil was on her heels —which, for all we knew, wasn't far off. I could hear her breathing: tight, fast, but steady. No panic yet. Good.

Ajax cut ahead of her, then back, circling like a satellite. He moved with a silent, deadly, controlled urgency that said everything I needed to know.

We weren't outrunning a four-legged predator. We were running from men.

Men with rifles and gear that didn't belong in these woods. Men whose camp looked too ordered, too permanent, too calculated to be anything casual. Men who hadn't flinched when caught on camera.

I glanced back, once. No visual yet. But I didn't need one. I'd heard the voice. That confident call—some command barked out to someone else. It was all the confirmation I needed that they'd seen us, and they were coming.

I caught Saoirse's eye as we crested a small rise. "Left," I breathed.

She veered with me without question.

Good. She was tracking terrain and threat as fast as I was.

We pushed downhill into thicker cover, roots slick and half-hidden beneath pine duff. I gritted my teeth as my right knee twinged—old injury, old reminder—but I didn't slow. Couldn't. Not when I had her to protect. Not when Ajax was flanking us. The last good thing I'd been entrusted with.

I wasn't losing either of them.

The trail narrowed, choked by brambles. Ajax shouldered through without hesitation, Saoirse right behind, and I took up the rear, resisting the urge to look back again.

If we stopped, we were done.

If we slowed, we were vulnerable.

My whole body was humming, electric, waiting for that first shot to crack the silence. For the hunter who didn't want to be seen to prove how far he'd go to stay invisible.

But for now—we ran.

And I knew, deep in my gut, it wouldn't be enough.

We were almost clear of the ridge, the terrain beginning to tilt downward again into a dense cradle of bracken and shadow, when Ajax's pace changed.

He stopped, hackles lifted, muscles coiled.

"Down," I barked—too late.

The man stepped out from behind a tree less than twenty feet ahead, like a fucking ghost conjured from bark and shade.

Mid-forties, lean build, face half-obscured by a beard that was too neat for someone living rough. Weatherproof jacket. Heavy cargo pants. One gloved hand rested casually near the grip of a holstered pistol.

But it was the blade he drew that set every nerve in my body on fire.

Curved. Broad. Not a hunting knife.

He didn't shout. Didn't raise the gun. He was there to block us, not bluff. To show control without saying a word.

And then Ajax moved.

The flash of teeth and muscle was so fast I barely registered it before impact. Ajax launched from the ground like a missile, hitting the man square in the chest, driving him back into a tree.

The hunter staggered but didn't fall.

The knife arced up.

"No!"

The blade punched down in a tight, brutal angle. Not deep. Not clean. But it struck.

Ajax yelped—sharp, shocked—and twisted away.

Something in me fractured.

I didn't think. There was no time to think. My body was already moving.

I hit the bastard a second later with everything I had.

We went down hard, me on top, my knees pinning his hips, one hand already closing around his knife wrist. He bucked. Grunted. Tried to punch upward, but I shoved my forearm across his throat, crushing his airway, jamming the heel of my palm into his nose.

He tried to reach for the sidearm. Bad fucking move.

I grabbed his wrist, twisted. Heard something pop.

He screamed, but I didn't stop.

I swept the knife away with one hand, drove my elbow into his jaw with the other. He sagged beneath me, stunned—but not out.

"Dinna. Touch. My. Dog." Each growled word was punctuated by a punch.

He came at me again, slower now, sloppy. That was all I needed.

One knee to the gut. Another blow to the throat. Then I flipped him, slamming his head sideways into the base of the tree with just enough control to avoid killing him.

Not enough to be gentle.

He crumpled; out cold.

Blood smeared my knuckles. My own chest heaved. But I didn't look at him again.

I turned, dropping to my knees beside Ajax so fast I barely remembered hitting the ground.

"Jesus, no." My voice broke.

Blood soaked into his fur along his left flank, glistening dark and thick against the lighter guard hairs. Not a puncture—too shallow. A slash. Still bleeding, but not gushing. Not arterial.

Okay. Okay.

He was breathing. Too fast, but steady.

"Hey," I whispered, one hand hovering an inch above the wound before I dared to touch. "Hey, mate. I've got you."

Ajax blinked slowly. Dazed, but conscious. His ears twitched at the sound of my voice. He didn't try to rise.

My hands wouldn't stop shaking.

I pressed my palm gently to his ribs, feeling for breath, watching the rise and fall. His pupils weren't blown. His gums were pale but not gray. He flinched when I touched his side—good. That meant the pain hadn't taken him under.

"You stay with me, mate." My voice cracked on the last word. "You hear me? You stay."

The blood was already soaking into my shirt, warm and awful. I tried to breathe around the knot in my throat. This was too familiar—too fucking close. It was Kandahar all over again, blood on the ground and the split-second between life and—

"Finn!"

Saoirse's voice cut through, sharp and breathless.

I turned toward her. She'd scrambled halfway back up the trail, eyes wide and locked on us.

"We have to move," she said. "There could be more."

I nodded, but couldn't make my body let go.

Not yet.

Ajax groaned—low and exhausted—but he shifted. Alive. Still here.

I closed my eyes for a second. Just one second. Then I pressed my hand flat over the wound to slow the bleeding and looked up.

"Help me get him up."

We weren't safe yet. But we were still together, and I wasn't leaving anyone behind.

I didn't feel the weight until I stood.

Ajax wasn't heavy—not for a Malinois—but he was dense, all muscle and tension and blood-soaked fur. My arms locked around his chest and hind legs, pressing him tight against me. I felt his ribs flutter against mine. Too fast. Too shallow.

It didn't matter.

I turned toward Saoirse. "Go," I rasped. "Find cover. I've got him."

She hesitated for half a heartbeat—only long enough to look me over, eyes catching on the blood across my chest, the wild edge I could feel in my own breathing.

Then she nodded once before pivoting on her heel to run.

I followed.

Every step jarred something loose in my back. I was off-balance, favoring my bad knee, and Ajax wasn't helping—he shifted slightly with every stride, a low groan vibrating through his body.

But I didn't let go.

The forest blurred around us, branches lashing at my arms,

my face, the exposed skin of my neck. I could taste iron—maybe from my split lip, maybe from fear.

Saoirse wove ahead of me, ducking under low-hanging limbs, her voice low and fast. "This way. There's a blind. It's not far."

My legs were cramping. I adjusted Ajax in my arms, gritting my teeth. I could feel his blood soaking through my shirt, hot and steady.

"Keep talking," I gasped. "Please keep talking."

"I think it's off the ridge. Northwest face. I saw it last year on a survey hike with Isla. It's not far, I swear."

"Good."

I didn't have the breath to say more.

We stumbled down a gully, sliding sideways through the bracken, and finally—finally—I saw it. A weathered structure tucked against the curve of the hill, half-collapsed on one side but still mostly intact. A hunting blind or old poacher's shelter, walls reinforced with stone and timber, roof barely holding up.

Saoirse shoved the warped door open. I staggered in behind her, dropped to my knees, and laid Ajax down with all the care I had left in my body.

His flank rose and fell.

Still alive.

Still with me.

I braced my hands on my thighs, head hanging. My breath came ragged and useless. The world tilted around the edges.

But we'd made it.

For now.

The second Ajax was down, I crouched beside him.

But that was all I did.

I didn't reach for my kit. Didn't peel back his harness. Didn't check the bleeding or clean the wound.

I just... stared.

His eyes were open. Cloudy. Pain-bright. He was panting, ribs fluttering too fast under blood-matted fur. The wound along his flank seeped crimson, dark and steady, and I knew— knew—what I was supposed to do next.

But I couldn't move.

My hands hovered uselessly above him, fists clenched too tight to function. I'd carried him through half a mile of brush and broken terrain. I'd fought off a man with a knife. I'd run on a knee that hadn't been quite right in years. But now?

Now I was paralyzed.

Because this wasn't merely a cut.

This was Charlie's blood again.

This was the woman I'd tried to save.

This was failure.

Ajax shifted slightly and let out a low, pained whine, and that noise cut deeper than the blade had.

"Stay with me," I whispered, voice shredded and raw. "You stay with me, mate."

I reached out, finally, to touch his side, but my hand was shaking so hard I didn't trust it. Couldn't trust it. My pulse thundered in my ears, drowning out everything but the voice in my head, the one that said *you let him down, just like the last one, just like always.*

A hand touched my shoulder. Steady. Grounding.

Saoirse.

She crouched beside me, her breath still coming quick from the run, but her hands didn't shake. Her voice didn't break.

"You have to move, Finn."

I didn't. I couldn't.

She looked at me—really looked—and said, soft but firm, "Let me help him."

That was enough to break the paralysis. I nodded once, barely able to manage it, and shifted out of the way.

She was already reaching for her kit.

And I sat there, useless in the corner of that shelter, hands still stained with blood, watching the woman I couldn't stop thinking about save the dog I couldn't afford to lose.

The crack in the mask didn't split all the way open.

But I felt it.

And for the first time in years, I didn't try to patch it back up.

CHAPTER 18

SAOIRSE

I didn't remember dropping my pack, but my fingers were already at the zipper before I'd fully registered that we'd stopped moving. The poacher's blind around us was narrow and musty, the wood damp with age and the faint stench of mildew, but it would hold. For now.

Ajax whimpered low as I knelt beside him. Finn hovered at his side, hands clenched at his thighs, chest heaving like he couldn't quite remember how to breathe.

Focus. Prioritize.

"Okay, sweetheart." I shifted into the soft tone I used in surgery, in emergency calls, in any moment where panic had no business being. "Let's see what we've got."

Ajax's flanks were rising too quickly, his sides trembling with the effort of staying still. I murmured nonsense as I ran my hands over his ribs. Palpated gently. The muscle on his left side twitched under my fingers, hot and wet. Not arterial. Not spurting. But bad enough to soak into Finn's shirt on the way here.

"Good boy." I whispered more words of praise as I checked for signs of internal bleeding, shock, obstruction. "You did so good."

His pulse was elevated, but not ragged. His gums were pale but not white. He was still tracking, eyes flicking toward Finn every few seconds like he needed him in view. Like he needed the tether.

I felt that, deep.

"Stay with me now." I tried to project calm into his bones. "You're in good hands. You're my patient now."

I reached for my trauma kit, tugging the roll open with a practiced snap. Gloves. Sterile gauze. Clotting powder. Local anesthetic.

The harness had to come off. I sliced it free with my pocket blade, pulling the shredded straps back to reveal the wound properly.

A deep slash—knife, definitely. Sharp, deliberate. Not a wild tear. I bit back a curse. I hadn't seen precisely what had happened because I'd been flat on the ground, barely out of harm's way, while these two had saved our arses.

"Missed the artery," I muttered. "Lucky lad."

I poured saline over the wound to flush it. Ajax flinched but didn't pull away. God, what a dog. I dusted the clotting agent into the cut, watching the powder fizz slightly as it did its job. Pressed gauze in place and held it, counting down from twenty under my breath.

Behind me, Finn didn't move. Not even when I asked, "Can you hand me the syringes from the red pocket?"

No response.

Ajax whined again, so I leaned closer, brushing his ear back from his face. "You're okay. It's almost over."

Painkiller next. I drew it up, found the muscle, and injected smooth and clean. Then the pressure bandage. Tight, but not too tight. A clean wrap. Containment.

The worst was done. I sat back on my heels, breath catching as I pressed the back of my wrist to my brow. Sweat, blood, bark fragments—I couldn't tell which was which anymore.

Ajax blinked at me, eyes glassy but calm now. He let out a low sigh and shifted slightly toward Finn.

"Of course you want him," I whispered. "It's always the stubborn ones."

I reached down and stroked his side, slow and careful. "You're going to be okay, sweetheart. I've got you."

Then I looked up.

Finn hadn't moved an inch.

Still kneeling, still staring at Ajax like if he blinked, the dog might vanish.

His hands were red with blood that wasn't his. His jaw locked tight enough to crack. His expression wasn't blank. It was far too full for that. Like if he let go for even a second, the whole thing would come apart.

Triage definitely wasn't done.

I reached for him next.

I stayed on my knees, shifting to close the space between us. Finn didn't flinch, didn't look at me—only continued to stare at Ajax, as if his will alone were keeping the dog here.

"Finn." His name was soft on my lips. Not the professional tone, not the vet's voice. Mine.

No response.

I reached out, slowly, and laid a hand on his forearm. His skin was hot and tacky with blood—Ajax's, not his, I was pretty sure—but he didn't react to the touch.

"Your turn."

That got his attention. He didn't look at me, but his shoulders stiffened, jaw grinding.

"I'm fine."

"Bullshit."

That made him blink. He still didn't look at me, though.

I let go of his arm long enough to grab the gauze again, then shifted in closer, scanning him. He had a long scratch running down his right biceps, caked with dirt and blood. Not life-threatening, but it needed cleaning.

There was blood at his temple, trickling from a shallow scrape hidden under his sweat-damp hair, and likely bruises on his knees from their fall into the blind.

"You're a mess," I said, gently. "Sit still."

"Saoirse—"

"Sit. Still." I didn't raise my voice, but I didn't back down either. "Let me check you."

He exhaled through his nose. Almost a laugh, if it hadn't sounded so damn broken.

He didn't fight me, though.

I cleaned the worst of the blood from his temple, then cleaned and wrapped his arm quickly. Nothing needed stitches. Nothing critical.

But his hands were still shaking.

I pressed the edge of a sterile cloth into his palm, to see what he'd do. He didn't close his fingers around it. Merely sat there. Motionless. Empty.

"Finn," I murmured, and then did something I hadn't done since we started this trek. I reached out and placed my hand flat against his chest.

His shirt was soaked—Ajax's blood, sweat, dirt—but beneath it, I felt the thud of his heart, fast and irregular.

"You're in shock," I said.

Still, he wouldn't look at me.

Then, so quietly I almost missed it, he murmured, "He's all I've got left of Charlie."

My throat tightened.

The words weren't for me, not really. They were just... loose. Uncontained. The way confessions sometimes slipped free when your guard cracked enough.

Ajax shifted beside us, letting out a breath through his nose, not quite asleep but fading fast from the painkiller. Finn's hand finally twitched—once—and settled lightly against the dog's side.

"I swore I'd take care of him. That I'd do it right."

Guilt radiated off him like heat.

"And you have." I infused my voice with as much reassurance as I could muster. "You are."

He finally met my eyes.

And God, there was so much pain in that look. Pain and self-recrimination and the barest flicker of something like hope —like maybe he wanted to believe me.

But he didn't say anything.

I let my hand rest over his heart a beat longer. Then I shifted slightly, leaned my shoulder into his just enough to remind him he wasn't alone.

We sat like that for a long moment, surrounded by trees and shadows and breathless silence, while Ajax slid into sleep beside us.

Finn's breathing eventually evened out, the shake in his hands mostly stilling. Not gone. But manageable.

I gave his arm a light squeeze, then rose, knees stiff from crouching so long. The blind was narrow, barely wide enough for the three of us and our packs, but it was better than nothing. I nudged open a warped wooden panel—hinged with rusted nails and what looked like repurposed leather strapping

—and slipped out into the dense brush while Finn stayed with Ajax.

A slow circuit confirmed what I already suspected: the old poacher's hide was built into a shallow slope, its rough-planked walls nearly lost beneath bracken and low-hanging spruce. The wood was grayed and cracked with age, but still held together, reinforced in places with moss-packed seams and the occasional bit of netting or tarp half-sunken into the overgrowth. The platform floor inside had held—dry, though it creaked underfoot like something remembering its age. The brush coverage above and around was decent. Not impenetrable, but enough to break up our silhouette, especially in the dimming light.

I ducked back in and gave Finn the report. "It'll do. We've got decent shelter above and low visibility from the ridge. No signs of recent use. Should be safe until first light."

Finn looked down at Ajax, then back at me. "It's not ideal."

"No." I settled onto the edge of the pack I'd repurposed as a seat. "But moving him tonight would be worse. He needs rest. So do you."

He didn't argue, but he didn't agree either.

I could see the calculation running behind his eyes. Risk versus reward. Danger versus exhaustion. His whole body was still vibrating with the aftershocks of fight mode.

"We hold here," he said at last. Not quite a command. A decision. "I'll take first watch."

I tilted my head. "You're not doing anyone any good half-dead on your feet."

He started to protest, but I held up a hand. "I'm not saying sleep. I'm saying sit. For five minutes. With me."

His jaw worked like he wanted to argue, but he didn't. With a low, exhausted exhale, he slid down beside me.

The blind creaked faintly as he leaned his head back

against one of the supports, staring at the ceiling like he was trying to see through it. Ajax shifted slightly, nestled between us, his breathing slow and even beneath the gauze bandage I'd wrapped tight.

I let the quiet settle between us.

It wasn't the same tense silence from the trail. This one was softer. Worn in. Like the hush that followed a storm.

Finn's shoulder brushed mine.

He didn't move away.

Neither did I.

We stayed like that for a long time.

Not hours. Not full afternoon to dusk. But long enough for the heat to fade from my skin, for my breathing to level out, for the ringing adrenaline in my ears to quiet into something like thought.

Outside, the sky lightened and shifted—not toward evening yet, but far enough that the shadows grew more directional, the air cooler where it touched my neck. Summer in the Highlands made time feel strange, like the light was elastic.

The forest didn't settle, exactly, but it changed. Branches creaked in ways that didn't feel threatening, and birdsong slowly picked up again, cautious at first, then bold. A breeze filtered through the slats in the hide's walls, dragging the scent of moss, soil, and old bark across the air. Somewhere farther off, I thought I caught the edge of smoke. Not strong. Not close. But real.

Inside, the space felt tighter than before. The rough wood walls trapped our breath, our silence, our shared waiting. But the structure held. Still solid beneath the bracken and lichen, with enough coverage to keep us shadowed and small.

I didn't try to fill the silence.

He didn't either.

And maybe that was the point.

There was nothing more to fix for now. No trail to follow or plan to make. Only the warmth of a dog between us, the ghost of fear still clinging to our backs, and this unlikely pause in the middle of nowhere.

We weren't safe.

But we weren't alone, either.

And for now, that was enough.

CHAPTER 19

FINN

The light came first. That soft, blue-edged glow that crept in before the sun committed to rising, while the world stayed hushed in the liminal space between night and day.

I woke stiff, back aching, neck kinked from the way I'd slouched sideways against the rough timber wall of the blind. My shoulder throbbed from holding tension all night, and my right leg—still nursing that ancient tendon pull from training ops outside Muscat—had officially registered its protest.

Didn't matter. We were still breathing.

Ajax was curled in the space between me and the outer wall, blanket tucked around him where Saoirse had left it. His breathing was steady now—deep and even, chest rising and falling in a rhythm that felt like permission to exhale.

He twitched once in his sleep, ears flicking. But I didn't spot any signs of distress.

I watched him for a moment longer than I meant to. Let my fingers drift across the curve of his shoulder—a whisper of touch, careful not to wake him. I needed that contact more than I wanted to admit.

The crackling rush in my chest hadn't fully gone away. That thing that had nearly broken loose yesterday, when I'd thought that—

I cut off that line of thinking. Didn't need to go there again.

A rustle pulled my attention toward the far wall. Saoirse.

She was already awake, sitting cross-legged with her back to one of the beams, a foil blanket wrapped around her shoulders like a shield. Her hair was a halo of static-fine waves, and the light from outside painted her in silver and shadow.

She looked... still. Not peaceful, not relaxed, but focused in that way only she could be. As if she'd already catalogued every sound in the forest and was letting her thoughts work around them.

No words yet. Just the shared hush of survival and the weight of too much not said.

I didn't want to break it, but I knew I would.

I shifted slowly, careful not to wake Ajax, and crossed the blind in a crouch to join her. The ground was cold beneath me, but I sat anyway. Close, but not too close.

Saoirse didn't turn, but I could tell she knew I was there. The way her spine stiffened slightly, then eased. The tiny flex of her fingers on the blanket.

We sat like that for a few breaths. The kind of quiet that felt earned.

Then, because I couldn't keep it in anymore, I said it. "Thank you."

She glanced sideways. "For what?"

I swallowed. "You know for what."

Saoirse looked like she was going to brush it off—shrug or joke or say it was nothing. I stopped her with a look before she could open her mouth.

"No. Really. You saved him. I—I didn't know how to move."

There it was. The raw edge. I'd tried to keep it tamped down, but it slipped through the cracks.

She didn't speak right away.

"I've seen a lot of chaos," I said. "Fought through worse. But yesterday..." My voice dropped. "He's all I've got left of Charlie. And when I saw that knife—"

The words stuck.

I exhaled hard. Looked out through the open slats of the blind. The forest beyond was pale and wet with dew, morning light bleeding into mist.

"You're no' what I expected," I added, quieter.

That got her attention. She turned slightly, one brow lifted in that way she did when she was half-challenging, half-curious.

"You say that like it's a bad thing."

I gave a crooked smile. "I meant it as a compliment."

She studied me for a moment, her gaze heavier than it had any right to be at this hour.

"You're not what I expected either."

Simple. Soft. But it hit harder than it should have. Because coming from her, it didn't sound like an accusation. It sounded like... maybe she liked this version of me better. The unarmored one.

And that? That was dangerous.

The kind of thing that made me want to reach for more.

Our eyes met, and everything else dropped away. The birdsong, the dawn mist, even the dull ache in my ribs.

It was only her. The woman I'd underestimated. Who kept showing up and showing me I was wrong about her.

There was no distance left between us that hadn't already been closed by silence and blood and borrowed trust. And the quiet between us now wasn't empty. It hummed.

I didn't mean to move.

Or maybe I did. Maybe the second her words landed in my chest like something gentle and unexpected, I knew exactly what was going to happen next.

I shifted a little closer. A breath. Maybe less.

She didn't move away. Her gaze stayed steady on mine, eyes dark and clear, and when I leaned in, she met me there without hesitation.

Our mouths touched, and the world narrowed.

Warmth. The brush of her lower lip. The faint hitch of her breath as mine slid against it. No rush or urgency. Just the quiet, perfect pull of it. Like coming home to something I hadn't realized I'd been missing.

My pulse jumped, but not from shock. From recognition.

She tilted her head slightly, her mouth parting to deepen the kiss. Her fingers found the fabric of my sleeve, curled there like she was grounding herself. My hand rose to the back of her neck, fingertips catching in her hair and curving around her nape.

The kiss wasn't demanding. It didn't need to be. It held.

And in that held breath—her mouth, my hand, the space between heartbeats—I felt something sharp and bright and real, blooming behind my ribs with the kind of ache I couldn't run from.

Because this wasn't the beginning. This was us, already in motion, already falling.

A twig snapped.

Loud. Close. Too close.

The crack was unmistakable. A single twig, brittle and careless beneath a boot that didn't belong.

I pulled back instantly, muscles locking tight, head tilting toward the sound. All softness vanished. The soldier in me rose without a word.

Saoirse froze, her breath caught halfway between the kiss

and the new threat. Her eyes met mine, wide and sharp, and I saw the shift in of awareness slamming into place.

I held up a hand. Flat. Silent. Stay low.

Ajax stirred beside us, ears twitching, nose lifting slightly, but he didn't make a sound. Good lad. Still with me.

The air changed. Again. Heavier now. Close and watching.

We were no longer alone.

The taste of her was still on my lips, sweet and unfinished, but survival had no patience for sweetness. It was a lesson I knew all too well.

I reached for my knife and crept toward the edge of the blind, every step measured, senses stretched to their limits. The birds had gone silent. Nothing moved. Not even the trees, as if they were listening, too.

No shapes moved between the trunks. No breaths sounded that weren't ours. Whatever had snapped that twig was gone now. Or watching. Either way, we were back in the waiting place.

After long, long minutes, I eased back down beside her.

Neither of us spoke.

Ajax shifted again, his head resting against her ankle like an apology. Or a promise.

The kiss still echoed in the air between us—unresolved, electric. I didn't look at her, but I could feel the hum of it, thrumming in the quiet, nestled in the space between our bodies like a live wire we both knew not to touch again. Not yet.

But it had happened. And the world had felt different while it lasted.

She didn't reach for me. I didn't move closer.

But we didn't pull away either.

CHAPTER 20

SAOIRSE

The temperature had dropped. Not cold, exactly, but cool enough to slip between layers. The kind of damp chill that settled in slow and stayed. Outside, the forest held its hush, branches barely stirring, the sky a soft, colorless stretch above the canopy.

Inside the blind, we hadn't spoken in a while.

And though we sat close, something between us had cooled.

Or maybe it had sharpened.

Neither of us mentioned the kiss. But it was there, suspended in the space between us like dew on a spiderweb—delicate, shimmering, impossible to ignore.

We moved through the morning in a rhythm that felt... different. Careful. The kind of awareness that came from knowing exactly what the other's mouth felt like, and having no idea what came next.

Not a thing I'd thought I'd have to consider when I'd set out on this expedition.

I crouched over the unfolded topo map, brushing pine needles off the corner. Finn knelt beside me, his shoulder bumping mine as he leaned in for a closer look. His hand stretched across the page at the same time as mine, our fingers grazing.

Static.

I felt it—sharp and electric—like my skin had a memory all its own.

I didn't pull away. Neither did he. When I glanced up, I caught him watching me. There wasn't a trace of that lazy smirk he usually wore like armor. No amusement or challenge, either. That steady, quiet gaze felt as if he was taking inventory of something new and didn't want to miss a detail.

I swallowed against a mouth gone suddenly dry and looked away, pretending to study a contour line I already knew by heart.

I wasn't someone who got flustered easily. I'd spent years cultivating the ability to hold eye contact through committee meetings, cocktail parties, and emergency surgeries. But this wasn't something I could compartmentalize.

Because the way he looked at me didn't feel like a beginning or an ending. It felt like a shift. And I didn't know where it would land.

We sat side by side at the entrance to the shelter, the last of the breakfast rations between us. A protein bar shared in silence. Dried fruit that tasted like paper. The comfort of food, even in small, bland doses, helped take the edge off.

Finn broke the silence first. "We missed our morning check-in."

I blinked. "What?"

"o800 came and went. With the sat unit destroyed, we're on our own."

I'd known that yesterday. But that had been before the mad dash to escape. The fight. The field treatment of Ajax's wounds. In all the ensuing chaos, it had simply bled out of my mind.

"What about the sat phone?"

He hesitated. "Gone."

"Gone? What do you mean, gone?"

"I think it must've come out when I went after the man who attacked Ajax." He said it evenly, but I could hear the self-recrimination underneath.

The implications hit me like cold water down the spine. We were off schedule. And not by a few minutes.

My chest tightened. "Someone's probably worrying about us by now."

It was the first time I'd let my thoughts drift back to Glenlaig. To the others. To my grandfather, likely pretending not to worry while obsessively cleaning surgical tools. To Parker and Pippa and the others, who would absolutely raise hell if they thought we were in trouble. I'd been so focused on the search, on Isla, on running, that I'd forgotten we weren't the only ones waiting.

Finn nodded. His jaw flexed, the muscle tight along the edge. "Protocols kick in when we miss two. They'll assume we're out of signal range at first."

"But we are out of signal range." The quiet words settled between us. "And we're alone."

It wasn't simply a statement. It was a reckoning.

Instead of offering false reassurance, he handed me the truth like it was a loaded weapon. "They'll start looking if we miss the next one. But that takes time. They won't scramble until they're sure."

Time we might not have.

My gaze drifted toward Ajax, still curled up with his head on his paws, ears twitching in his sleep. His breathing was slow and even, but the bandage on his flank made my stomach knot. We weren't only fighting against the clock to find Isla anymore —we were racing against the limits of our own isolation.

I looked at Finn. "So what now?"

His eyes flicked toward the trees, the unspoken answer already forming.

The cavalry wasn't coming. Not yet.

Whatever came next? It was still on us.

Finn spread the map across his thigh, but I wasn't really looking at it. My eyes were on Ajax, lying in the dappled shade near the blind's wall.

He woke as I crouched beside him and ran my hand gently along his side, checking the dressing. No seepage. No heat. The wound was clean. The swelling had gone down slightly overnight, and while he wasn't exactly eager to jump to his feet, he raised his head when I stood.

"He's good to move." After yesterday, I knew Finn would need that reassurance. "Stiff, but alert."

Finn didn't look up right away. His jaw was clenched, that tic pulsing beneath the skin. "Good to move" wasn't good enough for him. Not when it was Ajax. Not after what had nearly happened.

"He won't reinjure it," I added, softer now. "I won't let him push too far."

"I trust you." He said it without hesitation, but the words were taut. Like a rope stretched too tight. He was bracing himself.

But we both knew this wasn't about Ajax.

He dragged his finger across the map to trace our last known path. "Here's the dilemma. We keep pushing forward—

no comms, no backup—or we cut our losses and head back to get help."

The weight of the choice pressed against my chest like a stone.

"If we go back, that gives them time. Time to move her. Time to erase whatever evidence we've already seen. Time to make her disappear." Not that we'd seen evidence of that directly, but what was the alternative? Not one I cared to contemplate.

I didn't raise my voice, but my point landed nonetheless. I saw the way his shoulders tightened. Heard the low curse he bit back.

He hated this. Hated the lack of options. Hated the thought of moving blind. He was used to controlled operations. Orders. A safety net. A team on the line when things went sideways.

This? This was chaos.

He looked at me then, and I knew what he saw—mud on my boots, hair pulled back, fingers still stained with Ajax's blood. Not just a vet. Not just a client. A partner.

One who wasn't backing down.

I sat beside Finn, the weight of the decision still coiled tight in my chest. The silence between us wasn't hostile. It was thoughtful. Careful. We weren't arguing. We were both trying to figure out how not to fail someone we loved.

I ran my thumb over the edge of the map, the paper gone soft and creased from wear. The trails we'd marked, the notes we'd scribbled in the margins, all felt like echoes. Almosts. Nothing solid.

My eyes tracked the last location Isla had recorded. We weren't far now. If she was still out there—if she was still alive—then every minute we hesitated felt like a betrayal.

I looked down at Ajax. He'd laid his head back down, but his gaze stayed on Finn.

"Give him a chance to try to find her trail. If nothing turns up—if we're wandering blind—we go back. Together."

Finn didn't answer right away. His eyes stayed fixed on the horizon, the edges of his jaw flexing.

Then, slowly, he turned his head to me. Met my eyes. "One window. A short one. And then we get her help."

It was the most anyone could ask for. And the exact thing I'd needed.

I reached down and gently scratched behind Ajax's ear. "You hear that, handsome? This next bit's yours."

His tail thumped once against the floor of the blind.

Finn exhaled, low and rough, like he'd been holding his breath for hours. Maybe he had.

We had a plan.

It wasn't perfect. But it was hope.

We moved quietly, the hush between us threaded with the soft rustle of morning wind through the trees. There was no room for teasing or lingering glances after everything that had happened yesterday. We still had work to do.

I crouched beside Ajax while Finn knelt across from me doing... something with webbing. Then I realized. No harness now. He was repurposing the webbing from the pack straps to hold a light pouch of supplies and give us something to grab if Ajax faltered. It wasn't ideal, but it would do.

"We take it slow." Finn's voice still wasn't quite steady. "He sets the pace."

I stood, brushing damp leaf litter from my trousers. Our arms bumped as we both reached for our packs, and we both let the contact linger longer than it should have.

The memory of that kiss flickered between us like heat off sun-warmed stone.

We slung our packs over our shoulders, and Finn moved to

check the trail ahead. Ajax rose stiffly to his feet with a grunt, but there was no hesitation in the way he turned to follow.

Was this crazy? We had no backup. No comms. Ajax was mobile but still injured.

Then I thought of Isla. The fact that she was out here all alone. In danger. And I kept moving forward.

For now, that would have to be enough.

CHAPTER 21

FINN

We'd been moving for hours already.

The kind of hours that sank into your muscles. Ajax limped a little on the downhill, but he was focused, nose low and ears twitching with every faint shift in the air. He'd found something. I wasn't sure what yet—but it was enough to keep him pushing forward without needing my command. I was watching for any falter. Any hesitation. Any sign that I'd pushed him too far. I didn't see it. But that didn't stop me from looking.

Saoirse stayed behind me, close enough that I could hear the soft scuff of her boots and the quiet, measured pace of her breath.

And that damned kiss.

I hadn't let myself replay it. Not really. But my brain kept pulling me back to the shape of her mouth, the way she'd looked at me like she meant it. I didn't have space for that right now. And still, it kept carving one.

It hadn't been mentioned. Not even in passing. But it sat under my skin like a live wire, humming every time I looked at her. Every time I remembered how she'd looked at me before she leaned in. Like she was making a choice instead of a mistake.

That was the part that undid me.

Ajax slowed near a fork in the path. His tail flicked, then stilled. I gave a quick whistle, and he adjusted course, curving us northwest through a thicket of gorse.

I didn't let myself look back at her.

Because if I did—if I saw that look on her face again—I wasn't sure I'd be able to pretend like we hadn't crossed a line in that blind. And I wasn't sure pretending was the right call anymore.

We were in it now.

No backup. No sat phone. No plan but the next step forward.

And her. Always a half-step behind me, sharp as glass and as likely to cut if handled wrong.

I didn't know what we were walking toward. But if Ajax had his nose on the right trail, we weren't wandering anymore. We were hunting. And it was on me to make certain we didn't become the hunted.

We hit a narrow gully choked with slick mud and loose rock—half-scree, half swampy runoff that made every step a gamble. Ajax navigated it with his usual effortless calculation, adjusting for his injured flank like it was only one more variable. I, on the other hand, nearly went sprawling when my boot caught on a half-buried root.

My weight pitched forward. I caught myself hard, one palm in the muck, the other clutching a tree like it owed me money.

Under my breath, I muttered, "If I face plant and break my nose, promise to tell my team it was in hand-to-hand combat with a mountain lion."

Behind me, Saoirse huffed out a short, sharp laugh, clearly caught off guard.

Instead of pointing out that there were no mountain lions in Scotland, she declared, "I'll commission the statue myself."

I looked back, and there it was—that smile again. Barely there, but real.

It hit me sideways, like getting knocked in the sternum by something warm and ridiculous. It had been a long time since someone smiled at me like that. My chest did that traitorous thing where it fluttered like I hadn't seen war zones, hadn't buried people, hadn't spent the last twenty-four hours held together by duct tape and fury.

God help me, I liked making her laugh.

The trail narrowed as we climbed, a steep bend curling around a moss-slicked rock face. The trees thinned here, branches low and grasping, like the forest didn't want to give us up easily.

Saoirse ducked beneath a twisted pine limb, her balance hitching on a patch of uneven ground. Her hand shot out and landed on my forearm. A reflex more than request.

It was only the bare pressure of fingers, but my whole body stilled. I almost reached to keep her there. Stupid. Instinctive. I stopped myself before I did something I couldn't walk back. Again.

Her grip tightened for a beat, grounding herself. Then it loosened, and she stepped past without a word.

I exhaled only after she did.

She didn't look back. And I didn't move right away, because the way she'd reached for me without hesitation, like I was something solid in all this chaos, left a warmth that lingered under my skin longer than I'd ever admit.

Ajax froze.

One second, he was moving with that same steady pace

he'd held all morning. The next, he went statue-still. Head up. Ears alert. Nose twitching.

I felt it like a pulse under my skin.

"Hold." I lifted a hand. Saoirse stilled without needing to be told twice.

Ajax pivoted, low and silent, veering slightly off trail. I followed, every step measured now. Controlled.

We emerged into a clearing maybe twenty feet wide. Bordered by thickets on three sides and a natural windbreak of stone along the fourth. Perfectly tucked. Perfectly hidden.

And littered with signs.

Fresh bootprints in the mossy earth—deep enough to mark weight, splayed slightly at the toes. A broken branch at thigh height. Flattened grass. And near the stone outcrop, gleaming like a neon sign to anyone who knew how to look—an unburned cigarette filter, white and clean.

Too clean.

I crouched low, fingers brushing over the tracks. Still damp underneath. Hours old, not days. Something in my gut twisted. Wrong place, wrong time, wrong people. A reminder that this wasn't some amateur poacher's mess.

"Heavy tread," I murmured. "Loaded packs. Or body armor." I hadn't seen evidence of the latter, but I wasn't discounting anything.

Saoirse stepped up beside me, voice quiet but steady. "Could they have merely passed through?"

I shook my head once. "Not with this much ground disturbance. They stayed. Long enough to watch something. Or someone."

She didn't ask what.

She already knew.

As we backed out of the clearing, I checked my watch again without thinking, instinctively marking the time as part of the

silent inventory that was a habit from service and would probably never quite leave me. The need to know where you were,
what time it was, how long since the last check-in.

Two missed calls.

That meant protocol was kicking in back at base. Or
should be.

Saoirse must've been watching me, because after a while
she asked softly, "You think they're looking for us?"

"They will be." My voice was rougher than I intended.
"But right now, they're guessing. We missed two check-ins.
Best-case, they think the communicator's dead."

"And worst-case?"

"They're spinning up to organize a search and don't know
where to start."

She was quiet for a moment. "You trust them to come?"

I nodded. "With my life."

A breath passed. My eyes swept the tree line again, then
found hers. "But they're not here. You are."

Her gaze held mine.

"You've kept pace through everything," I added, quieter
now. "Most wouldn't have."

That earned me a sharper look than the others. As if she
was turning the words over before deciding where to set them.

She didn't smile.

She didn't need to.

Ajax's head jerked to the left, ears pricked sharp as his
body went still. One beat, two. Then he let out a single, low,
purposeful bark and began to move. Not fast, not reckless. But
with certainty.

Even limping, he had command in his stride. Like a switch
had flipped.

I was already following before I even registered the

thought. Eyes sweeping the terrain, pack shifting against my back as my boots found the narrow rise he was tracking along.

Saoirse fell in beside me without a word. No need for discussion. We both knew that bark. It wasn't confusion or distraction.

It was direction.

And suddenly, the air around us tightened. The quiet wasn't uneasy anymore. It was waiting.

Something had shifted. In the woods. In the rhythm of our steps. In us.

A part of me wanted to slow him. To ask—*what are you chasing, lad?* Instead, I followed.

We weren't hoping anymore.

Whatever we were closing in on, it wasn't far.

CHAPTER 22

SAOIRSE

We moved slow.

Ajax was the first to halt, his body stiffening as we crept along a natural ridgeline thick with gorse and pine. His ears twitched. Tail stiff, nose working the air in tight huffs. Something was close. Not prey-alert.

People.

Finn lifted a hand—*hold*—and I froze mid-step, crouched low behind a root-choked rise. For a long moment, none of us breathed.

Then Finn nodded once. We dropped to our bellies, crawling the last few meters through pine needles and moss. My palms were scraped, knees sore, heart thundering against my ribs like a trapped bird. I could taste soil on the back of my tongue. Every inch of me buzzed with anticipation and dread. Hope was a blade, and I'd carried it so long I couldn't tell if I was gripping the hilt or the edge.

Please let her be here. Please let her be alive.

We reached the edge together—Ajax low and silent, a ghost

in his own skin despite his injuries. Finn nudged a branch aside so we could see through the treeline.

And everything in me locked down.

Because I had *not* been ready for this.

It wasn't a smattering of tents. Not some rough-and-ready campsite thrown together by amateurs.

It was a freaking compound.

Muted canvas walls rose in neat lines between trees, every stake driven with precision. Tarps stretched taut over gear racks. Low-slung mesh netting broke up the visual shape of structures. Satellite dishes—three, maybe four—tucked strategically near the treetops, partially screened by foliage.

It was discreet. Non-reflective. Tactical, even to my untrained eye. Nothing to draw attention until it was already too late.

And for all the attempts at subtlety, the whole thing was unmistakably *luxurious*.

There were collapsible tables by the main fire pit, crafted of metal and dark wood—custom work, not mass market. I recognized the subtle signs of quality that couldn't be duplicated. Quarried stone encircled the fire, arranged not for function, but for aesthetic. Gear crates stacked beside weatherproof trunks. Nothing about it said "temporary." Everything said "money."

Finn made an indistinct sound in his throat. "This isn't weekend warrior bullshite. This took planning. And deep pockets."

I couldn't speak. I was too busy counting the tents. At least eight, possibly more tucked beyond sight. Guard rotations, too. Armed. Casual. Like they had nothing to fear.

Like they'd done this before.

There was too much. Too many bodies moving around the camp, all in muted gear that blended with the surroundings.

Too many high-end tents nestled between trees. Too much expensive camouflage pretending to be simple.

"Left of the fire pit." Finn's voice was barely a whisper.

And there she was.

Isla. My Isla. Sitting on the ground near one of the larger tents, wrists zip-tied in front of her. Her ankles too—tethered so she could still hobble but not run. A man sat a few feet away, rifle slung across his chest, watching her as if she were a stray dog he wished he could kick.

Her face was pale, streaked with dirt. One side bruised dark along the cheekbone. Her hair was greasy, pulled back in a makeshift tie that had half-failed. She looked exhausted. Starved for sleep. But her chin was up. Her back straight. She was still *her*. Even broken open, she had spine. My girl. Brave and bloodied and still fighting.

I didn't remember moving, but suddenly I was forward by a few inches, elbow buried in pine needles.

Finn's hand landed lightly on my shoulder.

I didn't look at him. Couldn't. Because everything inside me was screaming to run to her. To cut through the trees and the men and the rifles and *get her out.*

I pressed my fist to my mouth and held my breath. If I made a sound, I'd ruin everything. If I moved, I'd run. Because there was no part of me that wouldn't tear the world apart to get to her.

She was alive.

But she wasn't safe. Not yet.

I swallowed hard, breathing through the heat rising behind my eyes. And suddenly, I couldn't feel my hands. My pulse had gone somewhere I couldn't follow. Only the rage remained, humming under my skin like an electric current about to arc.

Finn's hand came to rest lightly between my shoulder blades. An anchor when I wanted to fly apart.

And then someone else walked into view.

Victor Sandhurst. He didn't look like a villain. He looked like a dinner guest. Like someone who would compliment your wine selection while auctioning off a life.

I'd seen him once already. But here—now—he was in his element. Chatting easily with another man in a field jacket that probably cost more than my entire vet school wardrobe. He laughed at something, gestured with his coffee mug like he was standing on the patio at Muirfield waiting on his tee time, not orchestrating whatever the hell this was.

He didn't even glance at Isla as he passed her. Because she was less than furniture to him. I wanted to reel back from the recognition of the world I'd been raised in. Not that my life had been this, precisely. Not everyone from privilege was like this. But there were plenty who wore this kind of power, this kind of entitlement, like a cloak. Men who always got what they wanted and saw no reason they shouldn't. Men who smiled while stepping on your neck and expected you to thank them for it.

Finn shifted beside me. I felt him looking at me.

"You okay?" His voice was almost subvocal.

I nodded once, too tightly.

His hand pressed slightly firmer against my back, a silent *I've got you.*

And I let it hold me steady. For one moment. Two. Because I couldn't afford to break. Not yet. Not with Isla still a prisoner.

I didn't want to move. My body refused, every muscle locked in place, as if sheer focus could act as a shield. Like if I looked away, she'd vanish. If I blinked, they'd hurt her more than they clearly already had.

My fingers dug into the dirt, breath shallow against the loam. Isla sat so still it scared me more than if she'd been crying. Despite the defiant angle of her chin, she looked... folded in on herself. Like someone who'd learned the cost of hope. It gutted me. Because I remembered that look. I'd seen it in the mirror the day after my father's funeral. That hollow place where faith used to live.

Finn shifted beside me, his voice barely more than breath. "If they were going to kill her, they'd have done it already."

I wanted to argue. To scream that he couldn't know that, not really. But I also knew he wasn't wrong. There was no chaos here. Everything was controlled, measured, and precise.

Isla was alive because they wanted her that way. For now.

Finn spoke again, steady. "We'll get her. But not like this. Not today."

His honesty landed like ice water—bracing and awful.

I knew he was right. There was no tactical advantage here. And we were only two people and an injured dog. We didn't have the upper hand.

But knowing that didn't make it any easier.

We crawled backward through the underbrush, elbows grinding against roots and pine needles, the weight of what we'd seen pressing harder with every foot of distance.

Ajax moved ahead, low and silent, like smoke through the trees. His ears flicked once, checking for us, and then he disappeared into shadow.

It wasn't until we were a good two hundred meters out—no voices, no movement in sight—that I let myself collapse back against a tree trunk. The bark bit into my shoulder, scraping through my shirt. I didn't even flinch.

My mouth tasted like copper and fury.

"He's not even pretending." My voice didn't sound like mine. "Sandhurst. He's not hiding."

Finn crouched nearby, eyes on the treeline. "They dinna think they have to." His voice was flat. Bitter. And he was right. Again.

I let out a breath that cracked something in my chest. "They're right. People like that don't get caught. They never pay. Not unless we do something about it." Saying it made my throat burn. Like daring the universe to prove me wrong. But I couldn't stop now. We'd seen too much. And I wasn't leaving her again.

Finn looked at me and nodded, slow and grim. "Then we will."

And God help them. Because now it was personal.

Reaching for him wasn't a decision. It was instinct. As if my body needed something solid to tether to before the ground gave way entirely.

My fingers brushed Finn's. He curled his hand around mine like it was the most natural thing in the world and pulled me close enough to lay his lips against my brow. I shuddered at the touch, let the tiny point of softness soak in as a counterpoint to all the horror. We sat like that for a breath too long, as the forest hushed around us, the ghost of the compound pressing like a bruise at our backs.

Then, softly, Finn said, "Come on."

I nodded, swallowing hard, and let him help me up.

But I didn't let go of his hand until the trees had fully swallowed the compound behind us. And even then, I felt the absence of his touch like a tremor in my skin.

CHAPTER 23

FINN

We made camp farther off, deep in a hollow where the trees pressed tighter and the world shrank to roots, stone, and the sound of our breathing. It wasn't fully dark yet—Scotland never gave up the light easily in summer—but the sky had dulled to a low, unbroken gray. The last of the sun was little more than a smear behind the ridgeline, casting no real warmth, only the kind of tired light that made the world feel older, worn thin at the edges. The air was damp and cool and heavy with the promise of rain.

Ajax dropped heavily beside my pack, his ribs rising and falling in a steady rhythm. He was holding up. Still stubborn, still game. But I'd seen the way he moved—careful now, measuring every step like it cost him more than he was willing to show.

Saoirse knelt beside him, brushing her hand down his side with a tenderness that cut deep. She didn't say anything about the way he favored his flank. She checked the bandages, changed the wrap with careful, practiced hands, and scratched behind his ear when she was done.

When she caught me watching, she gave a small nod. "He's good for now."

Good.

One less thing to break inside me tonight.

I shifted my weight, glancing toward the line of trees where the sound of running water whispered through the dusk.

"We should wash up." I kept my voice low and easy. "Blood and sweat'll give us away if they've got dogs. Or even sharp noses on two legs." Plus, cleaning up would hopefully help us both feel a little more human.

For a second, she hesitated, something flickering across her face. The collision of exhaustion and intimacy and the cold reminder that we were still in enemy territory.

Then she nodded once. Trusting me.

We dug out clean shirts and towels from our packs, the silence between us thick but not uncomfortable, and made our way toward the stream, Ajax staying behind to guard camp with a low, contented huff.

I tugged off my boots and wool socks, rolling up the legs of my trousers before stripping off my shirt and wading into the shallows. The water was ice cold, numbing. I welcomed it as I knelt to scrub the dirt and blood from my hands and arms. Let it chase the tremors out of my skin, the useless rage, the helplessness I hadn't been able to shake since we spotted Isla tied up like an afterthought in that damned compound.

Behind me, I heard Saoirse move. Boots scraping against pebbles, jacket rustling as she peeled it off.

When I glanced back, she was stripped down to a sports bra that showed off the shape of her arms and the smooth tone of her torso, her spine curving as she splashed water onto her skin.

I looked away fast. Not because I wasn't tempted to keep looking.

Because I wanted to. Too much.

Focus, Patterson.

I was half-distracted rinsing off my forearms when I felt her presence at my shoulder. Close. Closer than necessary.

"You're bleeding." Her voice was quiet.

I glanced down. A scrape—ugly but shallow—tracked across my upper arm. A twin to match the one she'd treated last night on my other arm. I hadn't even felt it.

"Sit." That voice stayed quiet, but I recognized an order when I heard one.

I waded out of the water and sat. Let her take the lead. Let her steady me in ways I didn't know I needed.

She crouched beside me, pulling a small first aid pouch from her belt. Her fingers brushed my skin, light and clinical, but they shook once before she caught herself.

I said nothing as she worked, letting myself feel the impossible smallness of the moment: her hands on me. Her care. The exquisite gentleness of it when everything else in this world right now was sharp and brutal and wrong.

The scrape stung as she dabbed it clean, but I barely felt it.

I was too busy memorizing the way her brow furrowed in concentration. The way her teeth caught her lower lip when she worked. Her slow and shaky exhale when she finally smoothed a bandage in place.

"You're going to be fine."

I understood the words were more to herself than to me. I heard the fear underneath. The promise she was trying to make real with her own two hands.

For Isla. For me. For all of us.

I caught her wrist before she could pull away. Not hard.

Just... enough. She didn't pull her hand away when the bandage was smoothed down and the job was finished. She stayed there, kneeling beside me, her fingers a small, trembling weight against my forearm.

For a long minute, neither of us moved. The stream burbled behind us. A night bird called somewhere up the ridge. Everything else—camp, compound, the monsters waiting in the trees —fell away.

"I'm scared for her."

The quiet words cracked open something between us. Raw. Honest. Unapologetic.

"I keep thinking..." Her voice wavered. She swallowed hard. "If we lose her—"

She stopped. Couldn't finish. But I understood, because I knew exactly what it felt like to have one person holding up more weight inside you than you ever let anyone see.

I shifted until I could see her face in the twilight. The damp strands of hair stuck to her brow. The tight set of her jaw like she was trying to brace herself against a storm she couldn't outrun.

And I said it the only way I knew how. The truth, hammered into something harder than fear. "We'll get her. I swear it." My voice and my gaze didn't waver.

Her eyes snapped to mine, wide and stunned, like she hadn't expected me to sound so sure.

But I was sure. Because there wasn't another option. Because I'd made that promise the second I let her hand find mine in the dark. And if there was one thing I still knew how to do, it was keep my promises. No matter what it cost.

I didn't think. I reached for her. My hand found the back of her head, fingers threading into the damp, tangled strands. I pulled her in slowly, giving her every chance to pull away.

She didn't.

I pressed my forehead to hers. A simple gesture of connection. Something older than words. Something that said, *I see you. I've got you. You're not alone.*

Her breath hitched against my throat. Then, slowly, she sagged into me.

All that brittle tension holding her upright gave way at once.

She folded into my chest like she didn't have the strength to pretend anymore. Like she'd been carrying too much for too long, with no one to catch her if she stumbled. And thinking of how she'd come to Glenlaig to help with her grandfather, how she'd thrown herself into helping all her friends without ever asking for anything in return, I knew it was probably true.

She was the helper, not the one who ever asked for help in return.

I wrapped my arm around her, one firm line across her back, pulling her in, anchoring her.

Her heartbeat thudded against mine, too fast. I tightened my hold, murmuring something—nonsense, maybe. I didn't even know what.

The rest of the world faded to a dull, distant hum. Right here, right now, there was only her. Only us. Only the way she breathed against my chest like it might be the first full breath she'd taken all day.

Eventually, she eased back, passed me my shirt, grabbing the clean one of her own.

In silence, we pulled our outer layers on again—damp sleeves sticking to chilled skin, boots sinking into the soft give of river mud. The air between us had thickened and grown heavy with knowing.

When I straightened, she was already watching me. Seeing me. The way I'd been seeing her for days without letting myself admit it.

I gave a small jerk of my chin—ready?—and she fell into step beside me without hesitation.

Every brush of her arm against mine—small, unintentional—felt seismic. Like a warning shot before the fall. The steady hum of inevitability followed us with every step. Like gravity had picked sides, and we were already falling.

I told myself to focus. To keep moving.

We hadn't brought much. Clean shirts slung over one arm, towels half-forgotten in the rush to get back. But every time her hand grazed the fabric near mine, the ground seemed to pitch a little steeper beneath my boots.

I could hear her steady breathing. The kind of sound that filled up the hollow spaces in your chest without asking permission.

I curled my free hand into a fist, knuckles tight. I wasn't carrying gear. Wasn't carrying weapons. Wasn't carrying anything to hide behind anymore. And God, it felt terrifying.

And inevitable.

I turned before I could second-guess it.

She looked up, and everything else slipped out of orbit. She watched me, wide-eyed, steady, like she was seeing all the wreckage inside me and choosing to stay, anyway.

I lifted a hand—slow, deliberate—giving her every chance to step back. To stop me. It hovered near her jaw, not touching. My throat worked around the words.

"Tell me to stop."

She didn't. Instead, she stepped in the barest of breaths, tipping that chin up in a gesture that was as much a challenge as a promise.

So I kissed her.

In another time or place, I might have let what was inside me for this woman burn. Released the firestorm. But that wasn't what either of us needed right now. So I kept it simple. Easy. Mouth to mouth. Pressure and presence. The kind of kiss that didn't need to prove anything, only confirm what we already knew but hadn't said.

Her fingers tightened against my chest, right over my heart, which was slamming as if it wanted out. She made a soft sound, not quite a gasp, not quite a sigh. I felt it more than I heard it. The shape of it against my mouth. The way her breath caught when I didn't pull back.

God, she felt good. Steady and shaking all at once. Hands clinging like she needed something to hold her together. And maybe I did too.

I leaned in a little more and let it deepen. Not all the way. Because I knew what this was. I knew where we were, and I wasn't going to be the one to break the line she'd chosen to cross.

She leaned into me like I'd become the center of gravity.

Her lips parted slightly, and I couldn't stop myself from sliding just a little deeper. I caught the sound she made when my hand skimmed the edge of her jaw, thumb brushing the curve of her cheekbone. I could've gone further. God, I wanted to. My other hand already hovered too close to her waist, too ready to slide lower, to press in.

She shifted so our bodies aligned, heat meeting heat.

But then she stilled, holding exactly where we were.

And I matched it. Matched her, pressing my forehead to hers, breathing through the ache of it. That tension curled hot at the base of my spine. Want and warning tangled together. But I didn't push.

When we finally pulled apart, she didn't let go. Her forehead rested against my chest, breathing me in.

Without a word, I wrapped my arms around her and held

on, like she was the only solid thing left in a world that had been shaking itself apart for years.

Her fingers tightened in my shirt, and I knew in my bones that I wasn't walking away from her.

Not now. Not ever.

CHAPTER 24

SAOIRSE

The camp felt too quiet when we got back.

We moved through the motions—rechecking the perimeter, feeding Ajax from the last of our trail rations, setting the bedrolls—but it was all muted, mechanical. Like the real thing happening between us had nothing to do with these tasks at all.

Every time I glanced at Finn, I felt the aftershock of that kiss again.

It hadn't been desperate. It hadn't been messy. It had been... steady. Sure. The way I imagined falling should feel if you trusted the landing. I never had before, and I couldn't quite wrap my brain around the idea that somehow—with him—I did.

I curled inside my sleeping bag, oddly relieved we hadn't bothered with the tent as I stared up at the faint smear of clouds overhead, the gray deepening as evening slid toward full night. The trees whispered. Ajax snored softly at my feet in the space between us.

And I realized, with a hollow pang, that I wasn't ready to let go of that feeling yet.

I wanted—*needed*—to be close to Finn. Not merely to have him there across the clearing. *Here.* Holding the pieces of me still rattling loose after everything we'd seen today.

I turned my head. He was sitting up against the base of a tree, arms folded loosely over his knees, keeping watch even now.

I hesitated for the briefest moment, and then before I could lose my nerve, I whispered, "Will you... hold me?" God, those words felt so awkward and weak on my tongue. I wished them back almost immediately.

Finn turned slowly. In the low light, his eyes looked almost silvered over.

For a heartbeat, I thought he might say no. That it might be too much. That I might be asking for something he didn't know how to give.

But then he simply said, "Aye."

Rough. Quiet. Certain.

He rose, crossing the small space between us, and my heart hammered harder than it had back at the compound as he shifted his bedroll beside mine. He stretched out, opening his arms without ceremony, and I shifted, slipping into his space. Into the warmth of him.

When had I started craving it? Craving him?

He tucked me in against his chest like he'd been waiting to. As if it was the most natural thing in the world. His arms came around me, and I felt something in my spine finally unclench.

I rested my cheek against his heartbeat and closed my eyes.

We didn't speak for a long time.

The wind whispered across the clearing, carrying the clean bite of river water and pine needles. Somewhere in the distance, a wood pigeon cooed. Ajax shifted in his sleep but didn't wake. And through it all, Finn's hand traced slow, thoughtless patterns along my arm.

I didn't mean to speak. Not really. But the words slipped out anyway, soft against the rough fabric of his shirt. "For someone who claims he doesn't want to be responsible for anyone... you're really, really bad at it."

He huffed a sound that could've been a laugh—or maybe only a breath.

I tilted my head to look at him. "I mean it. You take care of everyone. Whether you want to or not." I hesitated. "I didn't see it before. Maybe I didn't want to."

His jaw tensed.

I saw the muscle jump there. Felt the way his arms tightened slightly, and I almost left it alone.

Almost.

But something about the way he held himself—this terrible, careful stillness—made me push the tiniest bit. "What happened, Finn?"

If he didn't answer, I wouldn't press him. But I could hold the space for him if he needed to get it out.

For a long moment, I thought he might let the silence close over the question like a wave, washing the shore clean.

Then he loosed a slow, fractured exhale. "There was someone—a woman—before the Royal Marines. Before all of this."

I stayed still. Didn't speak. Didn't even breathe too loud.

"Catriona. We broke it off when I enlisted. She wasn't made for being a military partner. We stayed friends. Close."

He paused long enough that I could feel him gathering himself, like it physically hurt to say. Or maybe he was bracing himself for what came next.

"She got involved with someone else. Seemed good at first. But it wasn't."

His hand had stilled against my arm now, resting warm and heavy there.

"She called me once. Needed help getting out. I wasn't..." A harsh swallow. "I wasn't there fast enough. Because of deployment. Duty. All the shite that had been why we'd split."

My heart fractured right down the middle.

"She died, Saoirse."

Three simple words.

Quiet. Flat. Devastating.

"The arsehole went to prison. But that disnae matter." A bitter sound. "I wasn't there. I wasn't enough."

The wind stirred the trees. I could hear my own heartbeat, heavy and hurting in my ears.

"I didn't trust myself to carry anything alive after that. Not until Ajax."

Oh, God. My throat burned. And still, I didn't try to fix it. Didn't tell him he *was* enough. Didn't tell him it wasn't his fault. Because if he was going to believe any of that, he would have by now. So I merely... stayed.

I tipped up onto one elbow, brushing the side of his face with my fingers. Gentle. Deliberate. And pressed a soft kiss to his temple. A silent vow.

"You carry more than you think." I whispered it against his skin. "And you haven't dropped me yet."

His breath hitched against my cheek. Barely audible. But I felt it, like the flicker of a match catching flame.

He turned his head slightly, and the stubble along his jaw scraped soft against my fingertips. I didn't pull away. I couldn't have if I'd wanted to.

And I didn't want to.

Finn's hand came up slowly, sliding through the loose strands of hair near my neck, curling there. Gentle. Anchoring. Asking.

I met his eyes in the half-light, and whatever permission he needed, he must have found it there, because when he kissed me, it wasn't a question. It was an answer.

Everything else fell away.

It wasn't slow for the sake of being gentle. It was slow because it meant something. Because we both needed to feel it, all of it. The warmth of his mouth, the sure touch of his hands, the way his breath shivered across my skin when I leaned in.

I pressed closer instinctively, my palm flattening over the steady beat of his heart. His mouth moved over mine with a kind of fierce patience, like he was memorizing the taste of me. As if he had all the time in the world.

And it unraveled me.

When he nudged deeper, I opened for him without hesitation. The slow slide of his tongue against mine made my whole body tighten, heat coiling low and certain. He pulled me further into his lap without breaking the kiss, cradling me like something breakable and wanted.

God, I wanted him, too. Not as a reaction. Not out of fear.

But because I was still standing. Because I could choose. And I was choosing him.

When the kiss finally broke, it wasn't relief. It was need. Space to breathe so we didn't drown.

His forehead touched mine, breath ragged. The press of it made something in my chest go soft.

"Tell me to stop." His whisper was low and strained.

I caught his gaze with mine and felt the answer already rising in my throat. "Don't you dare."

Whatever had been holding us back snapped.

Finn kissed me again—harder this time—and guided me down onto the bedroll with maddening, devastating care. His weight settled over me, heat and muscle and the impossible calm of someone who knew exactly what he wanted and wasn't in a rush to take it.

I reached for his shirt first, fingers clumsy with want. The fabric caught, twisted. He helped, dragging it over his head in one smooth motion, baring the planes of his chest, the long line of his body, the scatter of scars I'd tried not to look at in the stream.

Without thinking, I traced tip of my finger in a featherlight caress along the edge of a faded line across his ribs.

He shuddered, his breath hitching as he said my name in a low, quiet voice, as if it hurt and healed at the same time.

I didn't answer out loud. Just tugged him closer.

His hands found me, sliding under my shirt with reverence that made my whole body tense and ache. His touch was searching. Careful. Not because he didn't know what to do, but because he wanted to get it right.

When he pulled my shirt over my head, he stilled.

The air thickened. His breath caught sharp in his throat, and for a second he didn't move.

I made myself meet his eyes. Let him see all of me.

He didn't look away. Didn't rush. He looked like he couldn't believe I was real. Like he was grateful.

He lowered his mouth to my collarbone and kissed me there, soft, slow. Another kiss followed, and another, trailing heat along the hollow of my throat, the edge of my shoulder. Each one was like a spark struck against my skin. Gentle, but building. Lighting me up from the inside out, until I was trembling under him with the force of it.

Wanting. Anchored. Oh, so ready.

When his hand slipped beneath the waistband of my trousers, fingertips brushing along the curve of my hip, something in me sparked hot and low. I arched into the touch without thinking, breath catching hard in my throat.

His lips grazed my skin. "Okay?"

"More than okay." My fingers found his hair, curling there. "Please."

He made a rough, raw sound I felt more than heard, and then he was moving, stripping away the last of what separated us with a kind of reverent urgency. Then we were bare. Skin to skin. Heat to heat. No space left between us.

He didn't rush. He came over me like he was afraid to break the moment. His weight, his warmth, the sheer presence of him sank into me, careful and devastating all at once. When he finally slid into me, it wasn't a jolt. It was a breath stolen clean from my lungs. My mouth parted in a gasp I couldn't hold back.

He stilled, giving me space to catch up, brow pressed to mine, our breathing tangled and uneven.

I tightened my legs around his hips, pulling him closer, and the guttural, helpless sound he made lit something deep and dangerous in me.

He began to move. Slowly. Deliberately. Each roll of his hips sent sensation coiling higher, stealing thought, stealing time. My world narrowed to this: the rhythm, the burn, the beautiful weight of him. The way he held back like he was trying not to fall apart too soon. The way he kissed me like he didn't want to miss a second.

Then he froze. Breath sharp, body braced. "I didn't bring anything," he rasped. "Should've—"

I cupped his jaw, grounding him. "I'm on birth control. And I'm clean. Last test was in the fall. There hasn't been anyone since."

His throat worked hard. "Me too. I swear."

The relief that passed between us was almost physical. It shifted something in the air—thicker, heavier, closer.

He kissed me again, deeper this time. Rougher. Like nothing else mattered. When he moved, I met him for that slow, inevitable climb. Every inch of him dragging pleasure tighter and higher inside me until it ached. Until it trembled at the cusp.

I clung to him. To the heat of his body, to the wild, restrained strength of him. He held me like he was trying to memorize every part of me, touched me like he'd never forget.

There was no edge, no ending. Only the glorious pressure that built and built, until it finally shattered. I broke with a sob into his mouth, everything inside me catching flame and then fracturing into something soft and wide open. He followed not long after, his body seizing against mine, a sound I'd never forget rough in his throat as he buried his face in my shoulder and let go.

We didn't move. Still tangled, skin warm against skin, breath slowing by degrees. I reveled in the soft thrum of being held. Being here.

His hand moved in slow circles over my hip, not even thinking about it. Like the rhythm had always been there, waiting.

And for the first time in forever, I didn't want to move either.

Didn't want to let go.

CHAPTER 25

FINN

The world was still gray when I surfaced.

Not the soft gray of peace. The brittle, watchful kind.

I eased out of the sleeping bag as quietly as I could, careful not to jostle Saoirse where she was tucked against my side. Her breathing hitched once as the warmth shifted, but she didn't wake. No surprise. We'd barely slept since we'd left Glenlaig all those days ago.

Ajax lifted his head the moment I moved—ears pricked, eyes bright in the low light. Waiting for a command.

Good lad.

I pulled on my boots, shrugging into my jacket. Checked the combat knife at my belt, the weight of the multi-tool tucked into my pocket. No gun. No easy fallback if things went wrong.

When I straightened, Saoirse's lashes fluttered. Sleep-heavy, half-aware.

She blinked up at me, and I leaned in, keeping my voice low.

"Going scouting," I murmured. "Be back soon."

Her hand twitched like she wanted to catch me, and I

caught it, pressing a kiss to the back. Her fingers twisted to brush my cheek before she let it fall, trusting. That trust anchored something in my chest I couldn't afford to look at too closely. Not now.

I turned to Ajax, dropped to a knee, so we were eye level.

"Stay with her," I ordered.

It was the only way I could make myself go do what needed to be done. Knowing he'd protect her. Hold the line.

Ajax settled his head back on his paws, muscles coiled tight beneath him. Ready.

Good.

I slipped into the trees, the mist closing around me in ribbons of silver. Each breath ghosted in front of me, cold enough to sting. The forest wasn't silent. It never really was. But it held a different kind of hush in the early hours. Like the world itself was holding its breath.

I moved through it without a sound.

Predawn was a hunter's hour. And today, I was the one doing the hunting.

The forest thickened as I moved downhill, every step calculated. Old habits took over. The ones drilled into bone and blood long before I ever set foot back in Scotland.

Stay low. Move slow. Use the ground like it's working for you, not against you.

The mist was thicker here, clinging to the hollow like smoke. It muffled sound, blurred edges. A double-edged sword. Good for masking my approach, but bad if I wasn't the only one slipping through the dark. I kept to the tree line, body angling into natural breaks in the terrain. Crouching behind a rock outcropping, I caught my first glimpse of the compound again.

Faint golden glows dotted the canvas walls. Probably small battery lanterns or chemical lights. Enough for them to see each other without giving away their position from the air.

Smart. Experienced. Expensive. But none of that made them invincible.

I circled wide, veering up a slight rise to the east. Higher ground meant better sightlines, and a fighting chance if I had to move fast.

I didn't let myself think about Saoirse waiting back at camp. Didn't think about Ajax, lying vigilant beside her. Didn't think about what would happen if this camp caught wind of a shadow moving in the trees. I focused on my breath, on each deliberate step.

When I finally dropped into position behind a half-fallen tree, sapling growth veiling me from view, I went still. Listening. Watching. Waiting for the camp to reveal its cracks.

I melted into the underbrush, breath shallow, every muscle tuned tight.

The perimeter wasn't careless.

Guards were posted—four that I could see, maybe more deeper in. They moved often enough to suggest routine, but not pattern. Not strict enough to give more than the illusion of control. Weapons slung easy. Eyes moving. Posture casual, but aware.

Not amateurs. But not pros either. They wore their confidence like extra kit, and that kind of cockiness could be an asset.

I watched longer than I probably should've, tracking their movements, letting the rhythm settle into my bones. It wasn't military discipline. It was something looser. Maybe learned from hunting lodges or security contracts. The kind of training that made them dangerous but not airtight.

The gap wasn't in the men. It was in the ground.

A natural fold in the terrain curved along the northern edge of the site—low, tangled, thick with scrub and moss-draped timber. Looked impassable if you weren't paying attention. Too steep to drive through. Too cluttered to be worth crossing.

It read like a natural barrier.

They didn't patrol it. Not really. A couple of glances. A sentry posted too far up slope to catch anything moving low and quiet.

I ran the calculation in my head, accounting for distance, grade, and cover.

It wasn't easy, but it was there. A blind spot. A potential way in. Risky. Tight timing. But possible.

A ghost of grim satisfaction stirred low in my gut.

You built defenses for what you expected. Not for what you didn't want to see coming.

And I'd made a career out of being the thing they didn't see coming.

A flicker of movement caught my eye—two figures near the main fire pit, framed by the weak glow of coals.

They were relaxed. Coffee mugs in hand. Talking low.

I shifted a little closer and caught the edges of their conversation.

"... spotted a pair near the west ridge. Big ones, good summer coats. Healthy."

A chuckle. "Client'll pay double if he bags a true Highland wildcat. No one's seen a pure strain in years."

"Tracker said there's a golden eagle hunting over the cliffs, too. Might set a bait line. Easy pickings."

My gut twisted.

Wildcats. Eagles. Deer with antlers thick from good grazing.

Not survival. Not conservation.

Trophies. Ego. The kind of killing done because no one ever told them no.

I swallowed the anger trying to rise and stored it. I'd need it soon enough.

Heart steady, I eased back a fraction, mind already working the angles.

The trackers were out there now. Somewhere in the forest. Radioing in locations. It was easy to imagine intercepting one. Disabling him. Taking his comms.

But finding one tracker in thousands of acres of dense woods? That was a needle in a haystack. And if I missed—if one so much as got a garbled call through—the whole camp would go on alert. Isla would likely be the first to pay the price.

I ground my teeth, considering. Better odds inside. Better to wait for the camp to thin. For a shift change. Hell, did they even do a shift change? I couldn't count on them operating with that kind of discipline. They didn't move like hired mercs.

If I could slip in, find a radio. Maybe in a command or logistics tent, maybe where they stashed the high-end kit.

It'd be a hell of a risk. But it was cleaner. And it was the only way we were getting backup before this turned into a two-body recovery.

As I waited, the camp shifted around the edges. Small movements at first, barely more than a ripple. Tent flaps stirred. Figures emerged, stretching, shaking off sleep. Someone kicked life into the main fire pit, smoke threading upward into the heavy gray dawn. If they were rousing this early, they likely had a hunt planned and needed to get into position.

I stayed motionless, half-buried behind a fallen log, the damp moss seeping through my sleeves.

No alarm was raised. No shouting broke the morning quiet. No one scrambled for weapons.

Good. I hadn't left a footprint. Hadn't turned a single head. The hunters moved like men with no reason to hurry as they checked rifles, topped off fuel on the ATVs parked along the tree line, laughing low over whatever they thought the day would bring.

They didn't know they were already being hunted, too.

I pulled back in the same slow, deliberate the way I'd come, every footfall placed with care. No broken twigs. No slipped stone. Nothing obvious to catch a half-alert eye.

With every step, I logged what I'd seen. Positions. Movement habits. The dead space near the fire where two of them leaned too close, voices low and careless, bragging about what they'd "bagged" that day.

A thread of arrogance running through it all. Like they believed no one would ever get close enough to hear them.

That arrogance? That was the opening. The thinnest of cracks in the armor. But it might be enough.

And still, something twisted low in my gut. A weight I didn't let myself look too closely at. Because hearing those words, seeing them laugh scraped something raw.

I wanted to move now. Strike. Do something.

But I couldn't. Not yet.

So I tucked it down deep. Locked it beside every other instinct I'd had to ignore. And kept moving.

We had a window.

It wouldn't stay open forever. And when it closed, there likely wouldn't be a second chance.

CHAPTER 26

SAOIRSE

I sat cross-legged in the dirt, Ajax stretched out at my side, his breathing steady and slow. One hand ghosted over the bandage on his flank—checking it again, even though I knew I was wasting my time. The dressing was clean. No seepage, no swelling. Healing, against all odds.

I wasn't checking for him anymore. I was checking for something to do with my hands, because sitting still felt unbearable.

The forest creaked and shifted around us, every crackle of underbrush snapping too loud in my skull.

I hadn't slept since Finn left this morning. Not really. Dozed, maybe, in fits and starts. How could I when every rustle, every sigh of the trees jerked me back to full, brittle awareness. Every sound felt like it might be *them*.

Ajax lifted his head once when a raven croaked overhead, ears twitching, then slumped back down without concern.

I tried to pull comfort from that. If there were real danger, he'd be up. Alert. Instead, it was only me, brittle and frayed, breathing too fast because the man I somehow trusted most in the world right now was out there somewhere in the mist.

I rubbed the heel of my hand against the center of my chest, trying to press the ache down.

It didn't help.

A soft scuff against the earth snapped my head up. I twisted on instinct, heart leaping painfully into my throat.

For a half breath, the forest blurred—threat everywhere, muscles braced for the worst.

And then Finn was there. Stepping out from the shadows like he'd been woven from them. His steady presence cut through the jagged edge of the fear that had been my unwelcome companion since he'd slipped away.

Our eyes met across the few meters of distance between us.

He gave a small, grounding nod that seemed to say, *I'm here. I'm safe.*

Relief punched through me so hard my knees nearly buckled.

It was all I could do to stay seated, to keep myself from reaching for him like some drowning thing that had finally found the shore.

Ajax stirred at my side, his tail thudding once against the ground without lifting his head. An acknowledgment, not an alarm.

He'd known it was Finn. Trusted that he'd come back.

I pressed my palm flat against my ribs, feeling the thundering start to ease.

For a moment, neither of us moved. Our eyes caught and held, and everything from last night—the weight of his mouth on mine, the feel of him tangled around me like something solid and saving—rose up between us. Unspoken. Unavoidable.

I hadn't meant for this to happen. Hadn't meant for *him* to happen.

Once, not that long ago, I'd put so much energy into disliking him. Into sharpening every glance, every word, into making sure he couldn't get close enough to disappoint me. And now he was the only thing that made the world feel steady at all.

My fingers curled against the dirt, a futile anchor against the way something inside me kept slipping sideways. Part of me wanted to reach for him—to close that stretch of earth like it was nothing—but something in both of us held back. Not because we didn't want it. Because we knew how much it would mean if we crossed that line again.

I cleared my throat, forcing my voice to work. "Ajax is holding steady." It came out too soft, like I wasn't really talking about the dog at all.

Finn's mouth hitched at one corner. Not quite a smile. Something quieter. Sadder. "You too."

The words landed heavier than they should have. Because somehow, after everything—after all the ways the world had tried to break us—I *was* still holding steady.

Not because I was strong enough on my own. But because somewhere along the way, without asking, he'd stepped into the spaces where I was fraying and held me there. And somehow, impossibly, I trusted him not to let go.

I sat up straighter, scrubbing a hand over my face. Ajax shifted against my leg but stayed down, his quiet presence anchoring me.

Finn settled across from me, moving like the woods still clung to him. His voice stayed low. "Camp's active. Still locked down. Guards moving regularly. Enough to keep people from getting curious."

I swallowed hard. "And Isla?"

His mouth flattened. He shook his head once. "Didn't see her. Didn't get close enough to risk it."

The cold that had been sitting in my gut all morning bloomed wider. Not seeing her didn't necessarily mean anything. But fear didn't care about logic.

Finn shifted his weight, like he could feel me curling inward, trying to brace for worst-case.

Before I could open my mouth, he added, "I overheard some of them talking. Trackers went out early. They're after protected species. Wildcats. Eagles. Trophy deer."

I looked at him sharply. "So if they're willing to kill endangered animals..."

"They're no' poachers playing survivalist," Finn said grimly. "They're organized. And careful."

I gritted my teeth. "So why keep Isla alive at all?"

His answer was immediate. "Because she's leverage. A risk to them. But no' enough of one for them to rush."

It made a cruel, awful sense. They hadn't hurt her badly—yet—because they were still figuring out whether they needed to.

I stared at the dirt between my boots. "But you didn't see her."

"No," he said quietly. "But if something had happened overnight, the camp would look different."

I frowned. "How?"

"They're still operating under normal routines, not tying up loose ends or panicking." He met my gaze evenly. "They're still weighing their options."

The breath I dragged in tasted of pine sap and bile. "And we have to move before they decide she's not worth keeping."

Finn nodded. "Exactly."

I dug my fingers into the dirt, grounding myself. "We have to try." The words cracked sharper than I meant. "We can't wait too long."

Finn didn't flinch. He only watched me with that steady, maddening calm. "We canna rush it either."

I shook my head, the panic crawling higher under my skin. "She's in there, Finn. We know what these men are capable of."

"And that's exactly why we have to be smart." His voice stayed low, but there was steel underneath it now. "We pull her out without backup, without a clean exit, and we dinna just put her at risk. We put you at risk. All of us."

I hated that he was right. Hated more that it felt like I was standing on a cliff edge, watching the ground erode under Isla's feet, and all I could do was wait.

Finn shifted closer, enough that I could see the fine tension running through him too—the control he wasn't letting slip.

"You trusted me last night," he murmured. "Trust me now."

I closed my eyes for a beat, swallowing hard. Trust wasn't the problem. The helplessness was.

When I opened them again, he was still there. Solid. Unmoving. My anchor in all this bloody chaos.

I nodded once. "Okay. But not forever. We don't leave her there forever."

Something flickered in his expression then.Something raw and unguarded. "No' a chance. We get her out. I swear it."

And this time, I believed him without question.

I didn't think about it. Didn't weigh the consequences or second-guess the impulse. I let myself lean.

Finn moved instantly, like he'd been waiting for it. His arm wrapped around me without hesitation, pulling me in against his side. The warm, solid press of his body chased some of the jagged edges out of my chest. His hand found the back of my neck, fingers splaying lightly there. A tether I hadn't even known I was searching for.

I breathed him in. Earth and sweat and the faintest hint of

whatever soap he'd used back at the stream. The human weight of him grounded me better than anything else could have.

We didn't speak. For now, it was enough to sit there in the quiet, with the woods pressing close around us and the impossible task still looming ahead.

It was enough that we weren't carrying it alone.

Eventually, Finn pulled back and met my eyes. His hand rested at the nape of my neck, thumb brushing lightly along my skin like he wasn't quite ready to let me go.

"Tonight," he said, voice low and certain. "After full dark."

I nodded, my heart beating thickly against my ribs.

"I'm going to try to slip into camp. Find a radio. Get a message out." He said it like a foregone conclusion, like failure wasn't even an option he was willing to name. The conviction in his voice made something tighten in my chest.

"I'll need you and Ajax close, watching my six."

My breath hitched, but I forced myself to stay steady.

"If anything shifts—if anyone comes near—you warn me. And if it turns bad, you pull back. No heroics."

I opened my mouth to argue, but the look in his eyes stopped me. Fierce. Protective. Trusting.

"I can do that."

"I know you can." His thumb swept once more along my jaw—a fleeting touch, almost unconscious—and something in me clicked into place. Somehow, that small, unshakable belief did more to settle me than any battle plan ever could.

After that, we didn't talk. Not about what could go wrong. Not about what it would cost if we failed. We simply sat there, shoulder to shoulder, in the thinning mist, while the forest slowly creaked awake around us. High above, a few birds stirred into cautious song. The breeze shifted, cold and damp, stirring the leaves like a whisper nobody wanted to hear.

I leaned into him, content to feel his warmth through the layers between us.

Finn didn't move away. He turned his hand so our fingers brushed. A solid, silent promise that whatever came next, neither of us would be facing it alone.

CHAPTER 27

FINN

We moved slow, staying low, every step calculated. The trees thinned as we neared the outer limits of the compound. The muted canvas tents were barely visible through the dense mist.

I led Saoirse to a patch of thick brush a good twenty meters from the nearest fire pit. Close enough she could see me signal if needed. Far enough to stay hidden if things went sideways.

I hated leaving her here. Hated it with a ferocity that clawed under my ribs. But bringing her any closer wasn't an option. She wasn't trained for this kind of infiltration, and Ajax needed to be close enough to catch trouble before it found us both.

I crouched low, touching Saoirse's hand briefly—steady pressure, a silent promise. She nodded, small and fierce. Her trust gutted me. I'd do everything in my power to earn it.

I turned to Ajax, keeping my voice low, barely a breath. "Stay sharp, lad. Eyes and ears."

He shifted forward, settling halfway between us. Close enough to warn either way. A living tripwire.

I'd stripped down to the bare essentials earlier, back at our camp. Now it was only me, a blade tucked into my boot, another at my hip, and a stolen sliver of hope.

I touched two fingers to the ground between us—*hold position*—then melted into the dark.

Every instinct in me howled at leaving Saoirse unprotected. Of trusting a world I knew better than to trust. But this was the only way. Get the radio. Get the message out. Bring the cavalry. Then, and only then, get us all home safe.

I left Ajax where I'd planted him, still and silent, half-melted into the shadows. Every step I took toward the nearest tent scraped against instinct. My boots barely kissed the ground. My breath was shallow, my pulse steady.

The camp felt different at night. Quieter, but not dead. Like something coiled and sleeping beneath the surface.

I moved fast, hugging the tree line, slipping through the patches of deeper shadow between tents. No alarms sounded. Nothing moved.

Good.

The tent I was aiming for had a slight bulge at one wall. An equipment table, maybe. No posted guards. No obvious traps. This crew was arrogant enough they likely didn't think they'd need traps.

I crouched low, checked the approach twice, then slipped under the canvas with a practiced flick of my wrist.

Inside, it was darker still, thick with the smell of canvas, sweat, and gun oil. And somewhere under all that, the faint crackle of electronics.

Exactly what I needed.

If I was lucky, lucky enough to still matter, the comms would be active.

The field radio rig had been patched together with more money than skill. High-end civilian tech. Not military grade, but functional. I could work with that.

I moved to it, fingers quick. There were no lights on the exterior of the unit, which was good. Meant less chance of some idiot noticing activity that shouldn't be there.

I tuned the radio manually, one careful click at a time, until I hit the Out of Bounds emergency band.

No voice. No risk.

I tapped out the message in tight, clipped bursts of morse: *SOS. Target held. Hostile camp. Poaching. Approximate coordinates. Request extraction.*

I kept the whole thing short and repeated it twice, hoping like hell someone on our end was listening.

I didn't wait for a reply. Couldn't. Every second I lingered doubled the risk to me, to Saoirse and Ajax.

I twisted the dial back to neutral and ghosted toward the canvas flap, listening. I waited for one breath. Two.

Nothing. So far.

I had one foot out of the tent when I heard it. A low chuff. Barely a sound at all.

I froze.

Ajax didn't break silence unless it mattered. And that wasn't a bark for me.

Sliding along the shadowed side of the tent, I kept low, edging back toward where I'd left him. I caught sight of him through the underbrush, body rigid, head fixed in one direction.

Not toward me. Toward the tree line. Toward where Saoirse was supposed to be hidden.

A chill ripped through my gut, sharper than any cold. Something was wrong. And I was too far away.

I caught the first sharp shout a half-second later, echoing too loud in the stillness, and my heart seized.

Saoirse.

Ajax moved first. A low growl ripped out of him, and his

whole body coiled like a spring. Instinct. Pure and primal. He would defend her. He would *die* defending her.

And for one terrifying second, I almost let him. Almost let both of us charge headlong into the teeth of a fight we couldn't win.

But I caught him—arm wrapped hard around his chest, dragging him back into the shadows.

"Easy, lad," I whispered, voice shaking with the effort it took to hold him. "Not yet. Not yet."

Ajax strained against me, muscles bunching, paws digging into the earth. He whined low in his throat—angry, frustrated, *hurting.*

I forced myself to look past him, past the tree line, in time to see them dragging her out of the brush.

Two men. Rough hands. Her boots kicking up leaves as she fought them every inch of the way. She twisted hard, kicking out, catching one of them square in the shin. But it barely slowed him. The other man moved in fast, grabbing her arms, shoving her toward the center of camp like she weighed nothing at all.

I should've stayed closer. Should've seen it coming. Should've never let her out of reach.

And then she looked up. Through all of it—the scuffle, the shouting—her gaze locked with mine.

It hit me like a blow. The terror she hid behind clenched teeth. The trust she didn't even have to speak.

You'll come for me.

I tightened my grip on Ajax. "I'm coming. I swear it." I whispered it like a vow against the side of his head.

The shadows swallowed us as I dragged him back. Each step was a wound. Each heartbeat another tally mark of how badly this had gone to hell.

But I didn't look away. Not until the camp swallowed her, too.

CHAPTER 28

SAOIRSE

They had me.

The thought slammed through my head in time with every brutal jerk of my body, as two of them dragged me through the camp, my boots barely catching purchase on the uneven ground. My wrists were ziptied behind my back, plastic digging hard enough into my skin that it would leave marks—if I got out of this.

When.

When I got out of this.

The camp blurred past, shapes of muted tents and dark vehicles, flashes of motion at the edge of the gloom. There weren't many people awake. A handful of men at the perimeter, another few tending the dying embers of a fire. Most were asleep, oblivious to the fact that their precious compound had been infiltrated tonight.

And I'd been caught because I'd been so focused on the tent where Finn had disappeared that I hadn't been looking for someone to step away to take a piss.

The knot in my chest pulled tighter, hard and mean, until I couldn't breathe past it.

I stumbled over a half-buried root, and one of the guards cursed, yanking me up by the arm hard enough to make my shoulder shriek. I bit down on the inside of my cheek so sharply I tasted blood, desperate not to make a sound. Because if I gave them that—if I gave them anything—it would be like admitting this was real.

Fear wasn't a thing in the distance anymore. It was inside me, in my blood, thick and choking. It pressed against my ribs with every step, every shove. Not only fear for myself. For Finn and Ajax, still out there somewhere, and Isla locked away God knew where.

I couldn't lose them.

I kept my head down. One foot in front of the other. *Pretend you're nothing. Pretend you're already dead. Keep up the charade, survive long enough. Long enough for Finn to find me.*

They hauled me across a narrow clearing, flashlights bobbing erratically as they moved. The air smelled of wood smoke and something sharper. Gun oil, maybe. We stopped outside a larger tent with a small lamp glowing low inside. One of the guards shoved the flap aside and pushed me through without ceremony. Inside, a man hunched over a battered folding table, the surface littered with topographical maps, a few radios, a dented thermos. He didn't look up right away. Instead, he dragged a finger along a contour line, muttering under his breath like none of this was more than a mild inconvenience.

When he finally turned toward us, his face was unremarkable. Weathered, flat, utterly forgettable. Exactly the kind of man you'd never notice standing behind a trigger. His gaze skimmed over me like I was barely worth cataloging. A flick. A dismissal. Not a threat. Not even a problem yet.

"Put her with the other one. We'll sort them both out tomorrow."

The words hit harder than the shove that followed.

The other one.

A jolt of breathless, awful hope snapped through my chest. They wouldn't say it like that unless Isla was still alive. For a few moments, sweet relief cut through the fear. If she was alive, there was still hope. A slim one, given this rescue mission for one had turned into two. But so long as Finn was still out there, we stood a chance.

I staggered as they yanked me back into the night, heart hammering so hard it hurt as they marched me toward whatever cage they'd built. They dragged me across uneven ground, my boots slipping in the mud, flashlight beams slicing wildly through the misty dark. I stumbled twice, earning sharp jerks on my arms that set my shoulders screaming.

Ahead, a smaller tent was tucked away from the others. Nothing here was cheap or poor quality, but this one seemed a little dingier than the others. As if they'd had to dig it out of storage or something.

One of the guards yanked it open with a rough hand. "In," he snapped.

I didn't get a choice. A hard shove sent me sprawling forward, knees slamming into packed earth. The smell inside hit me first—damp canvas, stale sweat, fear ground into the dirt.

I caught myself before my face hit the ground, gasping through gritted teeth.

A soft click, and one of them shoved a narrow-beamed flashlight between his teeth, casting a wobbly cone of light through the gloom. Rough hands grabbed me under the arms, hauling me up. I struggled on instinct, but it didn't matter. I was no match for them, even if my hands hadn't been bound. They shoved me backward until my spine hit something solid and unyielding—a thick central pole that supported the tent.

The man with the light barked something low I couldn't make out. Another guard circled behind me, dragging coarse rope around my torso, binding me to the post without even bothering to remove the zipties cutting into my wrists. The rope was rough, scratchy, biting into my jacket and skin.

I could shift, lean a little, maybe slide my weight, but that was it. No real movement. No escape.

Hearing a noise, I twisted my head as far as I could, straining to see behind me. Past the wobble of the flashlight, out of the corner of my eye, I caught a glimpse of a figure lashed to the opposite side of the same pole. Slumped. Small. Bound at wrists and ankles, head drooped forward like a broken doll.

Isla.

It was her.

A fierce, shuddering relief and a sick, helpless fear crashed into each other inside me. She was alive, but barely, from the look of it.

I bit the inside of my cheek hard enough to taste blood, forcing myself not to call out. Not to say her name. Not to give them anything. I kept my head down, breathing shallow, pretending to be cowed and beaten. Across the pole, Isla shifted minutely. I couldn't see her face. Couldn't tell if she even knew someone else was here.

The guards muttered between themselves, a few words I couldn't catch. Then, without ceremony, they left, zippering the flap behind them, the flashlight beam bobbing away into the dark. Leaving us alone, tethered together. Waiting.

The silence in the tent was thick enough to suffocate. I sat rigid against the rough pole at my back, wrists aching where the zipties bit deep, rope digging into my ribs with every shallow breath.

Then, barely audible, a rasp, raw with fear and exhaustion. "Who... Who's there?"

The sound cracked straight through me. My heart slammed against my ribs hard enough to hurt, and for a second, I couldn't find my voice at all. I forced air into my lungs, swallowing the knot that had risen into my throat.

"It's me." The words scraped out rough and low. "It's Saoirse."

For a heartbeat, nothing. Then I heard it—a tiny, broken gasp, half sob, half disbelief—and my chest caved in like someone had plowed a fist through it.

There was a shift of movement behind me as she struggled to turn toward me. I twisted too, feeling the rough burn of rope against my skin, desperate to simply *see* her.

In the faint spill of light still leaking through the slightly unzipped tent flap, I caught the barest glimpse of the huddled shape lashed to the opposite side of the pole, hair dark and tangled, chin tucked tight against her chest.

Alive. Hurt. Bound. But alive.

I wanted to laugh and cry all at once, but I locked it down. Clamped my teeth against the well of emotion rising too fast, too fierce to manage right now. Instead, I leaned my head back against the pole—because I couldn't reach her—and forced my voice to steady.

"Well," I said, pitching it light, almost teasing, the way I used to when she'd stress about exams or broken gear, "this is a hell of a reunion spot. Five stars for ambience."

Across the shadows, I heard a breathless, broken sound on the trembling edge of a laugh.

"You're real," she whispered.

"Real enough to bitch about the accommodations," I

murmured back, throat aching from the effort of keeping it light.

Suddenly, I better understood why Finn was always the one cracking jokes. This faint moment of levity kept me from being crushed beneath the weight of the situation.

There was a rustle. The sound of Isla shifting against her restraints. "How?" she rasped. "How the hell are you even here?"

I swallowed against the knot in my throat. "Long story," I whispered back. "Short version: We figured out something was wrong. I came looking."

A beat of silence. Then, sharper, "We?"

I huffed out a breath that was almost a laugh because I knew how she was going to react to this. "Me. And Finn."

There was a pause long enough that I could almost hear Isla's brain grinding through the implications. The rough sound was closer to a laugh this time. "So I was right. You don't hate him."

I let my head fall back against the rough pole behind me, squeezing my eyes shut. "Shut up," I muttered, but there was no heat in it. Only a brittle, aching relief. "He was the most qualified to help me find you."

Another breath, rasping through the dark. Then a low tease, "Uh huh. And did this two-person rescue crew involve an only-one-tent situation?"

My silence was answer enough.

Another low, ragged laugh sounded behind me.

I shifted against the rope digging into my arms. "He's good. He's why I made it this far." There was no exaggeration, no defensiveness, only utter truth in my voice.

Silence stretched between us again, thicker this time, weighted with everything neither of us could say aloud.

The dirt was cold beneath me, the chill seeping through the

thin layer of fabric. The rope bit into my arms every time I shifted. My fingers were already going numb from the angle they'd bound me at.

But none of it mattered.

Because he was out there.

I closed my eyes and whispered it like a prayer into the dark. "Finn's coming. He'll find us."

Behind me, Isla let out a shaky breath. Part trust, part terror. I could feel it like a live wire between us.

And I clung to that one small, blinding truth:

Finn would move heaven and earth to get us out.

CHAPTER 29

FINN

I didn't know how far I ran. Only that it wasn't far enough.

Branches clawed at my arms, roots snagged at my boots, and still I moved, as if forward motion might somehow erase the sound of her being taken. Of her voice crying out before it was swallowed whole by the dark.

Ajax kept pace beside me, low and silent. His ears pinned back, head down, gaze flicking constantly toward me. He knew something was wrong. Knew this wasn't a drill or a mission or a game. But he didn't know how to fix it.

Neither did I.

When the forest thickened and the slope leveled out, I dropped hard to my knees. Dirt bit into bone. My palms hit the earth like I was bracing for an impact that had already landed. I stayed like that, doubled over, forehead nearly to the ground, trying to breathe through a storm that didn't have air.

Because she was gone.

And I had let her go.

It didn't matter that I hadn't had a choice. Didn't matter that going after her right then would've been suicide. That I'd be bleeding out beside her by now, or worse, dragging Ajax into the crosshairs too.

Because the outcome was the same. She was gone. They had her. And I hadn't stopped it.

My fists clenched against the mossy ground, dirt grinding into my palms like penance. My body locked tight, every breath a fight not to explode. Not with rage—though that was there, too—but with grief. With failure.

She'd been right there. I'd told her to stay hidden. I told her I had it under control.

And now she was behind enemy lines—alone. Except she wasn't alone. Because Isla was in there, too. Two women. One mission. One fuckup.

Mine.

I slammed my fist into the ground, bone to stone. Something split. Maybe the skin. Maybe something deeper. It didn't help.

Ajax didn't come in close at first. He held a few feet back, shifting from paw to paw, ears half-cocked like he wasn't sure what to do with me this way. Cracked open and breathing like I'd been gut-punched. We hadn't had long enough together to build routines for this kind of moment. No training for comfort. No protocol.

But eventually, he took a step forward. Then another.

And then he sat right beside me, close enough to touch.

I reached for him like a man drowning. Fisted my hand in the thick fur of his ruff and held on. Not because it helped, not because I thought it would fix anything, but because he was something tangible. Something solid and alive.

He didn't flinch away as my forehead came to rest against his shoulder.

"I know, lad." My voice came out low, broken. "It's no' your job to fix this."

It wasn't his job. It was mine.

And I was going to fix it, even if I had to burn the whole fucking world down to do it.

I sat back on my heels, hands scraped raw from the forest floor, the stink of pine and sweat clogging my nose. My pulse was still jack hammering in my ears like it hadn't figured out the danger had passed. Or maybe it knew better. Maybe it knew it hadn't.

I didn't take stock of gear. Not my knife. Not the terrain. That wasn't the inventory that mattered.

No, what I cataloged were failures.

Every breath too slow. Every decision that hadn't been enough. The half-second I'd waited when Ajax gave the warning. The time it took me to circle that last tent. The idiotic hope I'd clung to that if we were quiet, if we were *smart*, we could pull this off clean.

Like a fucking amateur.

I'd let my guard down. Let myself want. Let myself believe for a second too long that maybe this could be more than survival. And now they had her.

My voice came out low, shredded. "You dinna get to want things."

Ajax pricked his ears, as if the words were meant for him.

I swallowed hard. Shook my head. "You want things, people get hurt."

And God help me, I wanted Saoirse.

I started pacing. A tight loop at first, to keep the panic from rooting too deep. Ajax stayed where he was, eyes tracking me without judgment. Just maintaining presence and bearing witness as I tried not to lose it completely.

Fall back on the training. Take inventory.

I crouched beside a fallen log and unsheathed my knife. The blade caught no light, because there wasn't any, but I didn't need to see the edge to know it was sharp. Reliable. Not enough.

My multi-tool came out next. Not much more than a glorified paperweight in a fight. I set both beside me in the dirt and scrubbed a hand through my hair, breathing hard.

What did I have?

Me. Ajax, who, despite all his heart, wasn't at a hundred percent. Two blades. A few rations stashed back at our fallback point. Rope. Duct tape. No comms. No backup. No time.

A distraction? Maybe. But it'd need to be big enough to pull the guards off-center, and subtle enough not to alert the entire fucking compound. Could I ambush one? Knife to the throat, drag them into the trees, take their radio? Possible, but sloppy. Risky. One wrong step, and they'd move the women. Or worse.

I could feel the plan fraying before I even finished sketching it in my head.

But one truth remained solid. I wasn't leaving her in there. Not for a second longer than I had to. Not even if it killed me.

I sat down again, slower this time. Not collapsing. Centering. Trying to force clarity through the fog still pressing behind my eyes.

The forest around me held its breath, thick and waiting. Overhead, the sky was beginning to thin slightly at the edges—more slate than black. Not full light. Not yet. Maybe four hours, give or take, until the compound began to stir in earnest. It wasn't nearly enough.

Ajax shifted beside me, his body tense, alert. I reached out and rested a hand along his uninjured flank, grounding myself.

"We get one shot," I murmured. "One."

His only response was to watch me, as if waiting for me to be the man he believed I still was.

I grabbed my knife and dragged the point through the dirt,

carving rough lines—tent placements from memory, the sloped edge of the treeline. Marks where I'd seen the guards drift without any real formation or strategy. Just motion for the sake of intimidation.

I scratched out a possible route. A pocket of cover. A soft edge in the noise.

It wasn't solid. Hell, it wasn't even smart. But it was something.

If I could trigger some kind of distraction, it might shift the focus. Even for thirty seconds. A crack in their attention. That's all I'd need.

There were still supplies stashed back at the hollow. Not much. A bit of accelerant. A flare. Fishing line. Enough to make something that looked like a threat. Fire was a certain attention grabber.

If I could bait the far side of camp enough to pull eyes in the wrong direction, get someone shouting, moving, I might be able to cut through.

Thin. Too thin. But I didn't have the luxury of waiting on perfect. She didn't have the time.

I looked down at Ajax, my voice low and rough. "I'm going for her."

Not because she needed saving.

Because I did, and because she was mine.

I was done letting the world take from me.

I'd get Saoirse back. Isla too.

Whatever it cost.

CHAPTER 30

SAOIRSE

I came to slowly, groggily taking stock of my stiff neck and arms, burning with an ache that didn't go away when I shifted. Mostly because I couldn't shift. The ropes across my chest dug in when I inhaled too deeply. My shoulders throbbed from the zipties securing my arms behind me, and the post at my back felt harder than stone.

I hadn't meant to fall asleep. Hadn't thought I would. But exhaustion must have caught up with me when I wasn't looking, like it always did after too many hours on-call. This time, though, there was no phone or message service. Only rough restraints and a dirt floor.

Somewhere behind me, Isla shifted, making a low, pained sound that twisted in my chest. I turned my head slightly and caught the faint sound of voices outside the tent. Two men arguing. Not loud, but sharp. One voice short and annoyed, the kind of tone that said he thought this entire situation was beneath him. The other flatter, more clipped. Calm in a way that made my skin crawl.

I strained to listen. The words didn't quite make it through the canvas. The cadence and rhythm were enough to stir something sour in my gut. I didn't know what I was afraid of yet. Only that I was.

The flap of the tent tore open without warning. Harsh morning light slashed through the gloom, catching dust in the air and stabbing at my eyes. I flinched, instinctively turning my face away even before two sets of heavy, unhurried footsteps followed.

Boots crunched on the packed dirt. A flashlight beam swept across the space, grazing Isla first and then slanting toward my side of the pole. It hit me full in the face.

I blinked hard, vision swimming. The light dipped lower, scanning the ropes across my chest, then lifted again.

"Well, that explains the noise last night." The vaguely bored voice was smooth and polished.

I didn't have to see him to know. But I looked anyway.

Victor Sandhurst stood inside the tent, dressed in a perfectly fitted waxed canvas jacket, like he thought this was some sort of wilderness photoshoot. Not a fleck of dirt on him. His expression, as he looked at me, wasn't angry or surprised. It was faintly amused. Like finding me tied up in his secret hunting camp was a mild inconvenience.

"Well, well." Victor drew the words out like a toast. "Saoirse MacGregor. Didn't expect to find someone of your pedigree all the way out here."

The knot in my stomach cinched tight.

Of course he recognized me. Of course. That smooth, smug smile was the same one I remembered from the few tedious charity functions my mother had forced me to attend in my early twenties. The kind where the champagne was flat, the conversation dull, and the men twice my age leered at me like I was a canapé.

I met his gaze and didn't blink. Let him see the disgust. The defiance. The utter lack of fear I refused to let show, even if I was hanging on by threads.

The other man—older, broader, with the deep tan of someone who actually spent time outdoors—turned slightly toward him. "You know her?"

Victor didn't take his eyes off me. "Daughter of Marian Rothwell-Pennington MacGregor." He reeled off the information as if reciting from a social register. "The Rothwell-Penningtons are quite the name in certain circles. Old money. Old manners. Shame she's chosen to waste all that on mud and stray dogs."

My hands flexed uselessly behind my back, the zipties biting harder.

I wanted to lunge at him. Scratch that perfect façade until it bled. But all I could do was stare and breathe and promise myself that if I got out of this, I'd make damn sure Victor Sandhurst never smiled like that again.

Victor began to circle, slow and measured, the way a man might inspect a prize horse. Hands clasped behind his back, face the picture of thoughtful disdain.

"Your mother always did have such high hopes for you," he mused. "Marrying well. Hosting tasteful luncheons. Keeping the right sort of company."

He paused at my side, just out of reach, though I had no reach to give. His gaze swept lazily across my face like I was an inconvenience, not a person.

"I can only imagine what she'd say if she saw you now. Filthy. Tied up. Meddling where you don't belong." His voice dropped, the silk peeling back to steel. "It would be a terrible scandal, don't you think? The daughter of Marian MacGregor found trespassing in the wrong forest. So far from home."

My jaw clenched. I didn't respond. Wouldn't give him the satisfaction.

Behind him, the other man shifted his weight. "She's a liability."

Victor didn't look away from me as he nodded once. "Precisely."

Then, with that same easy chill, he added, "And liabilities... have a way of disappearing in these woods."

The words hung there, suspended in the musty air of the tent. Calmly stated, as though I were already half-forgotten.

A decision, not a debate.

My blood went cold. Not with panic. Panic would've been a mercy. This was something heavier. Thicker. A crawling, suffocating clarity that settled into my lungs and refused to let go.

They didn't intend to let us walk away from this.

Not me. Not Isla.

I didn't need to hear the words spelled out to understand what had happened. Without raising his pitch or lifting a hand, Victor had issued the order in that smooth, aristocratic voice. The same voice I'd heard at charity auctions and ribbon-cuttings. The same one that once tried to coax my mother into joining yet another of his insufferable foundations.

Now he was weighing my life like a line item on a balance sheet.

I turned my head, as much as the ropes would allow, and caught Isla's profile. Her eyes were wide. Too wide. Not with surprise. With recognition.

She understood too.

No one was coming back to ask more questions. No one was waiting to ransom us. We weren't hostages. We were problems. And problems in operations like this didn't get solved. They got erased.

My chest ached with how badly I wanted to reach for her. To put some kind of barrier between her and the fear crawling up her throat. But all I had was breath and the frantic drum of a prayer I hadn't even realized I was repeating.

Come on, Finn. Please.

I lifted my chin. The movement scraped the back of my head against the pole, but I didn't flinch. Didn't blink. I stared straight at him, locking my gaze with the man who'd signed my death warrant with the same tone he probably used to order wine.

"You won't get away with this." My voice came out raw but steady.

Victor smiled. Politely. As if I'd made a naïve but charming observation at a dinner party. "We'll see."

He didn't look at Isla or back at me before he turned on his heel, the guard following him out with a heavy shuffle of boots. The tent flap zipped shut behind them, the sound crisp and final.

And then the silence came crashing back in. Dense and suffocating, broken only by our breathing and the fading echo of their words.

We weren't prisoners anymore. We were prey.

The quiet settled like dust, clinging to everything. My arms ached. My throat burned. I'd long since stopped feeling my fingers.

Behind me, Isla shifted—barely. I heard the rasp of her jacket against the rope, the small hitch in her breath. She didn't speak.

So I did. "He's coming." My whisper cracked on the declaration, soft as a bruise. "Finn's coming."

For a moment, she said nothing.

When it came, her voice was smaller than I'd ever heard it. "You're sure?"

I closed my eyes. Let my head fall back against the pole. I

knew beyond a doubt he'd come. But he was only one man, bringing a knife to a fight against a whole lot of guns, and I could only pray he wouldn't become yet another victim of privileged men's egos.

CHAPTER 31

FINN

I crouched in the underbrush beyond the perimeter, my whole body drawn tight like a wire about to snap. From this vantage, the camp was little more than a smudge of movement and muted sound—voices, footsteps, the occasional gleam of sunlight against metal. Nothing chaotic or out of place. Which made it worse. They were still in control.

Ajax hovered at my side, his ears twitching with every shift of the breeze. He didn't pant. Didn't fidget. But I could feel the same tension wound through my own spine coming off him. He knew. Something had changed in me. The stillness was different now.

I wasn't waiting anymore.

I had one real knife. No backup. No comms. No real plan beyond *get Saoirse out.* A suicide run, probably. But the longer I sat here, the less that idea felt like madness and more like inevitability. I couldn't keep waiting. Couldn't stomach the thought of her in there, trapped, scared, maybe already hurt worse than I could let myself imagine.

My hand flexed over the hilt at my hip, breath shallow. One

man. One blade. But doing nothing? That would kill me faster than a bullet.

A whisper of movement cut through the stillness. Too deliberate to be wind, too quiet to be wildlife. Even as Ajax tensed beside me, I turned on instinct, blade already in hand, muscles locked for a strike. But before I could launch, a low voice threaded out of the trees.

"Easy, Nomad. You called. We came."

I froze.

Callum stepped out of the foliage like the damn ghost we'd named him for, camo blending with every shade of green. Alex and Ewan emerged behind him, just as silent, geared to the teeth, eyes sharp. All three were dressed for war, and I must've looked like hell—dirty, unshaven, wild around the edges.

Relief hit me like a hammer to the chest. For half a second, I thought I might drop. My knees wobbled before I got them under me.

I opened my mouth, but Alex held up a hand. "No' here. Too close. Come on."

I nodded, throat too tight for words, and fell in beside them, ducking low as we slipped back into the cover of the forest. Behind me, Ajax stayed tight to my flank, quiet and watchful, but I swore I felt him relax the faintest bit. As if even he knew we weren't alone anymore.

We pulled back half a kilometer before anyone said a word. Far enough that the hum of the compound fell away, and the forest swallowed us whole. Once we reached a hollow tucked behind a collapsed ridge, Ewan gave a short hand signal, and we stopped.

I turned toward him, already thinking through the next steps, but it was Alex who cut in first. "Where's Saoirse?"

I swallowed hard. "She was at the perimeter last night. I

went in for the radio. We had a fallback plan, but she got spotted."

There was a beat of sharp-edged, brittle silence.

"They've got her?" Ewan asked.

I nodded. "Dragged her in while I was slipping out."

Callum's jaw flexed. Ewan muttered something savage under his breath.

"She's alive." I was grateful I could still confirm that. "They put her with Isla. I didn't see them hurt her." Not that my brain had stopped producing increasingly horrific scenarios in the hours since she'd been taken.

Ewan didn't waste time asking what I'd seen or how I knew. He only nodded, a grim set to his mouth. "Then we move."

Without another word, we fell into the familiar dynamics of an op, as we'd done countless times before.

Alex dropped into a crouch and finally unhooked his gear. The waterproof pack unzipped in near silence, and he pulled out a tablet, eyes flicking to me like we were already mid-briefing.

"We didn't know what we were looking for until your signal came through." He tapped the screen. "After that? We started pulling every nearby satellite ping and flagged comms trace from the last seventy-two hours."

He rotated the screen toward me. A terrain map came up first, then layered data—pings, irregular signals, a faint heat signature cluster.

"You said poaching in the code. Then the location. So I started scraping. Found mentions on closed channels of high-dollar hunting excursions—invite-only shite, flown in by private heli, no permits, no oversight—tied to this ridge."

He flicked again, this time to a grid of blurred photos. Long-lens shots of marked animals. A wildcat with a radio collar. A red deer with a clipped antler tip.

"They're tracking protected species. Tagging them with signal trackers, calling in locations. Selling the kill slots to rich arseholes who want to brag without getting their boots dirty."

My jaw clenched. I didn't look away.

"They knew how to hide, but your broadcast told us where to look. So we did." Alex looked up from the tablet. "Authorities are looped, but let's no' pretend they're moving fast. Out here? We're it."

It wouldn't be the first time we'd been on our own. But I was beyond grateful I had my team. "Understood. Let's plan it right."

I crouched beside him, cleared a patch of forest floor with my palm, and started sketching with a stick. "The only tent with a posted guard is on the eastern side. It's small, tucked near the tree line, half-shielded by storage crates. I haven't seen inside, but it's the only one with traffic that isn't shifting gear or posturing. That's where they're keeping them."

I saw the flash of understanding move through all three of them.

"I haven't seen Isla since yesterday. Saoirse and I spotted her when we first found the camp. They had her restrained but untouched. Since then? Nothing. But so far as I can tell, they haven't moved her, and they added another body to their problem. That pressure's building. They'll want to clean house before anything slips."

"Which means they willnae sit on them long," Ewan concluded. "This isnae catch and release."

"No." My hand fisted. "It's control and cleanup."

Callum shifted beside me, already scanning mentally for angles. "What's their coverage?"

"Loose perimeter. Three walking the boundary. Most of them look bored out of their minds, but they're carrying rifles. Weekend warrior types rather than hired mercenaries. I counted at least two with comm units. Basic, unencrypted. They've got a vehicle stash. Three ATVs. I haven't seen a heli-pad, but based on what Echo already found, they're flying in somewhere."

"They're used to being above consequences," Alex muttered. "They'll assume no one's coming."

"Let's prove them wrong." I tapped the dirt. "They've got gaps. West side's the quietest—shallow incline, brush cover. No guards stationed there full time. Not that any of their security is exactly disciplined. Callum, you've got sniper elevation on that quadrant?"

He nodded once. "I can give you the entry window and cover the fallback."

Ewan spoke next, low and steady. "I've mapped two exfil vectors. Stream path south, or the gulley east. We lose high ground either way, but the brush is dense. We'll have to move fast if it turns on us."

"We will." And with my men at my back, I felt as if I could fucking fly. "We go in, get them out. No posturing. No speeches. Quiet and quick."

Alex looked at me. "You're sure they're still alive?"

"I am. Because if they weren't, the guard wouldn't still be posted."

He didn't argue.

Ewan nodded. "Then we move tonight."

Callum folded his arms. "It's a decent plan."

Alex shoved the tablet back into his pack. "We've surely operated on worse before."

Ewan shucked his pack and pinned his focus on me. "In the meantime, let's get you properly geared up."

But as I reached for the fresh gear, my hand paused.

A single, insistent thought cut through the motion. Getting them out was step one. But it wasn't enough.

I looked up at Callum. "If we can find leverage—intel, evidence, something we can extract or burn—"

"—we end it," he finished. No hesitation.

Alex's jaw set. "You want to kill this thing at the root."

"If we can," I said. "Without risking them. We keep the rescue clean. That comes first. But if there's a chance to tear it down while we're in there—quietly, surgically—we take it."

No one disagreed.

Not even Ewan, who usually played the voice of restraint.

"They've been doing this a long time," he said. "There'll be records. Comms. Maybe even footage. Bastards like this dinna build these operations merely to brag to each other. They keep receipts."

"Then we find them," I said. "And we make sure this place disnae rise again after we're gone."

The plan didn't change.

But the stakes had.

This wasn't only about saving Saoirse and Isla anymore.

It was about making sure no one else ended up in that cage.

"Thank you. All of you."

Short nods of acknowledgment from all of them.

The forest didn't feel quite so suffocating now.

I sat back on my heels, hands braced on my thighs, and let the quiet between us stretch. For the first time in what felt like days, I wasn't chasing breath. I could actually pull it in and let it stay. The tension was still there—God, it was never gone—but underneath it now was something else. A thread of steadiness I hadn't felt since Saoirse was taken.

Ajax nudged in close, pressing his shoulder against mine. I reached up and scratched behind his ears, felt the weight of his body lean in, steady as ever.

"Told you I wouldn't do this alone."

He huffed softly and rested his chin on my thigh.

Hope wasn't loud. It didn't burn bright or swell up all cinematic and grand. It was quieter than that. Slower. But it filled the cracks. Held the pieces in place.

And it reminded me what we were fighting for.

Another chance to feel the silk of her hair, the bite of her sharp tongue, and the peace of her kiss. Another quiet moment with nothing more than her warm silence and her hand in mine.

I'm coming, Saoirse. Just hold on.

CHAPTER 32

SAOIRSE

The barked order jolted me out of my anxious rumination. I jerked my head toward the sound. Boots hit the ground outside. Crunching gravel. Purposeful. Voices low and clipped. No more of the lazy, drawling disdain from yesterday. These men were alert and focused. Something was happening.

Before Isla or I could speak, the tent flap jerked open, and two figures stepped inside, flashlights flicking over me and Isla. My eyes adjusted fast in the dimness, registering the same two thick-necked, bored-looking guards from the night before. They were tenser now, their silence heavier than noise.

One of them moved to the post and began untying the rope from my torso, movements brisk and efficient. The zipties around my wrists remained in place, biting into already abraded skin. Behind me, Isla stirred groggily as her own ropes were unfastened.

"Let's get it done before the rain hits," one muttered, voice flat.

The other grunted in agreement.

Outside, the air had shifted to something denser, more

expectant. I could feel it through the canvas walls, thick with the promise of coming weather. Low clouds pressing down on the forest like a hand. The kind of gray that made everything feel like it was holding its breath.

I turned my head and caught Isla's eyes. She looked pale, pupils wide in the dimness, but lucid. Her jaw clenched when the guards hauled her to her feet, and I knew. We both knew. This wasn't a relocation. This wasn't containment.

This was removal.

The air hit like a slap when they dragged us out of the tent. Damp and close, thick with the weight of cloud-heavy sky. The world had gone silver at the edges—muted and colorless under the late-day gloom, the kind of midsummer dusk where the light sort of *dulled* rather than faded. Wind rustled the treetops above us, stirring needles and leaves in uneasy murmurs. I caught the scent of wet pine and something acrid underneath.

The camp was quieter than I expected. No laughter or chatter interrupted the scrape of boots and the low hum of idling engines. Even the guards moved differently. Brisk, tense, their usual smugness stripped down to something leaner. Meaner. No masks of civility now. Things were coming to an end.

They didn't speak as they marched us forward, one hand fisted in the back of my shirt, the other on Isla's arm. The ATVs were parked in a neat line along the edge of the camp, beyond the fire pit. Engines ticking under the low sky, headlights dark, like beasts crouched and waiting.

We weren't being brought to vehicles. We were being brought deeper *into* the woods. Were they planning to execute and bury us? Or would they simply leave our corpses for the scavengers?

My feet caught on a tree root, and I stumbled forward,

barely catching myself. One of the guards jerked me upright again with a grunt. "Watch it."

Somewhere high overhead, a raven let out a single harsh caw, the sound slicing through the stillness like a warning. My gut coiled.

I didn't need a map to know we were going somewhere no one was supposed to find us.

The closer we got to the edge of the camp, the more I felt the shift. The wrongness. It wasn't only fear twisting in my stomach now. It was something else. Tighter. Sharper. Like the air itself had teeth.

The guards weren't talking. Not even in muttered curses or shitty jokes. The kind of silence that wasn't natural in a place like this. One of them paused mid-step and scanned the tree line, his fingers tightening on the butt of his rifle. The other followed his gaze, subtle but unmistakable, his jaw ticking once as he reached to adjust the strap across his chest.

They were jumpy.

And they weren't the only ones.

The wind shifted again, bringing with it the faint sharp, metallic scent of ozone biting at the back of my throat. A low rumble somewhere far off might've been distant thunder or might've been nothing. But it didn't matter. The air felt charged, like it was waiting for something to break.

I swallowed hard, forcing breath through my nose, heart hammering against my ribs like it wanted to outrun everything.

Something was coming.

No. Someone.

I didn't have proof. Couldn't explain it. But I knew with every scraped up, trembling part of me that Finn was out there. Watching. Waiting. Close enough to feel the same pressure crawling under my skin.

I didn't know what his plan was. I only knew he was about

to strike. Because the alternative was too horrific to contemplate.

A sudden burst shattered the quiet. Not a gunshot—more like something exploding low to the ground. It cracked through the air and sent a rush of white light and smoke blooming across the far end of the clearing. My ears rang. The men around us flinched, half-blinded, shouting over one another as the haze swallowed their footing.

And then everything broke.

Figures moved through the smoke—fast and deliberate. One man surged in from the left, swept the legs out from under a guard so hard I felt the impact in my ribs. Another tackled a second guard from behind, dragging him into the dirt in a controlled, brutal motion. Fists. Elbows. A sudden, shocking silence as one man crumpled unconscious.

They weren't shooting.

They were taking the camp *apart*.

A guard lunged for me—reactive, uncoordinated—and I threw myself sideways, shoulder first, into the one still gripping Isla. He staggered with a curse. She jerked free, half-falling, half-running.

"Go!" I gasped, breath catching.

Isla limped toward the tree line, quickly lost in the smoke.

I turned, only to freeze as I spotted the rifle barrel leveled straight at my chest. The man holding it looked furious. Shaky. Like he might shoot from fear alone.

Time stuttered.

I didn't scream. Didn't run. There was nowhere to go. My body froze, knees locked, lungs refusing to work. The man holding the gun looked half-crazed, sweat slick on his brow, arms trembling like even *he* didn't trust himself not to pull the trigger.

A blur tore through the shadows, low and fast and utterly silent.

Ajax hit him like a missile, with a snarl I heard even over the chaos around us.

The rifle went skittering across the ground as the man toppled backward, a strangled yell ripping from his throat. Ajax sank his teeth into the man's forearm with a sound I'd never heard from him before—deep and guttural and *final*. The kind of growl that left no doubt about intent or the kind of lethality he'd been trained for.

The man screamed. Thrashed. Ajax didn't let go.

I staggered back, gasping, the shock still rippling through my limbs. My wrists throbbed in their restraints. My legs felt loose beneath me. But I was still upright. Still breathing.

Still alive.

Through the rising smoke and scattering bodies, another figure emerged. My heart clenched, and I braced to stand my ground before my brain caught up and registered the familiar tall frame moving fast.

Finn.

His knife was drawn, shoulders squared and eyes locked on me. One flicker to check me for blood and injury. Then he was on the man Ajax had dropped, kicking the rifle out of reach and slamming a knee into his ribs with brutal efficiency as he snapped an order I didn't catch. Ajax let go, teeth dripping, chest heaving, falling in at Finn's side like he'd never left it.

Behind us, a voice rang out, clipped and commanding. "Two down, eyes left!"

Ewan. I couldn't see him through the blur of movement and trees, but the sound of his voice cut through the noise like a blade.

A single rifle crack split the air—tight and fast. My heart lurched.

I didn't know where the shot came from or who pulled the trigger, but it didn't sound random. It sounded deliberate. Controlled. Not chaos. Precision. A sniper?

Someone darted past the edge of my vision. Another man in camo moving with silent precision. Alex. I recognized the way he moved even before my brain finished registering his face. He swept along the rear edge of the camp, checking shadows, covering angles. Never stopping.

They weren't shouting. Weren't scrambling.

They moved like water. Like they'd done this a thousand times before. Smooth and fast and terrifying in how efficient they were. It wasn't loud. It wasn't messy. It was *effective*.

One by one, the guards fell or scattered. Not dead. At least, I didn't think so. But down. Unconscious. Disarmed. Out of the fight.

And all I could do was stand there, still bound and breathless, watching the man I'd once called insufferable move through a war zone like he'd been born for it.

God help me, it was beautiful. Awful. And beautiful.

It ended faster than I could've imagined.

One minute, the camp was a minefield of shouting and stomping boots and snarled orders. The next, it was still. Quiet in that eerie, post-storm kind of way. I could hear the wind again, and the rustle of canvas. Somewhere, a rifle clattered to the ground. A voice barked, "Secure him," and another answered, "Got it."

The guards were down. Not all unconscious, not all injured—but every one of them disarmed. Contained. Tents were being swept, gear ripped open and searched. A man groaned nearby, curled against a tree, arms ziptied behind his back. The tide had turned, and it hadn't taken hours.

It had taken minutes.

My legs buckled before I realized I was swaying. I sank to

my knees in the mud, heart pounding like it still thought we were running. I couldn't catch my breath. Couldn't seem to blink the blur from my eyes.

Then Finn was there, dropping to a crouch in front of me like the world had narrowed to this exact point. His knife flashed once, clean and sure, and the zipties fell away from my wrists. The sting where they'd bitten in barely registered before he pulled me against his chest.

His arms wrapped tight around me, solid and grounding. I let myself sag against him for a single heartbeat, soaking in the reality of him. Alive. Warm. Here. My fingers curled into the fabric of his shirt before I could stop them.

"You came." The words were barely a sound. My throat was raw.

His hand cupped my face before I could finish the breath. His gaze searched mine with the kind of care that unraveled me completely. "Always."

But it couldn't last.

He let go slowly, carefully, before stepping back with a reluctant glance over his shoulder. "Stay here." Then he was gone again, moving back toward the heart of the camp where the others were still working.

I sat down hard on a felled log, my limbs shaking now that the adrenaline was draining away.

"Saoirse!" Isla stumbled over. Had she gotten turned around in the chaos?

She collapsed on the log beside me, every bit as spent. We slumped against each other, the contact the only thing holding us both vertical.

Around us, the camp shifted, from a place of control and cruelty to something being dismantled and logged for evidence. I saw Callum stacking weapons, sweeping for anything missed.

Ewan crouched by the fire pit, examining a steel box full of trackers and tags.

Alex returned a moment later, tablet in hand, expression grim but satisfied. "Vehicles are secured. Footage uploaded to cloud storage. Comms logs copied. And the GPS data's giving us enough to trace this whole operation. Dates, names, buyers, the works."

He didn't need to explain what that meant. The poaching ring wouldn't disappear into shadows. Not this time.

I exhaled slowly, pulse beginning to settle. At least until Alex added, "Only one missing."

My gaze snapped to his. "Who?"

"Sandhurst."

My stomach dropped. "What do you mean, missing?"

"We never saw him during the breach. Tent's still got his gear. But no sign of the man himself. He's no' in the compound."

My jaw clenched. Of course. Of course, the bastard had slipped away—quiet and early, like a man used to walking through locked doors untouched.

"Coward," I muttered.

Alex nodded once. "Probably. But he willnae get far. Not with this much heat."

"He'd better not," I said, low. "Because if he does, I swear —" And then I stopped. I looked around again. Callum, near the tent line. Ewan, by the fire pit. Alex standing right in front of me. But not the one face I needed to see.

"Where's Finn?" I asked.

The silence that followed wasn't long.

But it was loud.

CHAPTER 33

FINN

I didn't stay.

Once the shouting dimmed, the threats were silenced, and the camp was under control, I turned away. I didn't look for Saoirse. Didn't let myself. Not again. Not when I could still feel the echo of her voice in my chest, still hear the way she'd whispered, *You came,* like it meant something I hadn't earned.

The others were moving through the compound, securing weapons, zip-tying wrists, documenting everything for the people who would come later and pretend they hadn't seen, even as they took the next steps through all the proper channels. Alex was already on comms. Callum and Ewan had their zones. The place was locked down tighter than a bunker. A relatively clean op, considering. No casualties.

Saoirse was safe. So was Isla. That should have been enough.

But one man was still missing.

I didn't ask permission or say a word before I picked up my pace and melted into the trees. Ajax stayed close, quiet as a shadow. We both knew the drill.

Victor Sandhurst had slipped the net. And if anyone was going to drag him back to face what he'd done, it was going to be me.

I wasn't chasing a fugitive. I was hunting a man who'd dared to lay a hand on what was mine.

The guilt settled in my chest like coiled wire, hot and tight and impossible to shake. It had been there since the moment they dragged her off and I'd had to let them. Since I'd made the call not to charge in like a fool and get myself killed, and by extension, left her alone in that nightmare. Even knowing it was the right decision didn't help. Not when I kept seeing her face in the dark. Not when I remembered the tremor in her voice, the way her hands had shaken, the restraint she'd forced herself to hold together for Isla's sake.

She was safe now. Breathing. Whole.

But I'd seen the marks on her wrists.

And I wasn't going to let the man responsible walk away breathing easy.

I told myself this was about the mission. About tying off the last thread and making sure no one slipped through to start the whole damn machine up again. But that wasn't the truth. Not all of it.

This had a name. Sandhurst. He was the rot. The money. The arrogance and entitlement that allowed this whole operation to exist. Men like him didn't build cages. They paid others to do it and made sure their hands stayed clean.

He was the reason Saoirse and Isla were ever in danger.

He was the reason her voice had been hoarse when she said my name. The reason her hands had been shaking when I cut the zipties off her wrists. The reason there was still blood on my knuckles from how hard I'd gripped that blade.

I couldn't go back and undo what had happened. Couldn't give either of them back the hours they'd spent bound and terrified. But I could make damn sure the man responsible didn't walk away.

And maybe that would be enough.

Ajax padded at my side, silent as shadow, his body alert. He didn't need commands. He could feel my focus sharpened to a point, every sense angled toward the chase. We moved without speaking, slipping between trees and over root-choked ground as the light faded into that dense Scottish gray that passed for night.

The rain hadn't started yet, but the air was wet with promise. Mist slicked the undergrowth and beaded on my skin, making everything smell like loam and iron. And still, the signs were there.

A boot print in a patch of softened earth, barely catching the edge of my flashlight's low beam. A freshly snapped stalk of bracken. A half-erased tire rut leading into the tree line where no vehicle should've been.

Sandhurst knew these woods. I'd give him that. Knew enough to vanish before the lockdown hit. But he didn't know how to evade someone like me. How to move through them without leaving signs I could read. Didn't know what it meant to hunt while being hunted.

Didn't know what it meant to be hunted by someone who'd found the woman he loved bloodied and trembling and still trying to protect someone else.

I could feel him out there—close enough to chase, not yet far enough to escape.

And I was going to catch him.

The hours bled together, each step folding into the next until there was nothing left but rhythm: breath, footfall, breath again. The forest pressed close, branches snagging at my jacket, the sky above gone to ink. I didn't care. I wasn't looking up. My focus was forward, tunneled down to the pulse of movement, the next clue to tell me the shape of the trail.

We hit the stream bed around what must've been the middle of the night, though it was hard to tell in the gloom. The only reason I caught the shape tucked against the trees was Ajax's sudden halt, the deep rumble building in his chest. My light swept sideways and found a quad bike half-concealed behind a fallen branch, its tires still wet. When I laid a hand against the engine casing, warmth bled against my palm.

Close.

He'd gone to foot travel from here. Too narrow a route ahead, too risky with the engine noise. He was trying to disappear into the dark. But he hadn't counted on someone who made his living in it.

I crouched, signaling Ajax forward. He slunk ahead, soundless as a shadow, and I crept after him.

I caught a flicker again. A flashlight beam, faint and erratic, swinging low through the trees. The figure holding it didn't know how to move quietly. He was breathing hard. Footsteps too fast, too careless. Panic was starting to edge in.

Good. Let him run scared. Because I was done chasing.

He heard me too late. I stepped out from the trees as he angled his flashlight forward, and his whole body jolted, hands fumbling, boots slipping in the soft leaf litter. He caught himself on a low branch, but I was already moving. No words. No warning.

He threw up a hand like that would stop me. "You know who I am?"

I didn't slow. "Dinna care."

His mouth opened, probably gearing up for some bullshite threat, some name to drop, some lawyer he'd call. But none of it mattered. He was simply another coward trying to buy time with bluster, and I was fresh out of patience.

It was fast. I slammed into him with enough force to knock him off balance and sweep his legs from under him. He hit the ground with a grunt, and before he could roll or scramble, I was on him, knee to spine, zipties snapping into place behind his back.

He grunted again as I tightened them a little harder than necessary. Not enough to damage—just enough to make sure he felt it.

This was for her. For the fear I'd seen in her eyes. For the bruises and the abrasions. For every second she spent wondering if help was ever coming.

"Wait," he wheezed.

"Shut up." I yanked him upright by the collar and shoved him against a tree trunk.

He was panting now, jacket askew, mud on his knees. "You can't do this."

In the faint glow of the flashlight that had been knocked askew, I met his eyes, cold and level. "I just did."

He cursed me with considerable vigor and creativity, but I didn't hear most of it. I wasn't listening anymore. There was no satisfaction or adrenaline high. Only the solid weight of an ending that had taken too long to come.

Justice wasn't always clean. But tonight, it was handled.

I hauled him to his feet with a rough grip on the zipties and gave him a shove to get him moving. He stumbled, spat something about his shoes being custom made, and I didn't bother to hide my contempt. Ajax circled us once, then fell in on my left, silent, alert, steady as ever.

We moved through the trees in near-darkness, no flashlight, no sound but the scrape of branches and the soft crunch of leaves underfoot. The clouds hung low and thick above the canopy, hiding any trace of moonlight, but I didn't need it. I knew the way.

Sandhurst wouldn't shut up.

"This is kidnapping. Do you have any idea who I am?"

"I'll bury you. You and whoever you're working for."

"You don't walk away from this kind of mistake."

I didn't answer. Not once.

Let him burn out his voice, trying to reclaim the illusion of control. Let him pretend his name still carried weight in the dark. I kept walking.

Each step felt heavier than it should've. Not from fatigue—though I was running on fumes—but from everything this bastard represented. Power without conscience. Wealth without consequence. He thought he could buy his way out of anything. That the rules didn't apply to him.

But they did tonight.

Ajax gave a growl once, almost thoughtful, when Sandhurst tried to twist away. I tightened my grip on the tie and jerked him forward again.

"You're going to regret this," he muttered.

I met his gaze for half a second and smirked. "You already do."

We kept walking, with nothing more than the rustle of branches, the drag of his boots, and the sound of justice catching up.

CHAPTER 34

SAOIRSE

By the time I gave my final signature, my hand was shaking from more than fatigue. The interview room smelled like old coffee and institutional floor polish, and my brain felt scrubbed raw. Across the table, Isla leaned forward, murmuring something too soft for me to catch. Her statement had taken hours. Mine nearly as long. Not because the detectives didn't believe us, but because they wanted every detail. Every name. Every timeline. And we gave them everything.

The lead officer, MacLeish, was a tall, sharp-featured man with a no-nonsense voice and a surprising underlying gentleness. He flipped his notebook closed and gave us a look I couldn't quite name. Respect, maybe. Or sympathy he wasn't ready to voice.

"You've both done incredibly well. This is going to be a hell of a case. I willnae lie. There's a long road ahead. But what you've given us? It matters."

Beside me, Isla nodded stiffly. Her knuckles were white where she clutched the edge of the table. I didn't reach for her, but I felt the ache to. We'd had too many eyes on us for too many hours. Now that it was done, I didn't quite know what to do with my body.

The door opened, and one of the constables gestured that we were clear to go. For now, we were done with forms and questions.

They didn't offer us a ride. Thankfully, they didn't need to.

Callum was waiting out front, parked illegally on the yellow lines, arms folded across his chest and a flat expression that said he dared anyone to challenge him on it. He caught my eye through the drizzle-damp glass as Isla and I stepped out into the soft gray daylight.

His nod was small, but sure. A silent *It's done now.*

And for the first time in days, I almost believed it.

The drive home passed in silence.

Outside the window, the Highlands bled into themselves—soft, gray, and endless. Rain streaked the windscreen. Low clouds veiled the tops of the hills, brushing the landscape in mist and shadow. Trees blurred past, branches wet and bowed as we rolled along the winding road.

I curled my fingers into my sleeves, palms pressed against the fabric like I could ground myself through touch alone. Isla sat beside me in the backseat, head tipped toward the glass, her profile caught in fleeting reflections. Her eyes were closed, mouth slack with exhaustion. She wasn't sleeping, not really. But she was too shattered to fake being truly awake.

Neither of us had spoken since we'd left the station. Not even to Callum, who drove with one hand loose on the wheel, gaze never quite leaving the road. I didn't think I could've managed words if I tried.

Glenlaig looked exactly the same.

Stone houses pressed close to the winding road, windows flower-boxed and still. Hedges trimmed. Flags fluttering in damp wind. A garden gate swung gently on its hinge in front of the bakery like someone had stepped inside moments ago.

It should have felt comforting. Familiar. But instead, something inside me recoiled. The unchanged sameness of it—all of it—felt wrong. Like the village hadn't noticed we were gone. Like it couldn't possibly understand what had happened in the wild between then and now.

The 4x4 crunched to a halt in front of my cottage, tires whispering over damp gravel. The second we came to a full stop, the front door swung open.

My grandfather didn't wait. He was down the steps in a heartbeat, striding toward us, his expression thunderous with worry. He went straight for my door, and the moment I opened it, his arms were around me in a fiercely protective hug.

"I'm all right." My voice was muffled against his shoulder.

His hand cradled the back of my head. "No' the point."

The tension in my chest cracked a little at that. Simply split open and softened. I didn't realize how much I'd needed that hug until his arms had wrapped around me, familiar and solid.

When we pulled apart, his eyes flicked past me to the other side of the car. "Isla."

She was slower to get out. Tired. Still pale, still moving like every bone ached. I was sure they did after the days of captivity and the hours we'd spent in interrogation. But when she stepped around the vehicle, he was already there, pulling her into a gentler version of the same embrace.

"Good to see you in one piece, lass."

She managed the ghost of a smile at his gruff but heartfelt words. "Better to *be* in one piece."

"Let's get you both inside." He began herding us toward the house. "You're home now."

I didn't correct him. Isla was only visiting, but that didn't matter right now. The cottage was a safe place, and that counted for something.

Inside, everything looked the same. Too much the same. The familiar scent of lemon balm and old wood. The kettle still resting on the stove. The well-worn rug Pippin frequently claimed for naps on sunny days. It made the last week feel even more surreal. Like we'd stepped sideways into a story someone else had written, and now we were simply... back.

Grandda was back to the practicalities. "Have you been medically cleared? Checked out by anyone?"

I glanced around for my errant cat. "A quick going over by emergency services at the police station."

"I'll call Taryn." Granddad reached for the kitchen phone.

I wasn't about to object to a house call from one of the village doctors. "Thanks."

I helped Isla out of her borrowed coat and got her seated on the sofa, her frame folding down like her strings had finally gone slack. Pippin appeared a moment later, tail puffed to the size of a bottle brush, giving me a look like I'd personally betrayed the crown. I crouched to scratch his ears, murmured apologies he accepted with only mild disdain, and then flopped into the chair opposite Isla.

The relief was real. So was the exhaustion. But it still didn't settle completely. Because Finn wasn't here. And that silence—his silence—was the one thing I couldn't make peace with. But I couldn't think about that now. Not until I was alone.

The knock came about twenty minutes later. As Grandda was puttering in the kitchen making tea, I opened the door to find Taryn Donaldson standing there, rain jacket spotted with drizzle and her usual no-nonsense expression tugged a little tighter than usual.

"Hey." She gave me a once-over. "You alive?"

I resisted the vaguely hysterical bark of laughter that wanted to escape as I stepped aside. "Barely. Come in."

She offered me a faint smile as she brushed past. We weren't close, not really. Merely two professionals who happened to serve the same small village. But there was a quiet trust there. You didn't live in Glenlaig and not know who had steady hands in a crisis.

Taryn's gaze flicked immediately to Isla, still swaddled on the couch beneath half a dozen blankets. She didn't ask questions. The placid look on her face told me she'd seen worse and didn't need the whole story to do her job.

"I'll start with her. You sit."

I didn't. I lingered nearby, watching her work—thermometer, blood pressure, pupil response, a hydration check. Isla barely stirred, murmuring something that might've been "cold" or "tea" or both.

When Taryn finished, she glanced up at me. "She's dehydrated, bruised up, but no signs of concussion or serious trauma. Keep her on fluids. Let her sleep."

I nodded, something easing in my chest.

Taryn turned to me. "Let me see your wrists."

I held them out automatically. The skin was broken in places, raw and inflamed where the zipties had bitten in. They'd been cleaned and disinfected earlier, but that had been the bare minimum. She took my hands with a gentleness I wasn't quite prepared for and turned them slowly under the light.

"This'll heal." Her tone was clinical. Her eyes weren't.

I nodded, not sure if I believed her. Not sure if she meant the skin or everything else. Maybe both.

Once Taryn packed up her bag and left with a last reminder to push fluids and take it easy, the house fell quiet again. My grandfather lingered near the door, one hand braced on the frame like he couldn't quite decide whether to stay or go. His eyes moved between me and Isla, still curled on the couch under a heap of blankets, breathing steady but shallow. The guest room was just down the hall, but if she was finally resting, I wasn't going to disturb her.

Grandda looked like he wanted to say something. Maybe a dozen things. But instead, he stepped close and rested a hand on my shoulder, the same way he used to when I was small, and scraped my knee and tried not to cry. I leaned into it for a second longer than I meant to.

"We'll sleep. We're okay. Just... tired." That was perhaps not entirely true, especially for Isla. But it was where we were for now.

He gave a single, gruff nod. His hand lingered for a beat longer, then dropped. He stepped back, his boots quiet on the wood floor, and let himself out with no more than a soft click of the latch behind him.

The quiet that followed was deep and thick with the kind of stillness that only comes after chaos.

I didn't sleep.

Didn't sit either. I moved through the house like a ghost, checking on Isla, adjusting the blanket that didn't need adjusting, rinsing mugs we hadn't used. And when I finally ran out of excuses to keep moving, I ended up at the window. Arms folded tight across my chest. Forehead nearly touching the glass.

The sky stayed gray, same as it had all day. The rain had slacked off sometime in the past hour, but more would come. It always did. Now there was simply a sense of waiting. A low, endless pressure, as if the clouds were holding their breath.

Maybe that was just me.

Alex had said Finn went after Sandhurst. That he was fine. That he'd be back. And I believed him. Finn wouldn't vanish.

Not from his team, not from the village he'd built something solid in. His roots were here now. Tied down in people and routines and a job I knew he loved.

But that wasn't what twisted in my gut.

The real question that kept tugging at me like a frayed thread just shy of snapping was whether he'd come back to me.

Not Out of Bounds Scotland. Not the village. Me.

What had happened out there in the dark had felt like something real. Like it mattered. Like we did. But maybe it only mattered because the world had narrowed to survival and urgency and quiet touches in the cold. Maybe it wasn't enough to carry past adrenaline and stitched up wounds.

I pressed a hand to the window frame. Cool wood beneath my palm.

Was it real for you too, Finn? Or simply another mission you're already packing away?

CHAPTER 35

FINN

The rain was steady by the time I stepped out of the trees, the wet ground sucking at my boots as I crossed the trampled edge of the compound. The site was crawling with high-vis jackets now, Police Scotland moving through the debris of the broken camp with methodical, clipped precision. Evidence bags. Radios. A slow, quiet hum of containment.

Victor Sandhurst stumbled a half-step behind me, soaked through, mud streaking his jacket. He'd been running his mouth the whole way back, like he couldn't stand the silence. Threats. Legal jargon. Half-baked reminders of who he thought he was.

"They won't hold me," he muttered for the fifth time. "I've had drinks with cabinet ministers. Golfed with half of Parliament."

I didn't answer as I continued to drag him toward the authorities.

An officer near the center of the compound looked up, clocked me, and stepped forward. He was mid-thirties, square-shouldered, and clearly in charge of the field team still on-site. I stopped in front of him and gave the leash of zipties a small, sharp tug to draw Sandhurst up short beside me.

"Victor Sandhurst. He's the money. He ran."

The officer raised a brow at my declaration, but he didn't ask questions as he reached out and took hold, snapping the restraints into his own grip like he'd been expecting this moment all day.

Sandhurst straightened, water sliding down his cheeks in thin rivulets as he sneered. "I'll have your badge for this. All of you."

I was already turning away. Let him spit and sputter into the gray light. My part in this was done.

One of the constables nodded toward the back of a marked Land Rover. A silent offer of a ride. I'd take it. I was dead tired, and my canine companion had gone so far above and beyond. The officer waited for me to load Ajax in the back. The dog moved stiffly, favoring his wounded flank, but climbed in without complaint, like even he understood this last piece of the job had taken its toll. I settled beside him, boots dripping onto the rubber mats as the rest of me leaked rain into the seat creases.

The way back to the trailhead was long and roundabout, considering there weren't really roads for most of it. Eventually, we came out on a narrow and winding track. Mist clung to the verge and curled around fence posts. Inside the vehicle, the heater clicked on low and the wipers kept time with the ache behind my eyes.

When we pulled up to the trailhead, my 4x4 was right where I'd left it, parked off to one side and spattered with fresh rain. I gave a curt nod to the constable as I opened the door. "Appreciate the lift."

He tipped his head in return. "Glad you made it out."

I expected there'd be debriefs and more questions later, but

I was grateful for the fact that he was letting me go now. The past several days were starting to sink in and exhaustion weighed at my limbs.

I got Ajax loaded into the backseat as gently as I could, pausing to ruffle his ears once he settled with a sigh. Then I climbed into the driver's seat, shut the door, and exhaled into the hush of my own truck. The rain tapped softly on the windshield. For the first time in what felt like days, I let my grip ease on the wheel.

The drive back to Glenlaig didn't take long, but long enough for the weight in my shoulders to settle in deeper. It had been maybe sixteen hours since we took the compound. Far less since I'd handed Sandhurst over to the uniforms still picking through the wreckage. But it felt like days. Weeks. Like the wilderness had stretched time until I wasn't sure what hour it really was anymore.

The village emerged through the rain with the kind of quiet only a place like Glenlaig could hold. Stone walls damp from drizzle, windows glowing softly behind drawn curtains, gardens wind-lashed but tidy. Normal. Comforting. So far removed from rifles and blood and the hard scrape of zipties against skin that it almost didn't feel real.

I pulled up in front of my house and killed the engine. The silence after the hum of the motor was sharp and sudden. For a moment, I sat there, watching the rain streak down the windscreen, listening to the slow tick of the cooling engine and Ajax's even breathing behind me.

I wanted the quiet. The empty. A place to wash off the last of the hunt and pretend, for a few hours, that it was over. Except when I stepped out of the truck and rounded toward the front door, I saw the faint flicker of movement behind the window curtain, followed by the low rumble of male voices.

Shite. They were already inside.

The door creaked open under my hand, and I barely had time to register the warmth of the space before the smell of fried something, the faint hiss of oil, and the unmistakable clink of glass bottles knocking together hit me.

My kitchen had been raided. Fully, unapologetically raided.

Callum was sprawled on the couch like he owned it, boots kicked up on the old crate I used as a coffee table. Ewan had claimed an armchair, legs spread, a beer dangling from his fingers, and no sign he intended to move. Alex had taken over my kitchen like he paid rent, sleeves rolled up as he flipped something in a pan and reached for the last can of beer from the six-pack they'd already decimated.

"Look what the dog dragged in." Callum didn't even glance up, chin lifting to nod toward Ajax, who padded in behind me with the slow confidence of someone who knew damn well he was about to be fed.

I stood there for a beat too long, rain dripping, mud still clinging to my boots, and something in my chest cracked wide with the kind of relief that didn't have words. This mess of noise and sarcasm and too many boots on too few surfaces was home.

And it was exactly what I hadn't known I needed.

"Sandhurst?" Ewan asked it without preamble. Squad leader waiting for the final report.

I nodded once. "In custody."

Callum grunted. Alex didn't look up from the pan, but his voice cut in, even. "Good."

I stepped further into the house, peeling off my jacket and moving straight to fill Ajax's food bowl. Poor lad had gone far too long without a proper meal. "Glad we're all breaking and entering now. Too impatient to wait for a key? Or an invite?"

Callum gestured vaguely at the fridge with a bottle already in hand. "Your beer was going to expire."

I fixed him with a glare. "It's a lager, no' milk."

Ewan leaned back in my kitchen chair like he owned the place. "Still would've been a crime to let it sit unloved."

"Is that my last pack of bacon?" I narrowed my eyes at the stove as Ajax went nose first into his kibble.

Alex flipped the pan casually. "Was."

I groaned and ran a hand down my face. "You arseholes eat like you haven't had a meal since deployment."

"We saved your sorry arse from doing something stupid." Callum cracked open another beer. "You're lucky we didn't take your mattress, too."

Ajax gave a small, tired thump of his tail from where he'd already polished off half the bowl. At least someone here remembered whose house this was.

I dropped into the nearest chair, the kind of exhaustion that wasn't merely physical sinking into my bones. Ewan handed me a beer from a second six-pack they must've brought with them, and they continued to sling shite back and forth. The banter helped. For a second, it made everything feel almost normal. But only for a second. Because we all knew what was still sitting beneath it. Waiting.

The laughter didn't last. Like a fire without enough fuel, it burned out fast and left the air heavy behind it.

Callum sat forward, elbows on his knees. "Cleanup wasnae the only reason you went after him."

I didn't answer. I didn't have to.

"You went because you didn't want to see her."

The words landed square in my chest, sharp and clean. I looked down, fingers curled around the neck of the beer I hadn't even touched. The label was already damp under my grip. "I failed her. I failed them both. I promised I'd protect her. And I didn't."

"Bollocks." The snap of Ewan's tone had Ajax lifting his head from his bowl. "Look, every one of us has been where you are. Every one of us had our women taken in one way or another. You had our six in getting them back. We had yours. You did exactly what you were hired to do. You found Isla. You called us in. You held the line until we got there. That's no' failure, mate. That's the job."

I shook my head once, rough. "She still got taken."

Alex turned off the stove, silence stretching in the sizzle that followed. He leaned against the counter, arms crossed. "She wasn't expecting some perfect man. She was trusting the real one."

That hit harder than it should have. Because I knew exactly what version of me she'd seen out there, and it wasn't the one I'd spent years building armor around. It was the raw one. The one that didn't have the right words, but still tried to give her something to hold on to in the dark.

And that was what scared the hell out of me.

Callum's one-eyed gaze locked on mine. "You're scared. Good. Means it matters."

I didn't deny it. Couldn't. And maybe I was a little afraid of exactly how much Saoirse MacGregor had come to mean to me.

Ewan tipped his beer back, then gestured with the bottle. "You gonna be a coward about it?"

I flinched. An unacceptable betrayal of emotion, but I was beyond masking anymore, and these were my closest mates.

Alex pushed off the counter, wiping his hands on a tea towel like the whole conversation wasn't gutting me open. "And Ajax still needs a checkup. Pretty sure we know someone qualified."

I stared down at the dog who'd curled at my feet, his ears twitching as he lay, head on paws, watching me.

Yeah. We did.

I leaned down to scratch him beneath the jaw. "Aye. But she'll be resting now. Tomorrow is soon enough."

And maybe by the time the sun rose again, I'd have some idea what to say to her.

CHAPTER 36

SAOIRSE

I woke early, long before my alarm. If I was waking, that meant I'd slept, which I hadn't truly expected. For a moment, I lay there, tangled in my covers, staring at the ceiling and trying to locate myself in my own skin.

My body ached in ways that didn't make sense. Muscle knots and bruises that hadn't quite formed, nerves that didn't know whether to calm down or stay on high alert. But the heaviest ache settled somewhere else entirely. In my chest. Under my ribs. A slow, quiet pulse of dread that hadn't dulled overnight.

Finn still hadn't come back.

At least, I hadn't heard from him. Hadn't gotten confirmation from anyone else. Not a message. Not a knock at the door. And yes, Alex said he'd gone after Sandhurst. Said he was fine. But that was yesterday. And silence had a way of twisting in my gut like wire.

A soft thump broke the quiet. Pippin hopping down from the couch. I pushed the covers back and padded into the living room, the floor cool beneath my bare feet.

Isla was still asleep, bundled in every spare blanket I owned like some grumpy little cryptid. Her mouth was slightly open, one arm flung out across the cushions. Pippin made a show of hopping right back up beside her, tail flicking as he nestled in close.

I narrowed my eyes at him. "Seriously?"

He didn't look at me. The sense of betrayal was palpable.

Apparently, it was going to be awhile before I was forgiven for vanishing off the face of the earth.

Back in my room, the air felt colder somehow, as if the cottage had exhaled overnight and forgotten to warm back up. I pulled open a drawer, the movements mechanical, and started getting dressed without really thinking. Jeans. A long-sleeved shirt that still smelled faintly of cedar and laundry soap.

I paused at the mirror, caught off guard by the woman looking back at me. My face looked the same. A little paler, maybe, a little more drawn around the eyes. But still me. Still standing.

I pulled my hair back into a tie, fingers fumbling more than they should have. Then I reached for my boots, tugging them on with the same kind of urgency I tended to feel before emergency farm calls or surgery delays.

My body was tired in ways I couldn't name. A bone-deep exhaustion that hadn't come from mere physical effort. But sitting still didn't feel like rest. It felt like drowning. I couldn't do it anymore. Couldn't keep pacing the same loop in my head, waiting for a knock on the door that might never come.

I'd go into the clinic. Animals would need feeding. Overnight patients checking. Something in my world had to still work the way it was supposed to. If it wasn't going to be my heart, it might as well be my hands.

A familiar knock sounded on the front door. Two quick raps, then the soft creak of the hinges as Grandda opened it only far enough to let himself inside, lest my cantankerous cat make a run for it. He moved with his usual slow, deliberate rhythm, a battered thermos in one hand and a paper bag in the other, as he made his way down the hall and past the lounge. He paused briefly, noting Isla still on the couch, before stepping into the kitchen.

His face didn't show surprise at seeing me up. "Brought you something hot." He set the thermos and paper bag on the counter. His voice was low, rough around the edges, and he didn't look at me directly. Just scanned the room like he was checking for damage.

I reached for the thermos and poured the tea into a mug. The warmth helped ease the trembling in my hands.

He stayed where he was, leaning one hip against the counter. "Did you sleep at all?"

"A little."

He nodded like that was enough, but I could feel his eyes on me.

"You're back," he said quietly. "But you havenae landed yet."

That made something in my chest hitch. I didn't look at him.

He kept his tone even. "I've seen that look before. No' often. But I know it. Like you're bracing for something to hit— only you're no' sure whether to duck or run straight into it."

I swallowed hard, throat dry.

"I dinna ken what happened out there," he added. "Dinna need to. No' really. But I know you. And I know the difference between when you're tired and when you're scared."

My breath wooshed out, as if the observation had been a direct blow to my gut. "I don't scare easy."

"No," he agreed. "But you care harder than you let on. That's always been the part that rattles you."

I looked at him then. That surprised me. "What do you mean?"

He gave a faint snort. "You keep people at a polite arm's length until they bleed into your ribs and you dinna ken how they got there. And when that happens, you get a certain look. Like your whole body's already leaning forward—like you're about to chase something or lose it."

He broke off a piece of oatcake and took a bite, chewing like we were talking about the weather.

Then he swallowed and said, matter-of-fact, "So. If this man—this Finn—means something to you, the question is simple." His eyes met mine, steady and unblinking. "What are you going to do about it?"

The room felt smaller. Thicker. Like I'd walked into the middle of a conversation I hadn't realized I'd started.

He reached for the thermos again, tipped it slightly in good-bye, and headed for the door. "Dinna wait too long to decide," he said. "Not everyone sticks around forever."

The door clicked gently shut behind him.

I stayed where I was, the steam from my tea curling in slow, aimless spirals.

He didn't know what had happened. Not really. Not the details. Not the guns or bindings or nights where the dark pressed too close. But somehow, he'd still seen it—that I wasn't merely tired or out of sorts. That something inside me hadn't found its footing again. That I was trying to hold together something that hadn't even begun to settle. He hadn't asked for names or explanations. But he looked at me like he'd already guessed where the fault line ran, and asked me what I was going to do about it.

I stared at the mug in my hands. It had gone lukewarm, untouched.

He'd made it sound simple. But nothing about this felt simple.

I wasn't used to wanting like this. Not openly. Not without knowing how the other half of the thread would hold. I'd spent so long managing expectations that the idea of stepping toward something without a guaranteed outcome felt like walking out over frozen water and waiting to hear the crack.

And still... I couldn't stop listening for the knock. The footstep. The sound that said Finn was back.

I set the mug down, the faint clink of ceramic against the countertop louder than it should've been. In the living room, Isla shifted. Pippin chirped once and settled again.

Still no knock. Still no sound.

I rubbed my palms over my jeans and reached for a pen. Found a scrap of paper.

Gone to the clinic. Back later.

I left it by the kettle—somewhere she'd see it—and grabbed my keys.

Outside, the sky was heavy and low, the kind of gray that blurred the edges of everything. But there was work waiting. A routine to slip back into. Some small rhythm I could move with, even if the rest of me didn't know where it stood yet.

I couldn't control whatever Finn was thinking.

But I could show up. Keep showing up. Until I figured out what it meant to stay.

CHAPTER 37

FINN

The engine clicked quietly when I shut it off, but I didn't move. My hands stayed wrapped around the steering wheel, thumbs rubbing at the worn leather like that might give me a different outcome than the one I was walking into. Ajax sat harnessed into the passenger seat, ears up, weight braced forward in that alert-but-still pose that meant he was watching me as much as anything outside.

I stared through the windscreen at the clinic door. I hadn't expected to feel this twitchy about coming here. I'd told myself it was the responsible thing to do. Get Ajax looked at properly, now that we were back in civilization. Give her the clean close of a follow-up. That's all.

That wasn't all, and I knew it.

I exhaled hard, then finally popped the door and stepped out. Came around to the other side and opened his. "Come on, lad."

Ajax hopped down carefully, still favoring the injured flank. He moved better than he had two days ago, but I could tell it pulled. He didn't whine—hadn't once—but he moved like a soldier under orders. God, I loved this damn dog.

The bell over the clinic door gave a soft chime as we stepped inside, and I stood inside the threshold for a second, letting the familiar scent of antiseptic and fur settle into me. This place had been the start of something. I didn't know if it would be the end.

Saoirse emerged from the back hallway in slate-blue scrubs, a clipboard balanced in one hand, a pen tucked behind her ear like she hadn't noticed it was still there. Her hair was back in one of those low, no-nonsense ties, a few loose strands curling around her temple. She looked... tired. But steady. Whole. And of course she was here, as I'd known she would be. She was about as capable of staying at home and resting as I was.

Her gaze landed on me first, then dropped to Ajax. And for a breath—no longer than a blink—something in her face softened. Unmistakable relief. But she shut it down quickly, flipping back to the cool, detached professionalism she'd wrapped around herself the first time I met her.

"How's he holding up?" Her eyes scanned Ajax's stance like she could read everything that mattered from posture alone.

"Surprisingly well. Considering."

She nodded once. "Let's get him up on the table."

Her voice was crisp, her movements efficient as she turned toward the nearest exam room and pushed the door open. I followed, Ajax close at my heel, the quiet click of his nails the only sound for a few seconds.

She didn't look back at me or ask why I'd come instead of calling. Instead, she pointed to the table and retrieved gloves. The distance in her tone wasn't simply habit. It was armor. And I couldn't blame her for wearing it.

Not after the way I'd left.

Saoirse worked in silence, her hands moving with that steady, no-nonsense rhythm I'd come to recognize. More instinct than conscious effort. She peeled back the bandage gently, eyes narrowing as she checked the healing wound. Ajax stood still beneath her touch, tail giving a slow wag as she murmured a soft, "Good boy," under her breath.

I stayed silent as she worked.

She never looked at me. Not once. After a beat, she spoke, still focused on Ajax. "The wound's healing clean. No signs of infection."

"He had good treatment in the field."

Her fingers hesitated for a fraction of a second, but she didn't respond. Didn't take the bait. Instead, she set to applying a clean bandage to the wound.

When she finally replied, she was all business. "Given the circumstances, it'll scar, but it won't cause any lasting damage. He should be back to full strength in a few weeks."

She stepped away to dispose of the bandages, stripping off her gloves with quick snaps. I watched her back as she moved around the room, cleaning, resetting instruments that didn't need it, like she needed something to do with her hands.

But her shoulders were tight. Her posture too straight. And I could feel the pressure building beneath her skin, as though if I even breathed wrong, the dam would break.

She didn't move away. Didn't retreat to the safe distance of professionalism. Instead, she crossed her arms over her chest and looked at me with something sharp and level in her eyes. "You, though—I'm not sure how long your recovery's going to take."

I blinked. "What?"

"Considering how far you've shoved your head up your arse."

It hit like a slap and a laugh at once, but before I could

react, the words were already tumbling out of her—fast, unfiltered, thick with everything she'd been holding back.

"I waited. I *believed* in you. I knew you'd come. And you *did*. You came for me. You dragged me out of hell. You dragged both of us out. And then you *left*."

Her voice cracked faintly, and it twisted something in my chest. I opened my mouth to explain—to give her the one truth I had. "I had to go after Sandhurst—"

"I don't *care* about Sandhurst." She cut me off with a fierceness that silenced everything else in the room. "I care about *you*, you *idiot*."

The bare, blistering truth vibrated between us in the space she refused to step back from.

Her chest rose and fell in sharp bursts, tears bright but clinging stubbornly to those mile-long lashes. She didn't blink them away. Didn't back down. Her chin lifted like a dare sharpened on grief and fury and something infinitely more fragile.

"So if this was just adrenaline and proximity—if I was only a mission to you—say it. Say it now."

The silence that followed shimmered between us like heat on pavement, charged with everything we hadn't said. Everything we were too scared to say first.

I stared at her. And I smiled. "I am so in love with you."

She froze. Eyes wide. Guardless in a way I hadn't seen since the woods.

I stepped in slowly, voice low. "I think it started the first time you used that sharp tongue of yours to draw blood. Refusing to take any shite. Not from me. Not from anyone."

Her lips parted, but no sound came out.

"Or maybe," I continued, "when you wouldn't leave. When you looked at Ajax and then me and decided we were worth staying for. When every instinct in you screamed to run, but you didn't."

Another step. Close now.

"Or maybe it was when you looked at me like I wasn't broken. Like I was something worth saving. Long before I ever believed that for myself."

She blinked once, slowly, like she couldn't quite trust what she was hearing.

"It wasn't the danger, Saoirse." I let her name roll off my tongue slowly, simply for the pure joy of feeling it in my mouth. "It wasn't the mission. It wasn't adrenaline, proximity, or circumstance." I leaned in, my voice a whisper now. "It was *you.*"

I reached up, brushing her hair back from her face, the gentlest contact I could manage without falling apart.

"I'm done fighting it. I'm in love with you." I let it hang there between us. A promise and a question in one. "What are you going to do about it?"

She surged forward, fisting both hands in the front of my shirt, and hauled me down into a kiss that punched every thought clean out of my head.

There was nothing tentative about it. No testing the waters. Just heat and teeth and the sheer, furious relief of two people who had nearly lost their chance and weren't wasting a second more.

Her mouth was warm and fierce, tasting of salt and adrenaline and something uniquely hers that I'd never be able to forget. She kissed like she fought—unapologetic, all-in, no room for half-measures.

I groaned into it, hands coming up instinctively to anchor at her hips, to feel that she was solid and alive and, against all odds, still mine. Her fingers twisted tighter in my shirt, dragging me closer, like she couldn't get enough, like distance itself was the enemy.

Ajax barked once, sharp and smug and deeply satisfied, his

tail thudding against the floor like a gavel delivering judgment. *Finally.*

We broke apart only when breath demanded it, breathing hard, our foreheads tipping together. I barely had the space to form words, but they came anyway, because they were true, and she deserved to hear them.

"So," I rasped, eyes locked on hers, "we're dating now?"

She gave a low laugh, her hands still clutching my shirt. "I intend to do a hell of a lot more than date you, Finley Patterson."

The words shot straight through me, bright and lethal and perfect.

I grinned like an idiot. "When do you get off work?"

She grinned back at me. "I'm not even supposed to be here right now."

"Then I definitely have suggestions on better ways to spend the rest of the day." I dropped my voice to a conspiratorial whisper. "All of them require significantly fewer clothes."

Saoirse rose to her toes and gave me a fast, nipping kiss. "I'll get my keys."

CHAPTER 38

SAOIRSE

The pub patio was full to bursting, the kind of summer night where the breeze carried laughter and the tang of ale, and the dogs—bless them—were all tangled beneath the table like someone had spilled a basket of fur and tails. Ajax had claimed his spot under Finn's chair, lean body stretched out and one ear twitching at every loud burst of laughter. Falkor had wedged himself beside him, tail thumping the ground every time someone passed with a plate of chips, while Maeve curled with catlike efficiency near Ciara's boots, gnawing on a chew toy. Ewan's dog Havoc—really Isobel's now, as we all knew—was stretched out beside his lady's chair, heaving the occasional contented sigh as she reached down to stroke his fur.

Our table had no right to still be standing, groaning under the weight of pints, plates, and far too many elbows. I was squashed between Isla and Finn, legs tangled somewhere with his beneath the bench, and across from me, Alex and Callum were arguing about whether you could use sheepdog training techniques on stubborn humans. Ewan kept muttering something about lost causes and handed off another bowl of chips to Jade, who sat beside Parker with a look that said she was used to managing chaos with one eyebrow raise and a well-timed eyeroll.

Parker had her arm looped comfortably through Callum's, her chin tipped toward him as she said something that made him huff out a laugh before pressing a kiss to the side of her head. It was all so domestic, so casual, like this was any old night—which, in its own way, made it all the more profound.

Locals filtered past in a steady stream, half of them using the excuse of dropping off fresh drinks to ask questions they had no business asking. "You lasses all right then?" "They say it's going to be in the papers, is that true?" "Heard you clocked a man in the jaw with a rock. Any truth to that?"

I offered vague smiles and noncommittal hums, and every time I started to tense, Finn's fingers brushed lightly against mine beneath the table.

I didn't need to answer the questions, not really. We were here. Whole. Together. And that said enough.

Alex leaned back in his chair with a pint in hand and a grin too smug to be anything but trouble. "You do know you're offi-cially the most interesting thing that's happened to Glenlaig since the sheep parade ran wild down High Street."

I arched a brow over my glass. "Please. We didn't even get a scandalously blurred photo. I feel cheated."

Across the table, Callum snorted. "Be grateful. I had to dodge three reporters and a drone on the way into town. You think I wear this face because I like people?" He pointed at the fearsome scar that bisected his eye, as if he'd donned it for cosmetic purposes instead of receiving it in battle.

There was a ripple of laughter, and then, as often happened in these conversations lately, the tone dipped slightly. Still light, but edged with the weight of reality. Isla, quiet until now, lifted her glass in a small toast. "To the arrests. And the fact that it's no' our problem anymore."

Alex raised his pint in kind. "Multiple warrants. Seized assets. Every name we handed over is either in custody or sweating their passports."

I had to ask. "Sandhurst?"

Finn nodded beside me. "He's no' talking, but he disnae have to. The records Alex pulled are airtight. Financials. Satellite tags. Communications. He's going away for a long time."

"And the rest of it?" Ciara nudged a half-empty plate of chips toward Isla, who pretended not to be starving but didn't hesitate to snag one.

Ewan kept his arm around Isobel. "Media's being managed. Too many protected species involved for the story to be ignored completely, but it's being framed as a wider crackdown."

Finn's hand brushed mine again beneath the table, and I held on to that quiet relief as I exhaled.

It was over. Really over. And the only thing anyone in Glenlaig had to gossip about now... was us.

The bell above the patio gate jingled, and I glanced over as Rory Fraser, the Glenlaig constable who'd been liaising with the assorted other legal agencies to wrap up the mess, wandered in with his uniform jacket unzipped and rain still clinging to his boots.

"Afternoon." He nodded toward the table with a casual confidence that somehow didn't tip over into cocky. "Heard the full roundup went through. Every one of them charged. You lot made it easy for the Crown. Paper trail's a mile long. They willnae be seeing daylight anytime soon."

Finn lifted his pint slightly in acknowledgment. "Glad to hear it." Pressed against him as I was, I could feel the subtle relaxation in his posture as full relief settled in.

Then Rory's gaze slid to Isla, still half-curled at the end of the bench with a lemonade in front of her and a faintly haunted look she hadn't quite shaken yet. "Might want to consider bringing backup next time you're out chasing wildcats, though."

Isla's brow arched, sharp and skeptical. "You volunteering?"

Rory didn't blink. "If you're asking if I hike—aye. Pretty well."

I raised my pint with a smirk. "Careful, mate. She bites."

Isla leaned forward to smile over the rim of her glass. "Only when provoked."

Rory's grin was small, but unmistakable. "Good to know."

The entire table leaned a fraction closer, collectively tuning in like wolves catching the scent of something juicy.

Rory tipped his hat to Isla and left us to our celebration. My friend smiled into her drink and snagged another chip from the basket in front of her.

The second round of pints had settled in, and the table was humming with the loosened joy that only came after survival and relief. Someone made a joke about Ewan's tragic attempts to take over the last time Dom Bassey, the pub cook, had been out sick. Then Alex tipped back in his chair, eyeing me over the rim of his glass with all the delicacy of a sledgehammer.

"Not that I'm judging, but you two really thought you were being subtle?"

That earned a fresh round of snickers and raised brows from the rest of the table.

Callum didn't even look up from his pint. "Subtle? They were about as subtle as a sheep in heat."

Parker snorted. "The entire village knew before they did."

"I'm pretty sure even Pippin knew," Ciara added, deadpan.

I rolled my eyes and offered the table two middle fingers with a generous flourish, trying for unimpressed. But my cheeks were already warm, and my pulse had done that betraying flutter it always did now when Finn was near and looking at me like I was the only thing in the world worth watching.

With a smile, he leaned in and kissed me—unapologetic and slow, his hand curling lightly at the back of my neck like he didn't care who was watching. Like I was his center of gravity, and he meant to prove it.

The noise around us blurred.

All I could feel was the heat of his mouth on mine, the solid press of him close, the sense that I could let go of every doubt because this—*this*—wasn't going anywhere. I relaxed into him, letting myself soak in the heady warmth as he made silent promises with that mouth.

When he finally pulled back, I was breathless, smiling despite myself and already making plans for exactly what I wanted to do with him when we left.

Ajax thumped his tail against the ground in lazy approval. Someone groaned. Someone else cheered.

Isla folded her arms. "Honestly, we deserve a group apology for having to wait this long."

I arched a brow in the look of disdain I'd perfected by ten. "Oh, because our relationship has anything to do with you lot?"

"We were the ones who had to listen to you hiss and spit at each other for the past year and change," Parker pointed out.

"And to all your denials that there was nothing there, and you were each the last person the other would ever date," Ciara added.

Finn glanced around with a faux sober expression and nodded. "Aye, you'll get your apology. Sometime after never."

And that was it. This was us, tangled up in the middle of everything, exactly where we were meant to be.

The warmth of his shoulder settled against mine like it

belonged there. Because, impossibly, it did. We somehow fit, Finn and I. And I was so glad we'd managed to get out of our own way about it.

My hand found his without thinking, fingers slotting between his like they'd done it a thousand times before. His hand folded around mine in easy comfort, and he leaned over to brush a kiss to my temple. The moment stretched, a quiet perfection I hadn't known I needed.

Around us, the pub carried on. Dogs snored underfoot, twitching occasionally in their sleep. Callum had launched into a story that was either exaggerated or outright fabricated, judging by the way Parker rolled her eyes and muttered, "Lies" under her breath. Ciara laughed so hard at one point she nearly knocked her chair over, and Isobel offered to arm-wrestle Ewan over the last fried pickle.

But none of it pulled me from the center of the world that existed right there—Finn's thigh brushing mine, his thumb grazing the back of my hand, the quiet rhythm of his breathing beside me.

We'd fought so much to get here, and I didn't think I'd ever take what we'd found for granted.

CHAPTER 39

FINN

The door creaked open under my elbow as I shouldered it in, basket balanced against my hip, rain still dripping from the ends of my hair. "Heroic rescue of your laundry complete. You're welcome. I fully expect praise, baked goods, or at the very least, a medal."

Saoirse didn't look up right away, her hands deft as she folded a tea towel with the kind of efficiency that should not have been hot, and yet—there it was. There was something stupidly appealing about her like this: barefoot, hair tied back in a loose knot, an oversized hoodie slung off one shoulder, and that small furrow of concentration between her brows as she smoothed another shirt.

She glanced up at me finally, one eyebrow arched. "If you'd managed it before the rain started, I might've made scones."

Ajax didn't even twitch from his spot by the hearth, sprawled on his side in the same position he'd been in all morning. Pippin, meanwhile, was perched on the windowsill, looking personally offended by the weather, tail flicking like the clouds had wronged him by taking away his sunbeam.

I set the basket down with a dramatic sigh, letting it thump against the bench. "Truly, no one suffers like I do."

I moved in beside her and reached into the basket, fishing out one of my own t-shirts and giving it a token shake. "See, I fold. I'm helpful."

She side-eyed my attempt, then made a noise that could only be described as unimpressed. "That's not folding. That's... vaguely creasing and giving up halfway."

"Pretty rich from someone who color-codes her socks like they're part of a military op." I held up a carefully rolled pair. "Do these get filed under navy or 'psychologically alarming'?"

Saoirse bumped my hip with hers, grinning. "They get filed under 'functional adult.' You should try it sometime."

We kept folding in a loose sort of rhythm, our elbows brushing now and then, the occasional nudge turning into half-hearted shoves. Her hands moved fast and sure, stacking neat piles while mine definitely leaned more toward casual suggestion than structural integrity.

I dropped a sweatshirt squarely on top of the wrong pile.

Saoirse huffed. "You're going to undo all my work,"

"I consider it a challenge. Or an invitation to chaos."

She rolled her eyes and lobbed a towel at my head.

It hit with a satisfying *thwap*, trailing over my face before landing in a crumpled heap at my feet.

"Oh, you're *done* for." I scooped it up and launched it back.

It hit her shoulder and slid off harmlessly, but her gasp was pure scandalized drama. "You absolute menace."

"You started it."

She lunged for another towel, and I backed up, arms raised in mock defense as I laughed, already planning my next move.

She lunged for a sock, damp from the sudden turn in the weather, threatening me with it like a weaponized bit of wool. "I *swear* to God, if you come at me with that blanket again—"

I grinned and advanced anyway, holding the half-folded blanket like a net. "What, this? This is a tactical maneuver."

"It's a *trap*."

"You say that like it's a *bad* thing."

I feinted left; she darted right, and I caught her around the waist, spinning her toward the sofa as she shrieked-laughed and flailed, the sock forgotten, the blanket dropping to tangle around our ankles. She twisted in my arms, elbowing me gently in the ribs, laughing hard enough she could barely catch her breath. "That's *cheating!*"

"All's fair in love and laundry." My fingers slipped under the hem of her shirt as I tried to gain leverage.

"You're ridiculous." She shoved back at me, harder than necessary, playful on the surface but with that undercurrent I'd come to recognize. That slow melt of tension. That spark in her eyes.

We were still laughing, still half-fighting for ground when I hooked my hand at her hip to steady us and didn't let go.

She looked up at me through a fall of hair, cheeks flushed, lips parted. Her sweatshirt had slid slightly off one shoulder, rumpled from where I'd grabbed it mid-spin. She looked like chaos wrapped in cotton, and I couldn't get enough.

"You're distracting." Her breath was a little uneven, her tone dry. But her eyes gave her away as she flattened her palms against my chest.

"You're beautiful."

Her gaze flicked to mine and held at the lack of teasing in my tone.

I let my fingers trace the edge of her waist, slow and deliberate. She curled her fingers into the front of my shirt, pulling me closer.

I leaned in and kissed her—slow, deep, a little smiling at first, then not at all. Her hands slid up to my shoulders, her mouth moving with mine like we'd been waiting all day for this moment.

Maybe we had.

She rose to her toes, shifting closer, and I caught her hips, dragging her the last inch in until there was no space left. Her laugh was muffled against my mouth, low and breathless and entirely unfair.

And then I felt it.

Eyes. Judging ones.

I cracked one eye open and glanced to the side.

Pippin. On the windowsill. Staring. Unblinking. Furry, feline disapproval radiating from every inch of his ginger menace frame.

I broke the kiss and groaned. "We're relocating."

Saoirse blinked at me, dazed and pink-cheeked. "What?"

"The cat is looking at me."

Her laughter came in a startled burst as I grabbed her hand and tugged her down the hallway.

"You're a trained Royal Marine." She gasped the reminder between kisses as we bumped off the wall, and I paused long enough to yank her shirt over her head. "But God forbid the cat watches you get lucky?"

"He *judges*, Saoirse. I can *feel* it."

"You're such a coward."

"Guilty. Bedroom. Now."

She grinned, grabbed my belt, and tugged. "Then move, Marine."

And I did. Happily.

Somewhere between the hallway and the doorway, she pulled me in again, and my back hit the frame with a quiet thump. Her hands were under my shirt, cool palms against warm skin, and the sound I made had her smirking into my mouth.

"Distracting," I muttered again, voice rough now.

She bit her lip, utterly unapologetic. "You already said that."

"Still true."

I let my hands roam with the confidence that came from knowing she was mine, and I was hers. She made a soft, delighted sound when I scraped my stubble along her throat, and I filed it away like it was classified intel. Important. Irrefutable.

We laughed into each other's skin, half-drunk on familiarity and heat. We shed clothes between kisses, half on purpose, half by accident. She shoved my jeans down, and I tugged her underwear off with my teeth for the pleasure of hearing her gasp. We tumbled onto the bed, got tangled in the duvet, elbowed each other, swore under our breath, and laughed through it all. She called me a menace. I called her one back. She kissed me to shut me up. It worked.

And still, somehow, it meant more than it should've—every grin, every stumble. Because this wasn't simple lust. Wasn't only muscle memory and momentum. It was trust. The kind you didn't ask for. The kind you were given.

When I finally moved over her—slow, steady, like I had all the time in the world—she arched up, wrapped herself around me.

"Right here. With you."

Not a question. Not a claim. Just the simplest truth as I slid into her.

Our rhythm wasn't frantic. It was deep. Intentional. The kind of pace you fall into when you already know the person beneath your hands. Matched breathing and tangled limbs, muffled moans and whispered yeses. Her fingers dug into my shoulders when I hit the right angle. I kissed the sound from her throat and felt her shiver all the way through—and I held on to it. To her. Like it was more than pleasure. Like it was proof.

It was the middle of everything. The middle of a life we were still figuring out. Only skin and breath and want wrapped in something I hadn't let myself believe I could still have.

When she came, it was with her head tucked under my chin, her breath catching, and my name on her lips like it belonged there.

And when I followed, it was with her hand over my heart. Like she'd put it there on purpose.

We didn't move for a while. Not because we couldn't, but because neither of us wanted to. The room was warm, the watery afternoon light slanting low through the curtains, and her skin was pressed to mine in a way that made the rest of the world feel optional.

Her leg was hooked lazily over mine, fingers tracing idle patterns along my chest. My hand rested at the dip of her spine, right where she fit against me like she was always meant to be there.

"You're crushing half the duvet." She muttered it into my shoulder, though there wasn't an ounce of complaint in her voice.

I kissed the top of her head. "It'll survive."

She hummed, amused, then went quiet again.

A few minutes later, the door creaked open, and we both turned our heads in time to see Pippin hop up onto the dresser with all the grace of a feline judge stepping into court. His tail flicked. His eyes narrowed.

"Oh, for the love of..." Saoirse sighed. "Do you mind?"

Pippin blinked once. Slowly. Like he absolutely did not mind, and also intended to report us to the proper authorities.

I couldn't help the laugh that rumbled low in my chest. "I think we've offended his delicate sensibilities."

"Again," Saoirse added, deadpan.

I turned to her, letting my fingers brush her jaw, slow and fond. "You're beautiful when you're scandalizing the cat."

That got me a snort and an affectionate shove. "We are never getting this laundry done, are we?"

I thought of the forgotten basket on the floor of the lounge, half-unfolded shirts and socks spilling out like they'd given up on us, and grinned. "Nope. But honestly? Worth it."

EPILOGUE

SAOIRSE

"She looked so gorgeous!" Ciara's voice sparkled like her earrings as she leaned toward me, one hand still curled around a glass of prosecco.

I glanced toward Parker and Callum, where they spun in a dance across the room and sighed. "She looks... incandescent."

Finn made a quiet sound beside me, one corner of his mouth tilting up. "You should see the way you look right now."

Ciara snorted. "Smooth, Patterson."

Alex, lounging nearby with a whisky and a grin, lifted his glass. "I give him ten minutes before he tries to sneak you off to a supply closet."

I arched a brow. "Please. He'll wait until after dessert."

"Generous." The feel of his murmur that close sent a warm ripple straight down my spine. His fingers brushed lightly against the small of my back. Innocent, probably. Didn't matter. My pulse still jumped like it had ideas of its own.

I took a sip of wine to regroup. The reception was in full swing now. Low music, the murmur of happy voices, Parker laughing in Callum's ear. The pair of them looked like they were holding court, impossibly happy and utterly themselves.

"I didn't think he could look like that."

Alex followed my gaze. "Like he's settled and happy?"

"Exactly." I smiled. "It suits him."

"He's not the only one." Finn's voice was so quiet I almost missed it.

I caught his eye. "Are you trying to start something?"

In answer, he slid his hand a little higher on my back.

Ciara elbowed me. "If either of you tries to pretend you weren't already disgustingly in love months ago, I'm throwing something."

Alex draped an arm along the back of her chair. "You'll have to beat half the village to it. I'm owed at least twenty quid."

I sighed. "I hate all of you."

Finn smirked. "But you love me."

"Tragically."

His grip tightened slightly. "Still lucky, then."

I thought of the last wedding we'd been to. To that canyon that had stretched out between us and the dislike I'd worn like armor against that charm I didn't know how to handle. I'd misjudged him so badly then.

Now he was the man who brought in the laundry when it rained. Who let me steal the duvet and always made sure the kettle was full. Who knew when I needed a cup of tea and exactly how I took it.

He laughed at something Alex said, his eyes crinkling, and I felt a smile tug at my lips, soft and satisfied. I wasn't always good with the big feelings. Still wasn't, most days. But this simple unshakeable joy? This I could manage.

Finn's hand rested against the small of my back, casual and

familiar, like he didn't even realize he was doing it. He probably didn't. That was simply how we were now. And who would have imagined *we* would end up as one of those couples who were easy and uncomplicated in the best possible way?

He glanced down at me, his thumb brushing lightly against my spine. I leaned into him without thinking.

"I hope you're feeling properly smug," I said.

He grinned. "Always."

The music shifted into something slow and low, all warm bass and longing.

Without asking, Finn took my hand and led me onto the dance floor. I went without resistance because it meant being in his arms, which was exactly what I wanted.

He slid one hand around my waist, the other settling in mine. His palm was warm against my back, thumb brushing the edge of my dress. We started to sway, bodies close enough that I could feel the steady rhythm of his breathing, the rise and fall of his chest against mine.

I let my head drop to his shoulder. Not because I was tired. Because I wanted to.

He smelled like sandalwood and evergreens—something sharp and earthy that warmed me low and deep. His hand tightened slightly at my waist, and I settled closer. We moved together, unhurried. The crowd blurred around us. Everything else faded.

"You know I was half in love with you before you ever stopped hating me, right?" His voice was a murmur, low and rough, near my ear.

I stiffened. Only slightly, but enough to make him notice.

"I didn't hate you," I said, keeping my head where it was. "I... moderately disliked your face."

He laughed, his breath hot against my neck. His hand slid a

little lower. Not enough to draw attention, but enough that I felt it.

I huffed a quiet breath, part exasperation, part something else entirely. His hand skimmed a little higher on my back—teasing now along the exposed stretch of skin revealed by the low back of the gown—and then he dipped his head to press a kiss to my temple.

"Come on, Doc." His voice stroked across my skin, warm with promise. "Let's go find somewhere private."

I rolled my eyes, even as a smile tugged at the corners of my mouth. "You're impossible. It's not even after dessert."

He leaned in, close enough to make my skin prickle. "It's no' my fault. You're wearing that dress, and I absolutely want you for dessert."

Heat flared low in my belly, but I kept my tone prim. "Oh?"

He lowered his voice even deeper as his palm skimmed over my bum. "I happen to ken you were verra interested in the easy access capabilities of this kilt."

Because that lit a fire straight in my center, I didn't dignify it with a reply. Just slipped my hand into his and let him tug me through the edges of the crowd.

We slipped out of the main hall under the cover of low lights and laughter, his thumb brushing against mine as we went. Silent promise of a door, a lock, and ten blessed minutes without an audience.

We barely made it into the room before the lock clicked shut behind us. Finn's hands were on my waist, warm and certain, and then his mouth was on mine, hot and coaxing. I pressed into him, fingers tugging his shirt from the waist of his kilt to find skin. He groaned against my mouth, shifting us back until my spine met the wall with a gentle thud. His thigh nudged between mine, and my whole body went taut, ready.

God, the things I wanted to do with this man.

His fingers skimmed the hem of my dress, already sliding higher, and all I could do was imagine the look on his face when he figured out I'd planned for exactly this.

No knickers.

Strategic planning at its finest.

I dragged his mouth back to mine, breathless now, already aching, already pulling him closer—

Then I heard it. A tiny sound, barely audible over the distant thump of music. Thin and high and wrong. A whimper.

I stilled.

Finn kissed along my jaw. "Dinna do it." His hands found bare leg and skimmed higher. "Please dinna be what I think it is."

There it was again. Definitely real. Faint, but close. Ignoring the heat he'd stoked, I slipped out of his arms and crossed the room to the second door, the one that led out to the garden. As I opened it, cool air spilled in, and with it, another soft cry.

I stepped outside, heels clicking on the flagstone path, and scanned the garden. There, beneath one of the benches, something small moved.

A puppy.

She was curled in a miserable little ball, half-hidden in the ivy. Her fur was matted with mud, ears too big for her face, ribs showing beneath a patchy coat, wide, wary eyes, and a body that shook with every breath. There was no collar.

"Oh, sweetheart." I dropped straight to the grass, not caring in the slightest what it did to the hem of my dress. "Where did you come from?"

The pup looked at me, frozen with fear and clearly exhausted. I held out a hand, murmuring soft nonsense, coaxing.

After a long, uncertain pause, she crept forward and collapsed into my palm.

Finn's footsteps crunched behind me. He stopped in the doorway. "Of course." Beneath the deadpan delivery, I could hear his amusement.

I ran a hand gently down her side. I could feel every ridge of her spine, every too-prominent rib. "She has to be a stray. No tag, no chip bump, underweight. Someone dumped her, or she got lost a while ago."

He crouched beside me, taking one look at the puppy now snuggled against my chest, leaving God knew what stains on my dress. "You've already named her in your head, haven't you?"

I grinned, stroking the pup's head as she gave a tiny, contented sigh. "Not yet. But she's definitely coming home with us."

Finn shook his head, but the smile tugging at his mouth betrayed him. "That's it. The menagerie begins." He reached out and ran a soft knuckle along her ear. "You couldn't have waited ten more minutes so I could take advantage of your new mum's lack of knickers?"

I leaned over to catch his mouth in another fast kiss. "Let me get her squared away first, and I promise I'll make it worth your while."

The heated look he shot me had me going damp between my thighs. "Then let's go make our excuses, Dr. MacGregor."

Choose Your Next Romance

I HOPE you enjoyed this conclusion to the Special Ops Scots trilogy! You can get one last visit to Scotland in Finn and

Saoirse's bonus epilogue. Grab that here: https://books.kait nolan.com/llprdus6rs

If you haven't read the adjacent Kilted Hearts series, it begins with *Cowboy in a Kilt*. Or you can get the full series bundle on my direct store. Happy reading!

OTHER BOOKS BY KAIT NOLAN

A complete and up-to-date list of all my books can be found at https://kaitnolan.com.

KILTED HEARTS
SMALL TOWN CONTEMPORARY SCOTTISH ROMANCE

- *Jilting The Kilt* (prequel)
- *Cowboy in a Kilt* (Raleigh and Kyla)
- *Grump in a Kilt* (Malcolm and Charlotte)
- *Playboy in a Kilt* (Connor and Sophie)
- *Protector in a Kilt* (Ewan and Isobel)
- *Single Dad in a Kilt* (Hamish and Afton)
- *Kilty Pleasures* (Jason and Skye)

SPECIAL OPS SCOTS
SMALL TOWN MILITARY SCOTTISH ROMANCE

- *One Fine Night* (prequel)
- *Before Highland Sunset* (Alex and Ciara)

- *Beyond Highland Sunrise* (Callum and Parker)
- *Beneath Highland Stars* (Finley and Saoirse)
  Coming June 25, 2025

BAD BOY BAKERS
SMALL TOWN MILITARY ROMANCE

- *Rescued By a Bad Boy* (Brax and Mia prequel)
- *Mixed Up With a Marine* (Brax and Mia)
- *Wrapped Up with a Ranger* (Holt and Cayla)
- *Stirred Up by a SEAL* (Jonah and Rachel)
- *Hung Up on the Hacker* (Cash and Hadley)
- *Caught Up with the Captain* (Grey and Rebecca)

RESCUE MY HEART SERIES
SMALL TOWN MILITARY ROMANCE

- *Someone Like You* (Ivy and Harrison)
- *What I Like About You* (Laurel and Sebastian)
- *Bad Case of Loving You* (Paisley and Ty prequel)
  Included in *Made For Loving You* (Paisley and Ty)

THE MISFIT INN SERIES
SMALL TOWN FAMILY ROMANCE

- *When You Got A Good Thing* (Kennedy and Xander)
- *Til There Was You* (Misty and Denver)
- *Those Sweet Words* (Pru and Flynn)
- *Stay A Little Longer* (Athena and Logan)
- *Bring It On Home* (Maggie and Porter)
- *Come Away with Me* (Moses and Zuri)

MEN OF THE MISFIT INN
SMALL TOWN SOUTHERN ROMANCE

- *Let It Be Me* (Emerson and Caleb)
- *Our Kind of Love* (Abbey and Kyle)
- *Don't You Wanna Stay* (Deanna and Wyatt)
- *Until We Meet Again* (Samantha and Griffin prequel)
- *Come A Little Closer* (Samantha and Griffin)
- *Just Wanted You To Know* (Livia and Declan)
- *A Love Like You* (Juliette and Mick)

WISHFUL ROMANCE SERIES
SMALL TOWN SOUTHERN ROMANCE

- *To Get Me To You* (Cam and Norah)
- *Know Me Well* (Liam and Riley)
- *Be Careful, It's My Heart* (Brody and Tyler)
- *The Matchmaker Maneuver* (Myles and Piper prequel)
- *Just For This Moment* (Myles and Piper)
- *Wish I Might* (Reed and Cecily)
- *Turn My World Around* (Tucker and Corinne)
- *Dance Me A Dream* (Jace and Tara)
- *See You Again* (Trey and Sandy)
- *The Christmas Fountain* (Chad and Mary Alice)
- *You Were Meant For Me* (Mitch and Tess)
- *A Lot Like Christmas* (Ryan and Hannah)
- *Dancing Away With My Heart* (Zach and Lexi)

WISHFUL MOMENTS SERIES
BITE-SIZED WISHFUL ROMANCE

- *Once Upon A Coffee* (Avery and Dillon)
- *Once Upon A Rescue* (Brooke and Hayden)
- *Who I Am with You* (Dinah and Robert)

WISHING FOR A HERO SERIES (A WISHFUL SPINOFF SERIES)
SMALL TOWN ROMANTIC SUSPENSE

- *Make You Feel My Love* (Judd and Autumn)
- *Watch Over Me* (Nash and Rowan)
- *Can't Take My Eyes Off You* (Ethan and Miranda)
- *Burn For You* (Sean and Delaney)

MEET CUTE ROMANCE
SMALL TOWN SHORT ROMANCE

- *Once Upon A Snow Day*
- *Once Upon A New Year's Eve*
- *Once Upon An Heirloom*

SUMMER FLING TRILOGY
CONTEMPORARY ROMANCE

- *Second Chance Summer*
- *Summer Camp Secret*
- *The Summer Camp Swap*

ABOUT KAIT

Kait is a Mississippi native, who often swears like a sailor, calls everyone sugar, honey, or darlin', and can wield a bless your heart like a saber or a Snuggie, depending on requirements.

You can find more information on this *USA Today* best selling and RITA ® Award-winning author and her books on her website http://kaitnolan.com.

Do you need more small town sass and spark? Sign up for <u>her</u> <u>newsletter</u> to hear about new releases, book deals, and exclusive content!